dream girl

Lauren Mechling

dream
girl

{delacorte press}

Published by Delacorte Press
an imprint of Random House Children's Books
a division of Random House, Inc.
New York

This is a work of fiction. Names, characters, places, and incidents either are the product of the author's imagination or are used fictitiously. Any resemblance to actual persons, living or dead, events, or locales is entirely coincidental.

Delacorte Press and colophon are registered trademarks of Random House, Inc.

www.randomhouse.com/teens

Educators and librarians, for a variety of teaching tools, visit us at
www.randomhouse.com/teachers

Library of Congress Cataloging-in-Publication Data
Mechling, Lauren.
Dream girl / Lauren Mechling.—1st ed.
p. cm.
Summary: When fifteen-year-old Claire Voyante's grandmother gives her
a cameo for her birthday, she starts having dreams that seem to be telling her
something that has to do with her new, wealthy friend being in danger.
ISBN 978-0-385-73521-6 (hardcover) — ISBN 978-0-385-90510-7
(Gibraltar lib. bdg.)
[1. Dreams—Fiction. 2. Clairvoyants—Fiction. 3. Schools—Fiction.
4. Family life—New York (State)—New York—Fiction. 5. New York
(N.Y.)—Fiction. 6. Family Life—New York (N.Y.)—Fiction.
7. Mystery and detective stories.] I. Title.
PZ7.M51269Dr 2008
[Fic]—dc22
2007034497

The text of this book is set in 12-point Joanna MT.

Book design by Angela Carlino

Printed in the United States of America

10 9 8 7 6 5 4 3 2 1

First Edition

I was breezing down the airport corridor, minding my own business and thinking about the new look I'd have with the liquid eyeliner I'd picked up at the duty-free shop in Paris, when I saw it in the distance: the pink combination lock.

It was bobbing from a burgundy tasseled handbag that was slung over the shoulder of a woman who'd been on my family's flight back to New York. She'd been in first class, and when we boarded I did a double take at the way she'd piled her chestnut hair into a perfectly disheveled updo. That's the French for you—even their disheveled is perfect. Only, now I was checking her out for a different reason. The lock on her bag was the same as the one I'd seen in my daydream in the waiting area before our flight.

Without a second thought, I peeled off from my family and tore ahead. As I neared her, I saw that she was younger than

I'd thought—probably not much older than me. She was one of those beautiful but deadly types, with cold onyx eyes and blade-sharp cheekbones. More Hollywood starlet, less French sophisticate. And there was no question about the lock. It was exactly the same as the one I'd imagined.

If she sensed me following her, she didn't show it. She just kept strutting along, her heels click-clicking on the hard floor. I picked up my pace, and when I got closer I saw that her trench coat was pulled tight around a huge and suspiciously uneven lump. What was she hiding in there?

I hung back and kept an eye on her as she wove in and out of the crowd. And then I must have blinked too slowly or something. She was gone.

I started to panic—no doubt, she was up to something fishy, and now I'd lost her.

Then another glimpse of pink lock—she'd veered off to the side of the passageway and opened a bathroom door. A flap of her trench coat rippled, and the door closed.

I glanced over my shoulder. My family was catching up to me, and I knew they wanted to get out of the airport as quickly as possible. But there had to be a reason why I'd seen that pink lock in my daydream. She looked shady, and I needed to find out what she was hiding under her coat.

I pushed past a group of stewardesses and darted over to the door. Gearing up for the worst, I pulled it open. The girl was hunched over a table by a row of sinks. In the mirror I could see her focused expression and the accordion-like folds that had formed across her forehead. Was she importing drugs? Assembling a dirty bomb? Or maybe she'd been hired by a black market adoption agency to smuggle in an illegal baby!

I crept up behind her, my eyes set on the pink lock. I still didn't have a plan, but I had to get to the bottom of this. And then, without really thinking about it, I reached out and grabbed her shoulder.

She pulled away, then whipped around. Her coat was unbuttoned, and a tiny dog was on the counter, barely balancing on its legs as it lapped water out of a plastic bowl.

"Can I help you with something?" the girl snapped at me.

"No, I . . . I thought you were someone else."

She glared at me, and the ominous lump—or, as it turned out, the thirsty little puppy—pulled its head out of the water and sneezed.

I could barely muster an apology as I stumbled away.

Me and my stupid visions.

{ 1 }

A Supposedly Beautiful Mind

"Claire!" Dad screamed down the airport hallway. *"Zeep zeep!"*

He was doing his best to sound authoritative, but with his French accent, he reminded me of Pepé Le Pew. My entire family had stopped walking and was looking at me as if I were personally responsible for how grumpy and tired they all felt after our eight-hour flight home. Mom made an exaggerated yawn, and my little brother, Henry, weighed down by his enormous backpack, crumpled against her legs.

The girl with the puppy emerged from the bathroom and cast me a wary glance. She coasted ahead of me, and I couldn't help taking one last look at the pink lock dangling off her bag. It was definitely the same one I'd seen in my mind before we'd boarded. Unfortunately, that was all it was.

It didn't mean a thing.

"I'm coming!" I screamed.

I'd been having visions ever since I was little, but they were usually stupid and meaningless, like Henry holding a green umbrella with a frog on it or, say, a bright pink lock—things that I'd later see in front of me but that never lead me to anything groundbreaking.

There was one time I saw something worthwhile: a picture of a tabby cat napping in a fedora. When I saw the same image on one of my grandmother Kiki's hatboxes, I peeked inside and found bundles of carbon-copied letters between Kiki and my mother from the time my mother was still in college. Suddenly everything made sense—my parents and Kiki didn't clash regularly just because of a difference in lifestyles, as they'd led me to believe. There had been a massive falling-out. Kiki had violently disapproved of Mom's getting engaged to her "penniless French professor," and when my parents went ahead and eloped, Kiki wrote my mom a soap-opera-worthy letter saying something along the lines of "Being excluded from my only daughter's wedding has been more painful than you, who do not yet have children, can imagine. I don't expect I will ever fully recover."

This revelation was huge—and not only because it explained so much about my family. It also gave me reason enough to believe that my next vision might lead to another monumental discovery. A hope I was hanging on to for dear life.

I never said a word to Kiki about the letters, but she already knew all about my visions. I had to tell her—the second you so much as think about a secret you're keeping from her, she sniffs it out. And she wasn't too weirded out when I told her. She said it was my parents' fault since they were the ones who'd given me my name. "You don't do that to a girl whose last name is Voyante," she'd moaned. "Not that Claire isn't a lovely name on its own . . ."

For their part, my parents said they'd named me after my dad's great-aunt Claire, who died in a Parisian heat wave the summer I was born. My little brother, Henry, is legally Henri, or as Dad pronounces it, *On-ree*. My mom, who thinks she's French, tries to pronounce it the French way, but she forgets at least half the time.

Down at baggage claim, Mom was channeling her inner Frenchwoman. "Voilà! There it is!" she cried, waving her Evian bottle across the carousel as if her luggage might be looking for her, too. Even when she's shouting, Mom's voice is light and girly, the polar opposite of my own husky rasp.

"You see it?" Dad asked. He squinted and perched on his tiptoes to look past the crowd. "Ah, there's mine, coming right along behind yours!" And then he pulled Mom in close and kissed her, as if their suitcases' being next to each other were the most romantic thing in the world.

I guess that's the way it goes when your mom isn't just beautiful but hot. And we're not talking hot-for-a-mom, here. She's unfairly, across-the-board hot, with huge drowsy eyes and chopstick-skinny limbs.

As fate would have it, I look like my dad, or at least the way he would look if he were a fifteen-year-old girl and not a middle-aged French professor. I'm short and blond, with a Cheerio-shaped mouth, a flat chest, and a megabutt—I'm keeping my fingers crossed for future developments. The only way I've figured out to wear my puffy hair is in a high ponytail. Most people say that the most distinctive thing about me is that I have one green and one hazel eye, but I think my friend Louis nailed it when he said I'm always scrunching up my nose like a confused duck. Attractive, I know.

As we gathered our baggage and headed toward the exit, we could see our friend and neighbor Cheri-Lee Vird waiting for us in her teal Honda at the curb. "Yoo-hoo!" She stuck her bright red bob out the car window. Mom and Dad don't believe in paying for cabs (or, for that matter, new books or name-brand cereal) and always arrange to have somebody pick us up at the airport. Cheri-Lee is generally that somebody.

"Sorry if we kept you waiting," Mom said when we were all squished inside the car. We had more luggage than the trunk could hold, so Henry sat on my lap in the oh-so-comfortable elbow-jutting-into-spleen configuration.

Since she'd taken us to the airport at the beginning of the summer, Cheri-Lee had done some decorating on her car. A flock of red plastic swallows was pinned to the felt covering the ceiling, and she'd affixed turquoise roses to the steering wheel. Over the last year she'd started to go through a crafty phase, dip-dying old nightgowns and attending potato-stamping seminars. Looked as though the party wasn't over yet.

"You must be exhausted," Cheri-Lee said, adjusting the rearview mirror. "Travel can be so *discombobulating*." As a poetry professor, Cheri-Lee feels it's her duty to trot out interesting words. "I was stuck in the library for the past three months. Nothing like fluorescent lighting to keep a summer glow away. For the love of the Dewey decimal system, tell me your summer was better."

"*Oui*," Dad said. "I think it was better."

"Care to *elaborate*?" Cheri-Lee cut into another lane.

"We went all over," I piped up. "Paris, the countryside, the

8

South. We saw family, old castles, unpasteurized cheese stores, nude beaches . . ."

"You wild and crazy Europeans!" Cheri-Lee tittered. "Now, Claire, I hope you've had your fill—wild and crazy isn't really Hudson's specialty. Still, there's nothing wrong with a bright new beginning! Sheila sure loved her fresh start."

Oof. Why did she have to bring up Henry Hudson ten minutes after we'd touched ground? Then again, if we waited a hundred years, I still wouldn't want to talk about Henry Hudson High, the school I was starting in a few days. It was a nerd school on the Lower East Side known for its competitive math and science departments, nationally ranked chess club, and recurring asbestos problem. It was also the school Cheri-Lee's daughter, Sheila, attended.

Sheila and I used to be close, so close that the summer after sixth grade I convinced my parents to let me skip our annual French vacation and join Sheila at Camp Maple Rock. The problem was, Sheila attended a two-day "precamp" for returning campers, and by the time I arrived, the former sword and sorcery fanatic had managed to become normal and befriend all the popular kids she'd been making fun of in her letters to me for the past two summers. I couldn't believe it— as soon as I showed up, she acted as if she barely knew me. And things didn't get any better when I became friends with Hayden Chapman, her cute shaggy-haired boyfriend from the summer before. Nothing ever happened between Hayden and me, but Sheila—and the rest of Camp Maple Rock—was convinced otherwise. Two years later, Sheila and I still barely spoke, but Mom and Cheri-Lee were constantly scheming to get us back together.

"You're going to get such a *phenomenal* education," Cheri-Lee hooted. Dad—Henry Hudson's biggest advocate—turned around and sent me an approving wink. Cheri-Lee went on, "Trust me, this school is nothing like Farmhouse."

I felt as if I was going to choke. Was this supposed to be encouraging? I had no desire to leave the Farmhouse School, my spiritual home for the last nine years. Farmhouse, a school for the "gifted and talented," was the best place ever. A few members of a communist theater troupe had founded it in the 1940s, and it had everything a kid could want in a school: tiny classes, no exams, a test kitchen where students could conduct their own chocolate fondue experiments. There was even an extended family of rabbits living in the backyard.

There was, however, one terrible thing about Farmhouse: since they didn't normally give tests, the school made its ninth graders take the entrance exam to Henry Hudson as practice. It was billed as a precautionary measure against future SAT disasters. If you bombed the Hudson test, you were required to go to standardized test tutoring until you got the hang of taking exams.

I didn't think much about the test, not even when I ended up acing it. It wasn't as if there was any chance I'd end up at a school like Henry Hudson. Farmhouse valued creativity, community, and eccentricity, the same things Mom and Dad stood for.

Supposedly.

That was before my acceptance letter came. Henry Hudson was free. Mom and Dad were cash strapped. You do the math.

There was no way I was going. A whole lot of kicking and screaming ensued. I burst into tears at the dinner table, on multiple occasions. When that didn't work, I went on a two-day silent strike. Mom and Dad still didn't back down, so I appealed to Kiki, but she wasn't any help, either. "I'm sorry, dear," she'd said, "but seeing that I'd only spend my money on a fine boarding school and I'm not interested in your living any farther away from me than you already do, I'm afraid I can't be of any assistance."

Of course Henry gets to stay at Farmhouse. In Mom and Dad's opinion, Henry is a genius who deserves a place at a school for the creatively gifted and talented. And I hadn't shown any signs of talent, unless you count knowing the words to most sixties girl group songs or chasing innocent girls and puppies into airport bathrooms.

Even though my friends from Farmhouse said they knew it wasn't my fault I was leaving, everything changed—and fast. I'd always been fairly popular, but after word got out that I was leaving, people started acting weird. My parents said it was because they were jealous that I'd done so well on the test, but I knew the truth: they were mad at me for splitting. And at the end of the year, when Sarah Blumenthal had a party and invited everybody but the class mute Cyd Federman and me, I wasn't all that surprised.

"Cheri-Lee's talking to you," Henry said, poking me in the thigh. I looked out my backseat window and realized we were already cruising down Houston Street. Labor Day was just a few days off, and people in shorts and flip-flops were shuffling around as if they had nowhere to go.

"You should come over and visit Sheila before school starts," Cheri-Lee was saying. "I'm sure there's gobs of advice she can give you."

"That would be wonderful," Mom chimed in.

"I'll see what I can do," Cheri-Lee trilled. "I know the school has a reputation for being a little dorky, but Sheila's posse is completely adorable. Not a single pocket protector in the bunch. Oh, and did you know you're in the same home-room? Talk about *serendipity!*"

"That's . . . great." Groaning internally, I folded my hands around Henry's waist and dug my nose into his shoulder. I didn't want to talk about serendipity, or anything else, for that matter.

{ 2 }

Cameo Appearance

We live in building number two of Washington View Village, a New York University faculty-housing complex whose name is an eternal mystery to me. None of the apartments have views of Washington Square Park, and all the buildings in the complex are over twenty stories tall—not exactly the first image that springs to mind when you hear the word *village*.

When we walked into the lobby, everything felt slightly unfamiliar, no one else in my family seemed the least bit disoriented and they started for the elevator as if it were just any other old day.

Upstairs, our apartment was a wreck, even more so than usual. In addition to the books and the rest of the summer's mail strewn everywhere, a couple of French country plates had fallen from their wall brackets, and there was a vaguely sour smell coming from the refrigerator.

Mom went directly for the mail and pulled all her missed issues of the *Planet* out, as if nothing were out of the ordinary and we hadn't just come back from the other side of the world. Mom supplements her career ghostwriting auto-biographies for C-list celebrities with writing a horoscope column for the country's second-most-popular gossip magazine. Don't get me wrong—Mom isn't a professional astrologer by any stretch of the imagination. When her old friend Tom Blakeson dropped out of grad school to move to Tampa and edit the *Planet*, he gave Mom her first astrology assignment as a joke. In her head shot—"Priscilla Pluto's" head shot, that is—she's posed over a pot of boiling water for a smoky effect with our blue floral tablecloth around her head like a turban. With her attention deficit disorder, she never could hold down a regular job, so her weird combination of jobs-you-never-knew-existed is perfect for her. Besides, it's pretty obvious she sees hero-worshipping Dad as her real job.

"There's no place like home," I said, ditching my suitcase and kicking my new Lacoste sneakers onto the shoe heap by the door. Mom and Dad say their no-shoes rule is to keep the rugs clean, though it's plain as day they think having everybody in socks or bare feet ups the place's bohemian street cred.

I aimed for Mom's left purple sandal. My right shoe skidded over to land by Henry's galoshes, but the left one was a perfect shot. If only this qualified as being athletically inclined.

Mom looked up from her magazine flipping and smiled in her hazy way at my stockinged feet. God, it was weird what made her happy. I cast Henry a remind-me-how-we're-related-to-her look, but he didn't notice. He was crouched by the coffee table, using markers and construction paper to create a new classification system for his dinosaur figures.

"Claire?" Mom said. "These came for you—a card and a couple of letters from Henry Hudson."

"What do you think the chances are that they're writing to say they realized they made a mistake when they let me in?"

"What do you think the chances are that you'll give it a chance?" Mom shot back.

I sighed my defeat and walked over to collect my mail. There was a flimsy envelope from my new school as well as a thick cream-colored envelope with Kiki's signature pink trim.

"There's only one thing from Hudson here," I told Mom.

"Oh," she said. "That's what I meant."

Her attention to detail was unbelievable. I ripped open the bargain-basement envelope first to see that Hudson's administrative office had sent an undersized sheet of paper that looked as if it had been xeroxed a hundred times. "Attention, incoming students," it read. "Our new metal detector system is highly sensitive. All students are advised to keep jewelry, hair accessories, and orthodontic contraptions to a minimum. See you on the fifth."

I trusted the cream envelope would be more fun, and headed into the living area to open it in privacy.

KIKI MERRIMAN
REQUESTS THE HONOR OF
CLAIRE VOYANTE'S PRESENCE
AT THE BELATED CELEBRATION OF
CLAIRE VOYANTE'S FIFTEENTH BIRTHDAY
SATURDAY, THE TENTH OF SEPTEMBER
SIX O'CLOCK
THE WALDORF-ASTORIA HOTEL

At the bottom, Kiki had written in her flawless penmanship: "When you get back, I'll be in D.C. visiting my dear friends the Lamonts. It would be unfair to deprive you of my company and your present. If you don't put it on immediately, I'll be most offended."

My confusion lifted when I realized the envelope was slightly heavier than usual. With my back turned to Mom, I stuck my hand in and fished out a rectangle of tissue paper with something stuck inside. Seeing that my grandmother lived uptown, only a short bike ride away, I was surprised that this present couldn't have waited, but as I pulled the paper off my gift, I realized why she'd sent it. It was a cameo pendant with the cream-colored silhouette of a woman on a black stone background. It wasn't the kind of thing you stuck in a drawer and waited to give to someone.

I'd seen plenty of cameos, but this one was different. It was as if it actually contained more than just two dimensions, and the longer I stared, the deeper I was pulled in.

"Anything good?" Mom asked absently, snapping me out of my haze.

"Not really," I mumbled, clenching the present in my fist. She and her mother had a weird relationship, and if I could avoid mentioning one in front of the other, I did.

Without further ado, I snuck into the bathroom and flicked on the light. I fumbled with the clasp until the necklace was securely in place, then let my arms drop to my sides and looked in the mirror. The chain was thin nearly to the point of invisibility, and the pendant hit the sweet spot just below my collarbone. I didn't know how it was possible, but set against my dehydrated, bleary-eyed, jet-lagged self, the cameo looked even prettier than it had before.

Sorry, Henry Hudson, I thought—the new metal detector was going to have to deal.

{ 3 }

Lawn Twister

Mom was too tired to go shopping that night, so she scrounged up some nonperishables for dinner. After I wolfed down my frozen ravioli and canned peas, I got a surge of energy and was crazily inspired to tackle my entire life at once. Why just unpack when I could unpack *and* hang up my new Folies Bergère poster *and* clean out my closet *and* check the Farmhouse Web site?

"Claire!" Mom yelled as I slid out of my chair and nearly crashed into Dad's wheeled desk. "Stay seated at the table and digest!" Digestion was a favorite topic of conversation among my parents' friends in France, so naturally Mom had developed an interest in it.

"The human stomach is a miraculous organ," I said,

17

backing away from the table. "It can do its work in any number of rooms." And this evening my bedroom would have to suffice.

Alone in my own little space, I got busy sorting dirty laundry and organizing the pens and scissors in my drawers and taking down a sunflower poster that had grown a million times uglier since June. I was running on all cylinders—until I wasn't, and my room melted away.

Everything was a whorl of motion—hundreds of circles were growing and bumping into one another like so many ripples in a lake. And I was floating in the middle of it all. I couldn't see up or down or tell what was spinning faster: myself or everything else.

The black and white circles slowed down and started to melt into one great sea of gray. I was still suspended like an astronaut when a tiny paper doll appeared before me. I reached out to touch it, but I just missed it. The doll turned on its side to reveal a paper-doll twin. The doll continued to roll over, leaving behind a dozen or so replicas, all linked by their little paper hands. And then another hand entered the picture—a human hand holding a pair of scissors. All it took was one quick snip for the string of dolls to break apart. And I started tumbling down, down through space until the dolls shrank to no more than little white specks in the distance.

I woke up with my clothes still on and my face buried in my fake polar bear rug. From this vantage point, I could see a family of chocolate bunnies hidden under the bed. I'd bought them at half off the week after Easter—a huge act of defiance against my parents' très French rule against snacking (we're only allowed a four o'clock goûter and it's always yogurt or, even worse, cheese). As I reached out for a bunny, the dream I'd just been having came back to me. It was definitely weird, and not just because it had been in black-and-white. It was exhilarating, more like an amusement park ride than my usual dreams, in which I'd find myself running around the Washington View courtyard in my underpants or on a Broadway stage with no idea what my lines were.

My clock said it was 3:08 a.m., and I felt like I'd run a marathon. I shuffled out to the living room, completely disoriented. All appeared to be normal—still and empty, with everyone else in bed. I poured myself a glass of water and sat on my favorite butterfly chair by the window. Almost all the other lights in Washington View Village were off, the curtains drawn, though I could make out a pixie of a woman in building one standing in front of a television set and lifting weights. Something creaked behind me, and I turned around to see Henry letting himself into the apartment, his Tintin backpack sagging to the backs of his knees.

"What on earth? Do you have any idea what time it is?" I cried through a mouthful of stale bunny tail.

"Relax," he said. "I was just walking the halls."

When Henry had started taking his walks, Mom and Dad had tried to lay down the law and forbid his wanderings, but eventually they came around. When a family lives in an apartment the size of an average Starbucks, everyone needs to get out from time to time. I had my bike, Dad had his classes, Mom had her coffee meetings with Cheri-Lee, and now Henry was free to go out whenever the mood struck, so long as he didn't go any farther than the corner. And starting at eight he could only walk around inside the building. Still—it was three in the morning.

"What floors?" I was testing him. When Henry lies, he gets nervous and makes up a million unnecessary details.

His curly silhouette drifted toward me, and he lowered himself onto the other butterfly chair, backpack still on. "Seven and nine."

I waited a beat to see if there was anything he wanted to add. Nothing. He was off the hook.

I broke off a bunny ear and handed it to him. "Okay, but if you ever go outside in the middle of the night and let yourself get kidnapped and beheaded, I swear I will track you down and kill you."

Henry coughed. "Wouldn't I already be dead then?"

I got up and started to stagger toward my room. "See you tomorrow," I said, yawning.

"You mean today."

"Hen," I said softly. "There's a very fine line between being smart and being a huge dork. Please tell me I don't have to worry about you."

"Whatever." Henry kicked his feet up to the windowsill, assuming the universal position of complete and utter unconcern.

The next time I woke up, the sun was beating through my window and the sky was a majestic shade of sapphire. I felt slow and groggy, but you would have to be a soulless cretin to spend such a beautiful day inside.

Or part of my immediate family.

When I cracked open my bedroom door, my parents were both in the living area, lost in their work. Mom was tapping away on her laptop, probably writing her latest astrology column. Dad was in the corner reading Émile Zola's Nana, one of the novels he was always rereading and marking up with different-colored Post-its.

I quietly closed my door before they could see me spying and logged on to my computer. Even if I wasn't going back to Farmhouse, I could at least pretend. As promised, my friend Louis had forwarded me the Farmhouse Summer Living

Agenda, the school's version of a summer reading list. It included teachers' recommendations for street fairs and day trips, and even the names and numbers of Farmhouse alumni who were open to receiving visitors at their offices. At the end of the summer, kids were supposed to go on the Farmhouse Web site and post photos and write-ups of what they'd done. Trust me, it's cooler than it sounds.

Some of this year's suggestions, like the International Tomato Day festivities and the Animate This! Film Festival, had already passed. And I had to rule out others, like the American Folk Art Museum and "Take the Q train to both ends of the line and take pictures of what you find," on account of the glorious weather. In the end, I settled on a visit to Brooklyn's Green-Wood Cemetery. Mr. Claxon, my history teacher from last year, had written a convincing recommendation: "You'll find trees full of wild green parrots, Gothic tombs, and tons of dead celebrities. Write a story there—it's the perfect setting for an Agatha Christie–ish mystery."

As if I needed more proof that I still belonged at Farmhouse. This trip was practically tailor made for me.

Back in sixth grade, when my love for Agatha Christie was verging on pathological, I got it in my head that I was a detective. I spent several months sneaking around the building trying to listen through people's doors. After a few complaints, the Washington View Village board banned me from going to floors other than my own for a year. To this day a handful of neighbors still avoid making eye contact with me on the elevator.

I got ready as quickly as I could, and Mom didn't look up from her computer until I was on my way out the door. "Claire, there's a departmental meet and greet in the Sunrise Room today, and people are bringing their chil—"

"I can't do it," I said too quickly. "I'm supposed to do this . . . write-up. It's for school."

It wasn't exactly a lie—I just left out the part about it not being my school.

"They already gave you an assignment?" Mom looked perplexed, but Dad was smiling at his diligent daughter. He'd been waiting fifteen years for me to embrace my studious side. Before Mom could ask any more questions, I blew them both a kiss and sailed out of the apartment.

I was walking my prize possession—my vintage red Schwinn—down the path outside our complex, congratulating myself on fibbing my way into what might be my last day of freedom, when I spotted a familiar pair of curly red bobs glinting metallically in the near distance.

Of all the thousands of neighbors to run into. Sheila Vird and her mom.

Without really thinking about it, I let my bike drop and ran into the courtyard. When I was younger, I always hid behind the hideous fake Picasso sculpture—I couldn't have grown that much since then, right? But just as I was sprinting across the patch of worn-out grass, our half-deaf neighbor Dr. Larson came out of nowhere and greeted me with what was possibly the loudest "Hi, Claire!" in history.

I was toast.

Cheri-Lee spun around, her eyes crinkling in puzzlement. "Is that our Claire?"

"Hi!" I squeaked from my spot on the grass, spastically bending down to touch my right ankle. I could feel how purple my face was, and I was reminded of when my parents went through an after-dinner Twister phase.

"I'm stretching," I peeped by way of explanation.

Cheri-Lee galumphed toward me, and Sheila followed, an

expression of annoyance washing over her potato-like face. She brought her hands to her hips and thrust out her whopping shoulders, a move she'd learned at one of the sword and sorcery role-playing conventions she'd gone to before she'd disowned that side of herself. If I recalled correctly, this pose was supposed to inspire fear in others. And it did, along with a tiny little bit of glee. Sheila was ridiculous.

Oblivious to her daughter's displeasure at seeing me, Cheri-Lee started yammering away about anything and everything on her mind. "Isn't the weather *resplendent?* . . . It just *harkens* back to the days I used to go back-to-school shopping with my mother. . . . Then we'll finish off with fro-yo at Bloomie's, the tangy natural-flavored one . . . don't you think?"

The sight of Sheila had instantly transformed me into a wobbling mound of idiocy, and I had no hope of following anything her mother was talking about.

"So what do you say, Claire?" Cheri-Lee brought her hand to her ear, and her rainbow-colored stars-and-anchors charm bracelet rattled.

I figured it would probably be a good idea not to keep talking to them with my face buried in my knee. I did one more toe touch for good measure and came up for air, only to be overwhelmed by the perfume Sheila had worn since fifth grade. Why had nobody ever told her she smelled exactly like a peach muffin?

"So," Cheri-Lee pressed on, "what are you doing tonight?"

Sheila shot her mom a loathing look.

"Probably taking it easy."

As opposed to my usual nighttime fare of nightclubbing and sitting on the backs of motorcycles.

"You're too young to take it easy." Cheri-Lee honked. "Sheila was just telling me about some *gigantic* party she and her friends are all going to."

"It's not *gigantic*," Sheila blurted out. "It's a little gathering at some kid's brownstone."

"So?" Cheri-Lee elbowed her daughter in the side. "Claire's small. I'm sure she could fit."

"Hilarious, Mom." Sheila stared at me as if I were made of millions of minuscule rat droppings. And then, as if she could no longer bear the sight of me, she blinked hard and reached down to tuck her sneaker tongue under her yoga pant leg.

"Where's the party?" Cheri-Lee persisted.

"I don't know." I could tell Sheila was working hard to drain her voice of any trace of life. "We're all going to Lauren's for an intimate get-together first."

"Great! That might be an easier atmosphere for Claire's big *debut*." She laughed at the term, clueless to what her daughter was really trying to say to her. "Why don't you give her the address and she can meet you there?"

I don't know if it was because I abruptly realized that I wouldn't mind meeting some new kids or because I was enjoying how much her mother's idea was driving Sheila crazy, but suddenly I wanted in.

"You know, that would be really nice." I shot Sheila a sickly sweet smile.

"I can't just . . . *do* that," Sheila sputtered.

"Oh, please," Cheri-Lee said. "Since when were you so uptight? If Lauren has a problem with Claire, tell her to call me."

It was a recipe for disaster, but before I knew it, Cheri-Lee was smiling and congratulating us on our freshly hatched plans.

{ 4 }

Meet the Beatles

I'll admit that a cemetery might be seen as a slightly odd destination, especially on my first day back in New York, but really, it wasn't morbid in the least. The sun followed me on the ride out there, and the grounds were more quaint than creepy—all rolling hills and overhanging branches and Gothic cathedrals. I only saw one person visiting a grave in the traditional sense—everyone else seemed to have come for a jog or, in one classy instance, to make out.

I got home a little after five, which gave me barely enough time to get ready for my big night with the Sheila posse. Mom and Dad were entertaining spillover from the French department meet and greet. My parents' scratched-up Jacques

Dutronc CD was playing, and the apartment was buzzing with French chitchat.

Hoping to drown them out, I went to my room and put on "Peanut Duck" by Marsha Gee, one of my all-time favorite songs. Without showering first, I threw on a black skirt and shirt and fastened a thick leather belt around my waist, a rump-concealing trick I learned from Kiki. Thanks to all the wine my parents' friends were drinking, the bathroom was occupied every time I tried to use it, so I used the mirrored Renault car poster in the living room to do my hair and makeup. I could barely see anything through all the lettering and had to lean in breath-foggingly close for my quick pony-tail and eyeliner job.

I must have been working hard on my eyes—I didn't notice that the phone had rung until I saw Mom's reflection holding the receiver. "Hello? Hello?" she said with growing agitation before hanging up. "Gus," she said to my dad, "it's happening again."

My parents are convinced that the reason Mom regularly gets hang-ups is that one of Dad's students is in love with him and is determined to harass my mother. Nobody ever stopped to consider that it could be Mom's mother calling for me.

Before the phone sounded again, I ran back to my room and waited. Didier and Margaux, my pet fish, were swimming around peacefully, unmindful of the irritating racket in the next room. I picked up before the first ring had completely played out.

"Hello?"

"There you are, darling," Kiki said grandly. "I've only got a minute to spare. It's almost time for dinner. We're having stone crabs and asparagus with hollandaise—I snuck a peek at the menu. Above and beyond the call of duty, those Lamonts. Though it sounded like there's a party at the Voyante residence, am I correct?"

"I guess," I said. "Mom and Dad are drinking Vouvray with some other barefoot professors."

"Delightful," Kiki murmured. "Now, I just wanted to confirm that you received your invitation."

"Of course—I've saved the date!"

"And the necklace? Is it to your liking?"

"Are you kidding? I'm never taking it off."

"I shouldn't if I were you. Apart from when you shower," she said. "It's an old good-luck charm, you know. It doesn't really take well to sporadic usage." This was the kind of remark Kiki typically followed with a spray of laughter, though this time she remained silent. "Oh dear—there's the dinner bell! Ta-ta, toodle-pip, and so forth. See you soon!"

Come again? Fifteen years into our bosom buddy–ship, I still have trouble distinguishing Kiki's important pronouncements from her jokes. Sometimes it feels as if she's on shuffle, her lines popping out with little relation to what has been said just before. Was she serious about the cameo's being a good-luck charm? Or was that just one of the comments she tosses around like table salt? I had to assume it was the latter—the only notable thing that had happened since I'd put on the necklace was my being roped into a night with Sheila and her nerd posse.

When I came out of my room, I saw that our family's favorite poetess had joined the fray. Cheri-Lee and my mom were over by the bookshelves, eyeing me as they drained their wineglasses.

"Big plans tonight?" Mom asked me, her voice laced with optimism.

"Yeah, I'm going to a party with Hudson people. Should be interesting."

Mom's face fell. "Claire, it won't be if you don't give it a chance."

"What did I say to make you so sure I wasn't going to give it a chance?" I protested. Just because I have a raspy voice, Mom thinks she can detect sarcasm in everything I utter.

Cheri-Lee leaned in to whisper something to her partner in crime, and the two started to smile and titter—there was no doubt Cheri-Lee had filled Mom in on our courtyard encounter. Shuddering at the realization that I was the petri dish for their social experiment, I made a beeline for the door.

Thirty minutes later, I was pulling up on my bike in front of the Upper West Side address Sheila had reluctantly handed over to me. It turned out to be one of those prewar buildings with beautiful details on the outside and gloomily lit hallways inside that smell faintly of meat. You'd think people living in multimillion-dollar apartments would go the extra mile and spring for a mop and a few lightbulbs, but the sad truth is they rarely do.

A chipmunk-cheeked woman who identified herself as the nanny answered the door and led me through a series of big dark rooms until we reached Lauren's bedroom. Sheila and her gang were stretched out on the floor, all dressed alike in black yoga pants, tank tops, and hoop earrings. With their heads close together and their identically clad legs splayed out in a circle, they looked like a giant starfish. And then there was me, sticking out like a birthday cake at a funeral.

I'd learned from Kiki that in the event you find yourself feeling shy at a party, you should approach the most uncomfortable-looking person in the room. "Princess Diana used to do it," she'd told me. "Buttonhole the biggest dud, and you'll immediately feel like the belle of the ball." But here, nobody else looked remotely anxious, which only made me feel worse.

"Hey," I said, trying to keep the discontent out of my voice.

"Hi," Sheila said without catching my eye.

Stop the presses: she'd acknowledged me!

"Everyone," Sheila said, "this is Claire, my old . . . acquaintance."

Of course. Saying "my old friend" would've been too much. Gritting my teeth, I waved.

Sheila started to point around the room. "This is Ariel, Janice, Lauren, and Lauren."

The girls were flipping through a stapled-together Hudson phone book and eating a bowl of pretzels. They all looked older than me, but the room seemed to have been decorated by an eight-year-old girl. Twin beds, pink walls, and even a shelf full of horse figurines. I sat on the edge of the nearer of the beds and put my bicycle helmet down by the pillow. I couldn't remember the last time I'd felt this badly accessorized.

And then, as abruptly as a car crash, the weird dream I'd had the other night came back to me. I was still looking ahead at the girls, but I could barely see them through the little paper dolls buzzing around my field of vision. A wave of exhaustion washed over me, and a spasm rocked through my left leg, which tends to happen when I'm falling asleep.

"You okay, Claire?" Sheila's tone was more catty than concerned.

"Yeah, I just . . ." I could see everything clearly again. "I haven't eaten in a while and I got dizzy."

"Help yourself." Ariel passed the bowl of minirods my way.

I did as told, and hammed up the munching for credibility's sake.

"Do you have a stomachache or something?" Ariel asked me.

"Me? No, why?"

"Sorry." She looked embarrassed. "It must be the way you're sitting, curled up like that." She turned back to her friends and I unfolded my arms and straightened my spine. One of these days I was going to develop perfect posture.

"Where's the book?" Sheila asked the rest of the social starfish.

"Oops, my bad," said curly blond Lauren. "I left it in my backpack." She flounced out into the hallway, then returned with a classic black and white composition book. The girls passed the book around and took turns writing in it. Silence descended on the room, and I felt as if I'd intruded on some ancient ritual.

Janice, a beautiful girl with dark sloped eyes, eventually motioned for me to join them on the floor, and I settled into the spot between her and brown-haired Lauren. "This is the Beatle book," Janice whispered conspiratorially to me.

I scratched my head. Last time I'd checked, Sheila was into symphonies—not old British bands.

Janice went on, "A couple of years ago a group of juniors kept a group diary. It got published and they all got into, like, Harvard."

"Not quite," Ariel scoffed. "Two of them got into Brown, one got into Penn, and the other went to Michigan for a year and dropped out."

"Whatever," Janice said. "It's still better than wherever my average is going to get me."

"Oh shut up, Miss Ninety-five Percent," Sheila hissed. I remembered how Sheila used to say she wanted to go to art school and be a ceramicist when she grew up. Something told me there'd been a change of plans.

When brown-haired Lauren took the book, I glanced at the cover. It said: "BDL Book," and in Sheila's loopy handwriting, no less.

My breath stopped. Janice hadn't been saying "Beatle," but "BDL," like Kiki's best-dressed list. The best-dressed list Sheila and I used to pretend to be a part of when we were little kids. How *could* she? Kiki had busted her butt to get on that list, hiring tailors and organizing shopping trips around the world. No doubt she'd be amused when I told her who'd anointed herself a member, but I was more than a little angry. I had to suck on my cameo to keep from saying anything.

Every time somebody was done jotting something down, the girls would pass the book around and titter.

"What are you guys writing?" I asked after they'd all examined a particularly hilarious entry.

"We can't show you," Sheila said. "It's between us."

"Like she won't see it when it gets published?" said Janice.

"Well, how are we going to publish it as a secret diary if we show it to every Tom, Dick, and Harry?" Sheila shot back.

Janice turned to me. "You'll see. It's just a typical diary. We write about the things we do together."

"Or we'll just debate about something totally random," Ariel offered.

"Yeah," curly blond Lauren giggled. "Like the pros and cons of see-through bras."

"And sometimes we write about important stuff." Ariel sounded defensive.

"Like your insightful entry on how blond guys are more likely to develop bacne than dark-haired ones?" Sheila said.

They all sounded infinitely amused by their witty project,

though I was suddenly grateful that I wasn't allowed to participate. I'd wait till it hit the bestseller list.

After the book had made a few more rounds, Sheila took control. "Okay, everyone's done writing, right?" She handed the book to brown-haired Lauren, the one whose room we were in. "You can keep it this week. Are we up for a round of telephone?"

"When are we not?" Ariel pulled out a cell phone, her eyes agleam.

Had I entered some time warp where we were all back in third grade?

"No, use mine," brown-haired Lauren said. "It's caller ID blocked."

"Who's going first?" Sheila scanned the group and pushed the phone into Janice's hands. "You didn't go last time." Sheila might have sworn off her former life as a sword and sorcery enthusiast, but her aggressiveness had found a new outlet.

Janice seemed uncomfortable. "Not me. I don't have any ideas."

"No wiggling out," Sheila said. "Besides, I have an idea for you. Call Dimitri Ossuraf and tell him you think the Jets sweatshirt he wore to school every day last year was really sexy." She laughed in a way that sounded like a flutter of hiccups.

Suddenly, the anger I'd thought had passed flared back up in me. This shindig had seemed fine when it was some lame powwow you would expect of a group of sixth graders. But I wasn't prepared for it to take such a mean direction. There was no question about it—these girls were awful. I could just see it: they had been nerds all their lives and had only recently schooled themselves in the art of acting popular by watching bad Disney Channel movies.

Janice took a steadying breath, then dialed a number.

"Um, is this Dimitri?" Her voice was shaky, and she stuck her fist in her mouth to keep from making any giveaway sounds. "Hi, this is, um . . ." When she looked at me, she came up with her pseudonym. "Clara." She looked at the pretzel bowl. "Clara Pretz."

Talk about creative.

The other girls were enthralled by her performance, and Ariel went to sit closer to Janice so she could listen in. "I wanted to tell you . . . I just love your . . ." She started to laugh hysterically and hung up the phone. "I couldn't! I was dying!"

"Would anybody care to explain what's going on?" I asked, but they were all too busy laughing to respond.

They passed the phone, taking turns making equally bewildering calls. One girl was asked to come try out for a modeling agency, and curly blond Lauren left heavy breathing on her math teacher's answering machine.

Then it was Sheila's turn. "I'm going to call Ian Kitchen." She was hiccup-laughing again. "The kid with the wheelie suitcase."

"Him?" Ariel groaned with amusement. "He's, like, nine, right?"

"You'd die if you saw this kid, Claire," Sheila said. "He's always shuffling around the hallways by himself." She paused. "He's like a high school version of your little brother."

Was she trying to be nasty, or did it just come naturally to her?

"So he's a cool loner?" I tossed back.

Sheila put her finger over her lips, then pointed to the phone to indicate that she'd already dialed the number. "Hi, Ian? It's, uh, Nina, Nina Papagiornas, from Hudson. . . ." I

33

knew Nina Papagiornas—but not from Hudson. She was a curmudgeonly biology professor who lived in building one, down the hall from the Virds.

At least Sheila was a better actress than Janice. "You don't? Oh, my locker was near yours last year. Listen, I know this is kind of random, but do you want to go to John's for pizza? On Bleecker Street? . . . So I'll see you in half an hour."

Sheila's friends were laughing so hard they were gasping for air, and she had to take a deep bracing breath to resist joining them. I had to take one to resist screaming.

"I'll see you there," she said. "Oh, and Ian . . . can you bring your suitcase? I think it's hot." She hung up and rolled onto her back. She was wheezing and kicking her feet in the air. "I think I nearly had a heart attack there."

If only.

Kiki always warned me against leaving anything too abruptly, but I couldn't stay there a minute longer. I peeled myself off the floor and scooped up my helmet.

"I'm sorry," I told them. "I . . . I have to go."

"What?" Sheila retorted. "What about the party we're going to?"

"I just . . . ," I said, backing toward the door, "I'm just feeling really dizzy. I should probably go home before I pass out or something. Maybe next time."

By the way all the girls were looking at me, though, I knew there wouldn't be a next time.

{ 5 }

Dinner Date on Wheels

Back outside, I could breathe again. I unlocked my bike and charged down Riverside Drive. It was one of those mellow late-summer evenings, and all the restaurants had set up tables outside.

I turned off Seventh Avenue and was forced to slow down. Just ahead of me, a couple was flouting the pedestrians-belong-on-the-sidewalk rule and moseying down the street with their hands stuck in each other's butt pockets. The one advantage to my being so short was that there was little chance I'd ever end up walking around in that lovely pose. Who would ever be able to reach my back pocket without looking like a hunchback?

Ian Kitchen was instantly recognizable, and not because of his wheelie suitcase. Not only was he the only person standing outside John's by himself, but he was also reading a comic book and wearing an army coat that was two sizes too big for him. It was the kind of getup that would lend most guys an air of creepiness, but to see somebody that scrawny dressed up like a countercultural renegade was almost touching. I jumped off my bike and walked it over.

"Hey," I said. "Are you waiting for Nina?"

"Yeah?" he said, looking at me suspiciously. "That you?"

"Uh, I'm Claire." I proceeded to tell him the story I'd concocted on my way down. "Nina told me to meet you guys here, but then she had to cancel at the last minute, so it's just you and me."

He looked confused. "I don't get it. Is this some kind of joke?"

"Do I look like some kind of joke?" Remembering I still had my helmet on, I took it off.

"That's kind of a loaded question." He slouched and stuck his comic book in one of his front pockets.

The pizza parlor was too crowded, so we ended up going to Great Hong, a hole-in-the-wall Chinese restaurant just above a leather shop on Sixth Avenue. They were playing terrible Muzak, and I wouldn't have been surprised if a cockroach had come crawling out of the napkin dispenser. And yet, it was certainly better than sticking it out with the BDLs or going home early and trying to read a fashion magazine while my parents and their friends guzzled wine and played French Trivial Pursuit.

We placed our order and small-talked for a little bit. He seemed skeptical of me, and rightfully so. But after a few mouthfuls of fried rice he warmed up and asked me where I lived.

"Around here, in Washington View Village. You know that weird complex where all the NYU professors live?"

He shook his head.

"Right by the Angelika movie theater?"

He shook his head again.

"How can you live downtown and not know the *Angelika!*" I exclaimed. "It's the theater where they show all the foreign movies with beautiful landscapes and no plot."

He shrugged. "I guess I'm not much of an art house guy. I'm more into movies with zombies and superheroes."

"I see." I took a bite and thought his answer over.

"And let me guess. You're not."

"A superhero?" I smiled. "As if I'd give something like that away so easily."

"That's true. They usually wait a few scenes before revealing their powers."

I smiled. "And what about you? What's your superpower going to turn out to be?"

He took a few seconds to think it over. "I've always wanted to be able to lift cars and buildings, but that's probably not going to happen." He dropped his egg roll onto his plate and pushed up his shirtsleeve to show me his pencil-thin upper arm.

"Well," I said, trying to cover up my amusement, "I bet you're a beefcake by Hudson standards."

He looked confused. "I thought you said you went there."

"I'm about to," I explained. "I'll be an incoming sophomore."

He shot me a look of pity.

"What was that for? You don't love Hudson?"

He looked up at the ceiling and followed a fly that was moving around in circles. "*Love* is a strong word."

"You hate it?"

"There you go with another strong word."

He looked back at me and leaned in over the dish of General Tso's chicken. "It's just not my kind of place. Maybe it's because I watched too many cheesy movies, but I always thought high school would be the time when I'd make a zillion friends and some out-of-my-league girl would spend three years ignoring me and then realize that I was the one she had loved all along. I guess you could say I'm still waiting."

"For the girl to come to her senses?"

"More like the opening credits." He drained his tea. "But then again, it's unlikely you have the exact same fantasy. Maybe Hudson will be everything you wanted."

"Do they have a bunny farm?"

He shook his head ruefully.

"We'll see about me and Hudson."

After dinner, Ian walked me to the No Parking signpost I'd locked my bike to.

"Too bad Nina couldn't come," he said when I was crouched down.

My hands shook and I had to restart the combination. "Next time." I turned the dial to its final stop. When I came back up Ian was looking at me with a pleading expression.

"You know," he said, "last spring I got stood up by somebody named Vera whose locker was also close to mine—or supposed to be." He blinked hard. "I still haven't met her. You wouldn't happen to know her, too, would you?"

And in one instant I knew that he was a whole lot savvier than he'd let on.

"Oh boy," I said after an awkward pause. "Don't look at me for answers. I just came to have dinner."

"Fine, but I'm not an idiot. Who's setting me up?" He shifted his weight to his other foot. "I'm not going to say anything. I just need to know."

I looked into his watery brown eyes and knew I could trust him.

"It's Sheila Vird," I told him quietly. "Know her?"

He gave a small nod and stuck his hands in his pockets. By the way he was looking at me, I thought he was about to say something else, but he just waved goodbye and wheeled his suitcase into the sunset.

{ 6 }

Roll Out the Red Carpet for #6013V

Our kitchen is too small to comfortably pour a bowl of cereal, but for some reason it didn't feel so congested anymore. There was enough room for a deluxe kitchen island, and—get this—a number of trees bearing fruit were growing out of the floor. It was all so beautiful it almost didn't matter that the color was missing.

I was at the island, constructing a fruit salad that could qualify as high art. Suddenly possessed of fluent knife skills, I was hacking the gray strawberries into cartoony hearts and carving elaborate palm trees out of dull mangoes.

From a line of strangers that wound all the way around the apartment, people came in one by one to relieve me of my sculptures. Domestic goddess that I was, I continued to shake fruit from the trees and carve edible sailboats and suitcases and cathedrals for my fans. It was amazing—all I had to do was *think of something, and after a few deft knife strokes, I'd have a piece of fruit the exact same shape.*

I woke up on my first day of school a nervous wreck. It was a different kind of anxiety than I'd ever felt before—as if every cell in my body were ticklish. I nearly mistook Mom's L'Occitane spray deodorant for my hair spray, and it wasn't until my jeans were up around my knees that I realized I'd stepped into them backward. I must have tried on and ripped off every top I had while the ladies in the vintage *Vogue* cover posters on my wall looked down at me with compassion.

Henry Hudson High School was much bigger than I remembered, a five-story concrete fortress that was covered in fresh-looking graffiti. Outside, the students milled about in a big noisy blur. I spotted a familiar group of girls clad in yoga pants and hoop earrings. They were standing at the top of the stairs by the entrance, calling everybody by their names and welcoming them with huge fake smiles as if they were a Hawaiian airport lei service. Steeling myself with a big inhale, I climbed up the front steps and, with lowered eyes, filed into the building and through the metal detector.

"Everyone to your homerooms," a stout woman in a security uniform bleated into a megaphone. "Transfers to the auditorium." I followed her pointed finger through a doorway and down a hall with glass trophy cases and ancient dean's list plaques.

The auditorium reminded me of a cavernous old swimming pool, with its mulchy smell and peeling blue walls. I was terrified, though slightly calmed, to see that the other fifty or so transfers looked pretty scared themselves. Scanning the back row, I located one free seat on the end.

The room was quiet, and it came as something of a relief

when a man with an outrageous comb-over took the stage and got going on his welcome speech. He introduced himself as Dr. Arnold, the assistant principal.

"Incoming sophomores, congratulations," he said. If I couldn't see I would have thought he was pinching his nose. "You all got into Henry Hudson, one of America's most challenging high schools, land of the gifted and the brave. Give yourselves a round of applause." He backed away from the microphone and waited for our clapping to trickle out.

"Well done," he said finally. "But let me remind you, for every Henry Hudson graduate who goes on to the Ivy League, there are twice as many students who don't make it to graduation."

I wasn't a math whiz, but I had to wonder if that statistic was valid. I looked around and noticed that most of my fellow students appeared too scared to blink, let alone question his statement. I was pleased to see a pretty girl down at the other end of my row napping.

"Nobody coasts through Henry Hudson," Dr. Arnold told us, and rambled on about the "once-in-a-lifetime challenge" that lay ahead. I scanned the crowd in time to see the sleeping girl wake up and stare at him incredulously. My eyes raked her over. She had brown hair with bangs that came down to her eyebrows, and when she raised her hand to cover up a yawn, I saw she had a thick silver ring with a big old-fashioned airplane on it.

"It's up to you," Dr. Arnold went on. "You can soar or you can fall. You can report to your homerooms." Nobody budged. Dr. Arnold leaned into the podium. "That means you're excused."

In no time, the other kids had pulled slips of paper out of their backpacks and pockets and scuttled off. I would have, too, if only I'd known where I was supposed to go. I'm not exaggerating when I say I was the only kid who didn't have a homeroom assignment postcard. It must have been the missing piece of mail Mom had mentioned the day we came back from France. I wanted to kill her.

I was left to wander the emptying halls, trying not to look lost. I rounded a corner only to nearly collide with a scary security guard who was yelling at the few stray students. Not wanting to get into trouble, I slipped into a stairwell. As I made my way up to the second floor, I saw the sleeping girl with the airplane ring sitting at the top of the landing. She was wearing the coolest pair of tall black boots with military-style buttons up the sides. I could tell she didn't want to be bothered, but just as I was about to slip through the door to the second floor, we smiled at each other and I felt a surge of happiness. Even if we didn't actually *say* anything, I'd take what I could get.

I floated around the second floor until I found an administration office. It contained little more than two desks and a cheesy poster depicting three floppy-eared puppies in a hot-air balloon, with a series of clouds overhead spelling out LET'S LEARN! A far cry from the racy Paul Gauguin nudes that decorated the walls at Farmhouse.

"Excuse me," I said, edging closer to the sole person in the room, an old lady with a hearing aid and messily applied coral lipstick. She looked up from her New York Times Magazine and watched me dispassionately while I explained my plight.

"Student ID number?"

"I don't know that either," I said. "All I got from this place was a note about the new metal detectors."

She made a sucking noise while retaining her mouth's tight scowl. It was quite the feat. "I'll need your student ID number. There are more than seven thousand students in the system."

"Are you sure my name isn't in the system?"

"I can try," she sounded exasperated. "Last name?"

Even though my last name is only seven letters long, she pressed at least fifty buttons on her computer. I was growing more impatient by the second, and a few minutes into my wait I couldn't resist gnawing on my fingernails. "Student ID number 6013V," she said at last. "Homeroom 3P. Do you want me to write that down for you?"

What a welcoming place.

Homeroom 3P was on the third floor in a chemistry lab whose windows started ten feet from the floor. I wondered if this was to keep the rest of the world from looking in or to keep us from looking out.

"Voyante?" asked the teacher, a tall man with thin hips and an improbable potbelly. "We were wondering what happened to you."

The redhead in the back row turned around to stare right through me. Now I knew what it felt like to wear a bodysuit of goose bumps. But then Sheila's mouth moved in what I could only interpret as a smile, and the world became a whole lot warmer.

The teacher handed me student 6013V's schedule. It was your standard sophomore-year fare: math, PE, homeroom, lunch, English, chemistry, global studies, French 2, and music appreciation. The classes met in the same order Monday through Friday—which meant I'd be sweating in gym class from 9:12 to 10:04 every single morning. Joy. Also, I only had five minutes to get to my next class, which meant there was no time for a postgym shower. Olfactory joy to the entire world. The final insult: I got dealt the earliest lunch period possible, at the ripe hour of ten-twenty-five.

I made my way to the only free seat in the room, front and center. I tried to pull my chair out from my desk only to learn it was bolted to the floor. "Hudson's no wrestling rule applies to the furniture, too," the teacher said over his shoulder.

And it probably also applied to faculty. Too bad.

All day long I was waiting for something good to happen. And all day long it didn't. The kids in the hallways seemed to be too preoccupied with being reunited with their old friends to acknowledge the new girl. And the teachers didn't even ask us what we did over the summer. Instead, they filled the time laying out seating arrangements and formulas for our final grades.

And then, at the end of the day, when I was getting my stuff from my locker and doing everything I could not to cry over my newfound invisibility, I heard the most beautiful sound.

"Hey, Claire."

Sheila was standing just a few feet away, her hair shellacked into a tight bun. Her quartet of friends hovered behind her, staring at me with more interest than ever before.

"Hi!" I had to struggle to hold back from thanking them for acknowledging my existence.

"You feeling better?" Sheila asked.

"Yeah, thanks." I stuffed my French workbook into my black and white striped tote bag.

"What was wrong with you again?"

"Just a headache," I fudged. "So how was the party? Late night?"

I could hear myself talking at double speed, the way I always do when I'm keyed up.

Sheila didn't dignify my question with an answer. "I was

just wondering something. I know you went home because you were feeling dizzy. What did you end up doing?" Her face was a funny shade of rose, and she wasn't blinking. At all.

I scanned the other girls' faces and saw that they were wearing the same icy expression. My heart lurched to my throat. Just because I didn't like them didn't mean I didn't want them to like me, and I certainly hadn't made enough friends here to start collecting enemies.

"At home? I don't know." I scrunched up my face. "I guess I just watched TV and read magazines. Why?"

"Oh, well, my mom was over at your place Friday night, and she said she didn't see you." Sheila squinted at me. "And she was there until pretty late. So unless she was really drunk or something . . ."

I laughed nervously. Not because she was right about her mom—though she probably was—but because I didn't have an alibi. "Well, I didn't go *straight* home. I—"

"I see," Sheila said sharply. "You didn't want to hang out with us and you didn't want to be rude. You've always been so conscientious about manners." She turned around to whisper something to her posse, and they all wagged their heads. "You won't have to worry about our feelings again. . . . We're not really planning on inviting you to anything in the next little while. And by *little while*"—she paused, taking her time to bite back a smile—"we mean *ever*."

Sheila tapped her sneaker on the ground and glared at me. I needed to think of something good—and fast. But the only thing that came to mind was the word *whatever*, a rejoinder that wasn't going to go the distance for me. And as if in slow motion, the girls removed their hands from their outthrust hips and turned around, leaving me in the dust.

"Wait!" I said to the space they'd been standing in. "Aren't you going to let me come up with a witty reply?"

But they'd walked off so fast they didn't even hear my lame comeback, if you can call it that. Demoralized, I leaned against a locker and started to slide down to the floor.

"I wouldn't worry about it," a chubby girl said, crouching down to join me. "Anything you said would have been lost on them anyway. They're a bunch of fools."

"I know." I sank even farther. "That's what scares me."

When I got home that day, I didn't say a word. I just put my *A Murder Is Announced* DVD on in the living area and plopped down on the couch for a much-needed session of self-pity. Mom and Dad must have been able to smell my misery: they didn't bug me about doing homework, and every so often Mom would come by the couch to make sure I hadn't strangled myself with her crocheted throw.

By dinnertime, they'd had enough of their own patience. They were ready to get the scoop. I was enjoying my first bite of creamed spinach and ham and cheese quiche when they launched their assault.

"I can tell you're not ready to talk, Claire, but the suspense is killing me," Mom said. "How was it?"

I shrugged.

"Give it time, *ma petite!*" Dad cut in, tipping a bottle of red wine into his favorite mason jar. "This is going to be a banner year. Hudson is a first-rate school, and you will love it. Did you know that the secretary of defense is an alum and they have more National Merit Scholars every year than . . ."

As Dad prattled on, citing Hudson's "high-caliber" alumni and "unrivaled contributions" to the scientific community, I stared at my plate, watching my mound of spinach turn cold and waxy.

I just had to take matters into my own hands. I could run away and join the circus—maybe there was an opening for a nonbearded lady. I could buy an armful of creepy self-help books. Or I could bite the bullet and make a friend or two.

Kiki was always encouraging me to stop waiting for people to introduce themselves to me. "What's the matter with your generation?" she'd say. "Introducing yourself is the easiest thing on earth. Just say, 'Hello, I'm Kiki Merriman and I'm a friend of Trudie's,' or, 'Hello, I like to eat lobster thermidor in the nude.' It doesn't really matter how you break the ice so long as you break it."

Assaulting strangers wasn't exactly my thing, or at least it hadn't been back when I'd had a choice. But I had to accept that that might not be the case anymore. Right then and there, as I glanced up at my parents' pitying looks, I resolved to change my tack.

At lunch the following day, I hastily scanned the cafeteria for the girl with the airplane ring before sitting down with three other girls.

"Hi," I said. "My name is Claire and I just transferred here."

"Hey," said a pretty girl with long hair and an eyebrow ring. She gave me the once-over before turning back to her friends and resuming their conversation. I knew I should have said something else—I could have asked what their names were or even for some advice about Hudson—but I was too uncomfortable and embarrassed, and I finished eating quickly and spent the rest of the period in the bathroom, pretending to fix my hair while working out a very important calculation.

Only 1,095 days until college.

{ 7 }

A Curious Incident on
the Thirty-eighth Floor

"I'm sorry I'm late!" I rasped when I hustled into Kiki's apartment on Saturday, twenty minutes behind schedule. I'd run all the way from the subway station—and not only because Kiki hated it when I was late. I'd barely made it through the week at Hudson, and never had I been so desperate for a visit with my favorite person on earth.

Someone had left the door open a crack, and through a forest of balloons I saw my grandmother and her four best friends clustered on the damask couches in the back of the room.

"The F train got messed up," I explained, preemptively thwarting any guilt trips. "Some lady tried to throw herself on the subway tracks."

"Life can be overrated," Kiki's friend Clem Zwart sighed. Clem is a melancholic man with a long white beard and a soft spot for silver biker jewelry. He used to be the errand boy at Andy Warhol's silver-walled Factory, and now he works as an interior decorator for Fifth Avenue ladies. His specialty is silver bathrooms. Clustered around Clem was the rest of Kiki's gang: Edie Wilcox, Kiki's oldest friend; Edie's unbelievably boring husband, John; and George Jupiter, who used to be the hotel's resident piano player.

"The subways are such an inconvenience—I don't see why anyone bothers with them!" Kiki hollered. She didn't sound too mad at me. My heart swelled with relief. Kiki rose to her feet and raised her arms. "Well, what are we waiting for, mademoiselle? Come and let me see my favorite grandchild up close."

I shrugged off my jean jacket and smiled at the ground, trying not to let it show how great it was to hear, for the umpteen-thousandth time, that I was her number one. It made her feel a little guilty to prefer me to Henry, and she often made sure to justify her favoritism by saying I was her only grandchild who will sit pretty while she drinks cocktails and gossips about dead people. "Boys are hard," she'd say. "They become interesting around their sixty-fifth birthday."

I started my approach, but it was cut short. "Fix yourself a drink, dear," she instructed.

So I turned back around and headed for the sideboard. Next to a pile of newspapers whose typos Kiki had corrected in red ink, I saw an ice bucket, a crystal glass, and a bottle of Orangina—my favorite.

Drink in hand, I joined the gang. The sun was sitting low against the skyline, and the silhouette of Clem's beard blended in nicely with the clouds. It had been a while since I'd seen Kiki, and she looked exactly the same, with her blond bob and a hint of a smile that suggested she was up to no good.

"Let's have a hug." Kiki put down her martini glass and wrapped her arms around me. Her body felt solid and her hands were cool on the back of my neck. "No need to hunch, my love. A little posture goes a long way."

I adjusted my shoulders and imagined that strings were pulling them up, as Kiki had recommended countless times.

"There you go! Now, that's what I call beautiful carriage!"

"Can we just call it 'not slouching'?" I asked her. "*Carriage* makes it sound like I'm being pulled around by a horse."

Laughter came from the shadows. Only then did I see a familiar nest of auburn curls. Slouched in an armchair and holding Kiki's ages-old IF YOU DON'T HAVE ANYTHING NICE TO SAY, THEN SIT BY ME needlepoint pillow was Louis, my one remaining friend from Farmhouse. He was wearing a jacket and tie, and instead of the wire-rim glasses he'd worn ever since I could remember, he had on a pair of heavy tortoiseshell frames. There was no question they were more attractive, but I missed his old glasses, the ones that used to fog up all the time. He'd even invented a character called the Man with No Eyes who would walk into walls and mistake armoires and coatracks for his girlfriend.

"When you stand like that, you remind me of Frankenstein," he teased me.

"If it isn't the crab apple of the Upper West Side," I answered with a smirk. It was all I could do to keep my excitement in check.

"Seriously," Louis said, still laughing. "You look like you just sat on something painful."

"Are you feeling left out?" I asked sweetly. "I can give you something painful to sit on." I looked around for a candle-stick, but there was none on hand.

"That's all hooey. Pay him no mind," Kiki told me. "You look smashing."

"Thank you." I gave Louis a pointed look.

"Who are you wearing?" This was Kiki's way of asking who had designed my dress. Not that she needed to. Ninety-nine percent of my clothes came from her closets.

Kiki has boatloads of stunning clothes from her Inter-national Best-Dressed List days (1963 to 1967)—Givenchy dresses, Halston coats, Yves Saint Laurent jackets—most of which she can no longer fit into. Luckily, there was somebody who could. Tonight I was helping her resurrect an old red hal-ter cocktail dress. It was perfect except for its high neck, which covered my new necklace.

"Still waiting," Kiki remarked.

"Um . . . ," I said, racking my brains. I'd seen the tag just hours ago, but sadly, my visionary powers did not extend to photographic memory. "Balenciaga?"

"For shame!" Kiki pshawed. "That's an Yves Saint Laurent original. And if memory serves, I wore it to Babe Parkhurst's fiftieth birthday party."

"Which one of her fiftieth birthday parties?" Clem asked with a chuckle. "The one in '65, '66, '67, or '68?"

"Oh, there weren't that many," Edie twittered.

"Maybe she was born on a leap year," Louis offered.

"Ha!" Kiki yelped.

Kiki used to be a big-deal socialite. And you wouldn't nec-essarily know by looking at her now, but she was also a cele-brated beauty—she was dubbed "the Gazelle" by the New York Herald Tribune. She still has the peacock-feather mask she wore to Truman Capote's Black and White Ball and pictures from her nights at Frank Sinatra's al fresco parties upstairs on the hotel's Starlight Roof. Still, she doesn't like to indulge her nostalgia. The last time she pulled out the bird mask for me, she was quick to point out that it smelled like the bottom of a pigeon coop. How she knew, I had no idea.

Once upon a time, back when Kiki was a Broadway showgirl, she and her mother, Clarissa, lived at Mildred Terrace, a residence for women in Hell's Kitchen. During a fateful Friday-night performance, Kiki caught the eye of a certain gentleman in the third row. Only two months later, she handed in her showgirl costume and married Joseph Merriman, my grandfather. As the wife of a diplomat, Kiki had to move to the capital, where she needed to consult *Things to Do and Things to Don't*, Washington's protocol guidebook, every time she wanted to open her mouth.

Kiki could only take so much of trying to memorize gift-giving and place-setting rules and cunningly told my grandfather that a pied-à-terre at the Waldorf Hotel, an Art Deco palace on Park Avenue, would be good for his "professional prospects." After a few weekends in their new suite, Kiki pretty much took up residence there. My grandfather died when I was three, and Kiki wasted no time in selling the D.C. home.

"Will somebody get a chair for the birthday girl?" John wondered aloud.

"I'm okay," I said, squeezing onto the couch between him and his wife. "It's cozy this way."

"I forgot!" George cried. "It's your birthday." He began to croon the birthday song. His voice was a little wobbly, and I tried to cut him off with applause, but he kept singing until the end.

George Jupiter (né Jaeweschi) inherited a suite on the

thirty-eighth floor when its sole inhabitant, a lonely auto magnate who lived for George's lobby piano performances, had a heart attack.

"Happy birthday, lamb chop," Edie peeped in her Betty Boop voice. Edie Wilcox and my grandmother had met back when they were both in the chorus of "Coney Island Follies." They drifted apart when my grandmother got married, though not for long: Kiki persuaded Edie to move into the hotel when Edie married John, a wealthy ad man who only got excited when speaking on the subject of avoiding toxins. Most of the time Edie seemed to be too busy gossiping to mind her husband's dull conversation.

"Well, what now?" Kiki asked. "Down to Peacock Alley for cake?"

Kiki is the hotel's formal restaurant's most loyal customer. Without her, it would have gone out of business long ago. To tell the truth, I sort of wish it had. There's a difference between fancy and stodgy, and Peacock Alley is pushing the limits.

"How about room service?" I asked.

"What is it with you and having your food rolled in on a trolley?" Edie tweeted.

"It tastes better that way," I said.

"You know it always gets here cold," Kiki tut-tutted.

"But it is Claire's birthday . . . ," said George.

"Well, technically it was a month ago," Louis pointed out.

"Ignore him," I said to Kiki. "Oh, can we, please?"

"Go on, then," she moaned. "Why is it that I can deny you nothing?"

Sometimes I wonder how different things would be if Mom and Kiki were on good terms. Or even semidecent terms. Though I probably shouldn't admit this, I'm kind of glad they aren't. There's no way I would get away with half as much as I do.

"Well, what are you waiting for?" Kiki said after calling down our order. "There's a table of presents that need to be opened."

"Oh, you shouldn't have!" I tried to sound as though I meant it.

Louis rolled his eyes at me and whispered, "You're shameless." I ignored him and skittered across the room to pour myself another Orangina.

When I came back, I started with Louis's present, a pair of yellow terrycloth wristbands. He cringed when I showed everyone his gift—which he'd obviously picked up at his tennis club at the last minute. With all his shrink appointments and tennis classes, Louis was busier than anybody I knew.

Edie was the only one who could muster a response. "Yellow is such a good color for you, Claire! So . . . brightening."

"Thanks, Louis," I said, examining them more closely. "They're very . . . stretchy?"

I looked over at Louis, who was smiling into the middle distance. I could tell how uncomfortable he was by how fast he was tapping his foot. I'm a sucker for Louis when he gets all awkward and bothered. He starts to look lost and skinny, like a runaway pet.

"I know, I know, I'm a terrible friend, but I'm not the only one." Louis was blushing profusely. "Remember the Statue of Liberty cookie cutter you got me last year?"

"I thought it was cute." I held down my laughter. I'd stayed up late the night before making a Motown mix on iTunes that was going to take up five CDs, but midway through burning disc three, my computer decided to crash, and I ended up having to run down the block to the Associated Supermarket to pick out a gift. "I also gave you that apron," I reminded him.

"Sure did." He looked at me over the frames of his glasses. " 'Kiss the cook.' And women's sized, I might add."

"What are you talking about? Aprons are unisex."

"Most are, but not that one. No worries. I'm comfortable with my masculinity."

"Why don't you two make up for lousy birthday presents and go to a basketball game?" Kiki suggested. "You can get seats, can't you, Louis? And Claire can buy the sandwiches."

"Sure." He shrugged.

Everyone else started oohing and aahing, but I could tell Louis was bluffing. Even though his dad is the general manager of the New York Knicks, Louis never asks him for things like that. In Louis's household, there's an unspoken rule that all favors are reserved for Louis's stepmother, Ulrika, the Swedish spa receptionist Mr. Ibbits married the year after Louis's mom died in a plane crash.

"Basketball would be totally wasted on me," I muttered to him. I didn't want him to worry about it. "Just promise you'll come visit me at Hudson sometime," I added under my breath.

"I'll see what I can do, Lemonhead."

I opened the rest of my presents—a Kate Spade wallet from Edie and John, a Dean Martin CD from George, and a watermelon-sized silver lump from Clem.

"It's an original disco blob," he told me. "More organically shaped than the typical disco ball. A collector's item—I used to sell them to Bianca Jagger and her set."

I was so busy admiring Clem's handiwork I didn't notice that Kiki had gotten up to open the door for our molten chocolate cakes.

She fingered the top of one and frowned. "They're room temperature."

"I'll microwave them," Louis offered.

"Not mine," John said, suddenly energized. "Don't trust invisible waves."

Louis shot me a look, and I had to bite my lip not to laugh as I got up to join him in Kiki's "kitchen"—a sink, a mini-refrigerator, a microwave, and Kiki's personal stash of electric kettles, toasters, and Crock-Pots.

"What about television?" Louis asked John from across the room. "Do you trust those invisible waves?"

"That's different," John said dismissively. "Though I won't watch prime-time network programming. Toxic in its own way."

"Convenient logic," I whispered to Louis. "Kiki told me that John is addicted to soaps. He watches them when he does his morning stretches."

Louis considered this. "I think that makes me like him a little bit more."

"I know what you mean."

"So?" Kiki said once we'd all gathered around the table and tucked into our birthday cakes. "You left for France two months ago. You must have something amusing to tell us."

I sifted through my reserves of anecdotes and shared a few, in increasingly scandalous order. I started off telling them about how I'd come in second at the teen dance contest at La Goulue, an outdoor disco named after a famous cancan dancer, and ended with how I found my Aunt Ségolène in a closet feeding Nutella to her supposedly gay work friend Jacques.

"Can't eat that stuff," John shared, glossing over the interesting part of the story. "I'm allergic to nuts."

"And how'd your brother get on?" Kiki asked, steamrolling over her friend's dud of a husband.

"Fine. He can read chapter books in French, so he stayed pretty busy."

"So bright, that boy." Kiki smiled. "And how are you getting on at this new school of yours?"

Why did she have to ruin my birthday party and bring up Hudson? I put down my fork and looked at the ceiling, trying to figure out how to phrase it.

"That great?" asked Louis.

"Let's see. Lobotomized teachers, metal detectors, and students who are so competitive they cry if they only get a ninety-four percent. But I'm optimistic." Everyone around the table started to smile at me, until I completed my thought. "I might flunk out."

"Don't say that!" Edie peeped.

"I wouldn't get your hopes up, dear," Kiki said knowingly. She looked at me the way she does when she's waiting for me to figure out something that's obvious to the rest of the world.

"You might warm up to the place," Edie said feebly.

"Yeah, and the place might warm up to me."

A sense of seriousness settled over the room as we finished our cakes.

"Well, you can't be a recluse forever," Kiki said when I was done with my last bite. "Let's go downstairs for a moment. Shall we?" She took hold of my arm and dragged me out of my chair and toward the hallway.

"What about everybody else?" I protested after the door had shut behind us.

"Oh, they can look after themselves for ten minutes. I wanted some private time with my granddaughter on her quasi-birthday. Is that so terrible?"

"Depends on what you want to talk to me about."

When we got downstairs, the big Art Deco clock in the

lobby said it was a little after eight-thirty, and the lounge was jumping. Everyone was gussied up, and it smelled of vacuum cleaning and new clothes.

Kiki put in our order with the maitre d' while we waited for our balcony table to be set.

"Um, do you want to explain why you kidnapped me from my party?" I asked. Kiki raised her hand and waited until the piano player had finished a song about putting all his eggs in one basket.

"I bet you don't even know that song. It was an old Fred Astaire number. Your grandfather was crazy about it."

"Really? What other music did he like?"

Apart from the fact that he was a big-shot diplomat who liked to get down on the dance floor, I knew pathetically little about my grandfather.

"Now, there was something I wanted to talk to you about," she went on, chatting away as if she hadn't heard a word I'd said. "The necklace I sent you . . ."

A dark expression crossed her face, and my heart started to pound. I felt like such a jerk—how could I have forgotten to send her a thank-you note? Kiki was an etiquette fanatic.

"Kiki," I said, my cheeks crimsoning, "I can't believe I didn't send you a card. It's just with school starting, it must have totally—"

She shook her head and chuckled. "Is that what you think this is about? I do expect a note, but that's not why I brought you down here." She reached over the table to pull my necklace out from under the dress. "I wanted to talk to you about the present. You should know it's no ordinary trinket."

"Obviously." I reached up to pull it out. "I've never seen anything like it before."

My words seemed to please her. "That's because there is

nothing else like it. Now, if you lose it, I'll be beside myself with sorrow."

"I won't. When I don't wear it, I'll keep it tucked away in my secret hiding spot." Kiki knew about the back corner of my underwear drawer.

"No, no, no, don't stash it away with those old potpourri sachets. It'll absorb that wretched smell. Promise me that you'll wear it at all times. And pay close attention."

"For thieves?"

"Thieves are the least of my worries. My point is, when I wore that necklace, well, all my dreams started to come true."

Now I was starting to understand why the necklace held a special significance for her. "And that's when you started to dance on Broadway?"

Her gray eyes glimmered in a way I'd never seen before, and she shook her head unsteadily. "Just promise me this: I want you to pay attention to your dreams. I'd be most surprised if they didn't lead you somewhere interesting. Don't let them waft away, you hear?"

Just then, a waiter's arm inserted itself between us and plunked another miniature round cake on the table.

"Oh, will you look at that!" she said, sounding like her normal self again. She tapped the top of the cake. "Now, this time it's warm, as it should be. Hurry up before it gets cold!"

The chocolate steam smelled delicious. I used my fork to shave off some cake and release the oozy center.

"How is it?" she asked after my first bite.

"Out of this world," I told her, feeling weak from the most heavenly mouthful I'd had since . . . fifteen minutes earlier.

"Out of this world," Kiki repeated, and let out a pleasant, almost fluttery sigh and eyed my necklace pointedly. "Yes, that is rather a good way to describe it."

I'd grown used to all of Kiki's sides—bossy, charming, flirtatious, melodramatic, and so on—but I wasn't used to this vagueness. I hoped it didn't mean she was coming down with a brain tumor or something.

"Oh, what was I thinking?" She lunged at me and tucked a napkin into my neckline. "Be careful or you'll smudge it!"

{ 8 }

A League of Our Own

Henry Hudson High School was guilty of many things, but unpredictability was not one of them. At 10:10 every morning without fail, Dr. Arnold made his daily homeroom announcement. His voice would come through the loudspeakers, and he would tell us about the upcoming fire drill or how to sign up for a flu shot. On the Wednesday of our second week of school, after letting us know about a ribbon cutting for the new Shuttleworth chemistry lab, he urged us to check out the Henry Hudson activities fair. "Sports, science, music, religion, debate. Clubs of all shapes and sizes. Come build your third dimension!"

At Farmhouse I had belonged to the Supper Club, a monthly dining society that invited special guests, and I was hoping to find a similar group at Hudson. But on Wednesday morning, when I trudged down to the cafeteria for my ten-twenty-five lunch (or was it brunch?), none of the club tables that had been set up by the cash registers—yearbook, blood drive, juvenile obesity foundation—looked remotely fun.

I made my way to my new regular table. A few days earlier, I'd found out that Ian Kitchen had the same lunch period as me. And it turned out he wasn't quite as lonely as he'd led me to believe: he sat at a back table in a crook by the recycling area with his friends Zach and Eleanor. Zach belonged to the Hudson JV football team, but he seemed more like a member of the Boy Scouts than any organized sports team. He maintained an aggressively sunny disposition; he actually claimed to like Henry Hudson—though Ian said this was because it was the only school where a five-foot-tall kid could make it onto the football team. Eleanor had thick black hair, thicker black glasses, and a unique ability to stay engaged in a conversation while not saying a single word. There was a palpable intensity to her, and our table's energy would droop every time she got up to buy a cookie or to pee.

"You going to sign up for anything?" Zach asked me when I sat down.

I told him I hadn't really thought about it.

"I can't do much because of football, but you should," he said. "There are some amazing clubs. Young Philosophers, Model UN, the Happiness League."

"What's that?" I asked, suddenly curious.

"They commit random acts of kindness to make Hudson a more cheerful place," Ian told me.

"Sounds like a worthwhile cause," I said. "Though considering how grim it is around here, I'm not sure they're doing a very good job."

"Baby steps," Ian said.

"So what do they do? Bring us new shoes and ice cream sundaes?"

Ian laughed. "What part of 'New York City public school' do you not understand? You're in the land of budget cuts. Or have you not been drinking from the same rusty water fountains as the rest of us?"

Eleanor made a disgusted face.

"The Happiness League has to make do," Ian said. "See?" He pointed to a pale pastel drawing of a rainbow hanging at a crooked angle on the wall. "They brought you that."

"Oh," I said, cocking my head to consider the artwork. I kept looking, waiting for the happiness to kick in.

Eventually, I gave up and got back to work on my lunch— leftover beet salad and lemon chicken that probably would've tasted good at a normal hour.

"Hey," I said a few minutes later. I was ready to ask the question I'd planned on my bike ride to school that morning. "Do any of you guys want to hang out this afternoon? There's a cool Italian ice place I heard about right by school."

Zach coughed and the other two froze.

"Or not!" I said.

"Don't take it personally," Ian said. "It's just not gonna happen. Zach always has football practice, I draw in the afternoons, and, well." He paused to nod at Eleanor. "She doesn't really do after-school hobnobbing."

Our quiet companion shook her head resolutely.

"But things can change," Ian assured me. "Give it time."

I threw him a disappointed look. Even though the sole occasion on which I'd tried to have a one-on-one conversation with Eleanor had been the most awkward social experiment of my life, I felt bummed. If persuading my new friends to join me for an Italian ice was something that would require more patience, we obviously didn't have much of a future. By the time they were ready to come to my place for dinner, our teeth would be too loose to enjoy Mom's *pommes frites*.

As if able to read my thoughts, Ian cocked his head and looked at me sweetly. "It's nothing personal. It's just how things are done here."

In music appreciation, my last class of the day, all I could do was stare at the bell and wait for its beautiful mosquito-buzz sound. At last, I ran down the back stairwell, the fastest route to the outside world and my bike, and I zipped through our school's first floor. Well, I zipped through the first few inches of it.

The lobby was as crowded as Ben & Jerry's on free cone day. Student groups had set up tables everywhere, though it was an older kid in a backwards baseball hat who was attracting the most attention. Inching closer, I overheard him promise a ring of potential customers that his "Payoff Guide" was well worth the five dollars. "We've compiled data on time required, potential awards, and the colleges each student group feeds," he announced. "For instance, I bet you don't know only one-eleventh of participants in student government go on to the Ivy League. As it happens, the Student Improv League has a much greater success rate."

I heard a round of gasps, and then a girl thrust a five-dollar bill at him. That girl, I realized, was the brown-haired Lauren. She must have sensed me lurking behind her. She turned around to glare at me and as I was loping away, I could have sworn I heard a deranged cat hiss.

The Happiness League had set up shop on the far end of the lobby, near the double doors to the gym. The yellow smiley face buttons that had been scattered over the table only served to underscore how unhappy the pair of club officials looked. The girl was frowning and pulling at a hole in her shirtsleeve. Her companion, a pasty-looking guy with orange hair that grew out of his head like foam, was watching a prospective club member flip through a binder.

I installed myself a few feet away from the table, close enough to see everything without having to join the conversation. I must have stood there for an entire minute before the most important fact hit me: the person flipping through the binder was the girl I'd been on the lookout for. Her face was practically curtained off by her long dark waves but I recognized the airplane ring—though it had moved to her other hand. She was dressed in a short-sleeved white sweater and a pair of jeans with a hole in the knee. By far the highlight of her outfit was her tan riding boots with dark brown wingtips. If only we were friends. And the same shoe size.

Going closer, I saw that she was taller and prettier than I'd remembered. With her rosy skin and delicate features, she reminded me of a child you'd see in one of those old Dutch paintings, sitting next to a water jug or a bowl of miniature pears.

"You should come to our meeting," the guy said to her, giving her a piece of paper.

"And you, too." He thrust the same flyer in my direction.

"Me?" I hadn't realized I was close enough to be noticed. I guess feeling invisible only works when you don't want it to.

The girl kept studying the flyer, and I realized I should look at mine. The last thing I wanted was to be charged with creepiness.

Happiness League. Room 705. Wednesdays. 3:30. Be there. Or despair.

"I don't get it," the girl said to the guy behind the table.

Her tone was matter-of-fact, and her voice was louder than I'd expected. "This is an official Hudson extracurricular?"

"Worth two extra credits," he responded. "That's as many as Paintball Physics and Welsh Clog Dancing."

"If only the Happiness League burned as many calories," I murmured.

The girl laughed, and the guy gave us the sad-eyed smile of a mime. "That's beside the point," he said. "What other club can give you the opportunity to bring joy to the world of Hudson? You two should sign up." He thrust out a clipboard. "Not to pressure you."

Ring Girl took a tiny step back. "Um, maybe later. I'm still shopping around."

"Me too," I added, "but it's high on my list."

The guy's face drooped and the clipboard fell to his side. "Don't turn happiness away."

"Thanks for the advice." The girl turned around and moved on without a second glance, leaving me to withstand the guy's philosophizing on my own.

"Why just be satisfied when you could be in seventh heaven?" He sniffled at me. "Why embrace contentment when you could . . ."

His words flattened out. How could I pay attention when the unbelievable was happening? The girl did a one-eighty and looked straight at me.

"What's the deal? You coming or what?"

"Me?" I asked unsurely.

"I thought we were activity shopping together."

"Sorry," I told the guy behind the table, trying to hold back a smile as I jerked ahead to catch up with her.

"What do I owe you?" I said when I'd reached her side. "I'm so bad at getting out of boring conversations."

"I hear you." She wended to the right to avoid bumping into a hand that was jutting out of the Chaos Theory Society's human pyramid, a maneuver that made her temporarily lose her balance. "That Prozac candidate kept me there for, like, fifteen minutes," she said, still wobbling.

I started to laugh.

"I know, I don't exactly have the grace of a ballerina."

"No," I said. "I was thinking of that guy. How weird is it that the Happiness League is run by somebody so . . . suicidal?"

"Who isn't at this school?" she asked dryly.

"So you're not completely sold on the Hudson experience?" I prodded. Until now, I'd felt alone in my misery here.

"You could say I have issues with it." She raised an eyebrow ever so slightly.

"You don't like having teachers who don't know your name?" I asked.

She smiled, probably at the realization that she'd found likeminded company. I had to put myself in a mental straitjacket to keep from hugging her. "Oh, it's the best," she said. "And I'm also a huge fan of the computers that read our essays. Why get graded on your ideas or writing style when a machine can measure your word count?"

"I can't believe it." I looked up at the ceiling, my heart skipping giddily. "Here I was thinking I was going crazy."

"I never said anything about not being crazy. I'm just not crazy about this place."

She turned around and led me up another row.

"The Zombie Club!" she cried, quickening her steps to approach a table. But as soon as she realized that ZOMBIE was a half-assed acronym for an environmental club—Zany Or Monotonous, we Believe In the Environment—she rolled her eyes and kept walking. She slowed down again to look at

Whatsits, a club that built mechanical toys out of discarded computer parts. A mechanical unicorn was galloping in place, and next to it was a one-eyed fur ball on roller skates. I was about to lean in to get a better look when the fur ball's stomach popped open to reveal a figurine that looked exactly like Dr. Arnold, hideous comb-over and all.

"League of the gifted and the brave," the mechanical Dr. Arnold said, and then the door shut.

Ring Girl grabbed my arm and jumped back. "Did you just see that? Is that the freakiest thing ever?"

Ever? Not if you include my dreams.

But I just stared at the beast and nodded.

"I kind of like it," she said.

"It's *unique*," I agreed.

"Excuse me," my new friend said to the Whatsits ambassador behind the table. "Is that for sale?"

"We don't put up any of our work—" he started to respond, but just then a kid elbowed his way in front of us.

"Quick survey," he squeaked. "In your opinion, who has more success placing students at MIT, Whatsits or the Robotics League?"

"That's tough to say," the kid manning the table replied with a straight face. "The short answer is, percentage-wise, we send more people to MIT than the Robotics League does. The long answer is, there's no causality. We have very rigorous standards, and in order to participate in our organization, you need to already be a highly functioning engineer."

"Wanna go to the land of low-functioning regular people?" I whispered to the girl.

She wagged her head in the affirmative. "A gifted and brave suggestion."

When we got outside it was breezy. She reached into her

brown leather satchel for a red and white striped scarf and I put on my jean jacket.

"By the way, I'm Claire," I said, closing a top button.

"Becca." She stopped to think about something. "Hey, congratulations. I think you're the first person who's actually introduced themselves since I've started here."

My mind reeled back to Kiki's suggestion that I take the plunge and tell people I ate lobster thermidor in the nude. "Introductions aren't really in style around here, are they?" I asked.

"Not this season," she said.

She started walking toward Delancey Street, to get a subway, I assumed, and I followed, glancing back at the bike rack. One night away from my Schwinn wouldn't kill me.

"To be perfectly fair," she went on, "there are a few girls here who I already knew, but they're seniors and they probably don't want to be hanging around with some sophomore transfer. What's your story?"

"I'm actually a sophomore transfer, too."

"Yeah, I thought you looked familiar," she said. "So why'd you come here?"

"I took the test as an experiment and got in by mistake."

She eyed me curiously. "What do you mean you got in by mistake?"

"It means I should've known better than to put down the right answers. My parents decided they didn't want to keep paying for private school."

"Ouch. That sucks. My parents forced me, too."

"Where from?"

"I used to go to Houghton, this boarding school in Massachusetts."

"I've heard of it," I told her. "My grandmother Kiki has mentioned it. It's full of high-society types, right?"

"Not as much as its reputation would make you think, but sorta. Despite its stuffiness, I liked it, but at the end of last year, I got into a little bit of trouble. . . . My parents wanted me to be close to home so they could keep an eye on me."

I knew I shouldn't pry, but how could I not? Talk about dropping a scintillating detail into conversation.

"What happened?"

"Nothing major." She looked at the ground and pushed back a stray hank of hair. "I just snuck out one night too many. . . . Lucky for me, my dad had a connection at this mental asylum," she said, indicating the school building. "So here I am."

As we talked, her tone kept shifting—one second she'd seem fascinated by me, and the next she'd appear to be bored out of her mind. Coming from somebody else, it would probably have smacked of rudeness, but with her, I didn't see it that way. She was different than most kids our age—I guessed complicated was what you'd call it.

"Any chance you can talk your way back into your old school?" I asked.

"Nah, I have to be here—my parents and I struck a deal."

"What's in it for you?" I asked.

"My boyfriend's here. Plus I want to study opera. This way I get to take classes at Lincoln Center."

"Got it," I said, trying to sound as if I did. The closest I'd come to attending an opera was the time I let Clem and Kiki drag me to the Metropolitan Museum's Costume Institute. We saw a show of Plácido Domingo costumes that Clem had dubbed "Through Thick and Thin." As for having boyfriends, well, they figured into my two greatest fears. The first was running out of things to talk about. The other was making it to my college graduation without ever putting my phobia to the test.

71

"Hey." Becca looked at her watch—a simple white face on a black ribbon. "I'm supposed to meet my brother and his girlfriend in a little bit, but if you're hungry, there's a place I'm obsessed with that's on the way to my train."

I sensed she was more interested in getting a snack than she was in hanging out with me, but I went along. It wasn't as if I had anywhere else to go.

The Doughnut Plant was an old-fashioned bakery on Grand Street full of old-world touches like a gumball machine that only took pennies and a cash register that went *ka-ching!* I bought two of their specialty square jelly doughnuts—one for me, one to give to Henry. Becca bought a half dozen and started eating a doughnut before she'd paid. "I'm trying to build a layer of fatty tissue around my larynx," she told me. "My voice coach says I sound like a mouse."

"Is that bad?" I said, following her back onto the street. "I was once told I sound like a moose."

"I didn't know they made sounds."

"Seriously, my little brother saw this *Nature* video about moose mating calls. I guess they were raspy, because then he started calling me Moose Mouth."

"Aw, that's still kind of sweet," she said. "My brother was always way too busy being cool and aloof to make up nicknames for me. I spent a lot of my childhood playing with an imaginary brother named Tyrone."

I looked down at my chipped nails and smiled inwardly. She hated Hudson. She had an overactive imagination. What was she going to say next—that she had weirdo visions and the occasional strange black-and-white dream?

She stopped to admire the window of a boutique that sold nothing but extravagantly priced custom sneakers. She looked up at me and seemed to be suddenly reminded of something. "Andy's not that bad. He's three years older than me and he's spent his life being a total jerk to me, but now he has this girlfriend and he got his learning disabilities diagnosed and he got into Columbia. He thinks he's a changed man or whatever, and he suddenly wants to be best friends with his lowly little sister."

"Are you falling for it?"

"Of course." A smile broke out on her face. "He's my cool older brother who wouldn't talk to me for fifteen years."

We walked down Grand Street, past the dilapidated old tenement buildings and kosher food shops, past the trendy teahouses and a French café.

At the corner of Grand Street and the Bowery, we waited for the light to change. A sanitation truck rumbled past, and the garbage men hanging off the back whistled at us. Not that there's anything wrong with sanitation workers, but it would have been nice to get that kind of reaction out of guys my own age every now and again. The last person to check me out had been an old man who was sunbathing in Washington Square Park. When I sailed by without responding to his "Sexy little lady!" catcall, he changed his tack. "Screw you! You're not even all that!"

Becca turned around and I realized the light had changed. "You coming?"

"So, wait," I said, scrambling to reenter the conversation. "It's just you and your brother?"

"As far as I know." Her eyes twinkled. "And what's your story? Is it just you and moose boy?"

As we walked to the subway station, I told her a little bit about the people I share a home and a last name with—Dad's makeshift café society, my hot mother and her ghostwriting career, and Henry's midnight strolls and homemade board games. "People who aren't related to them think they're very entertaining. You should come and meet them sometime."

Stupid Claire! Why had I just blurted that out? I wanted to kick myself for smacking of desperation.

"Sure, sometime." Her tone was polite but noncommittal. "Anyway, this is my stop."

A rumble from below indicated that a train was pulling into the station. With a quick goodbye, she scampered down the stairs, leaving me to feel like a dork who'd come on too strong.

"Hey! Claire!" she called out a few seconds later. She was running back up the stairs. "I forgot to get your number." I fumbled in my bag for a pen. "You don't have to write it down. My brain's wired like that."

And so I gave it to her, trying to sound as indifferent as I could.

"That your cell?" she asked.

"Home," I said quietly. "I'm one of the five American teenagers without a cell."

"You should consider yourself lucky," she said, picking up on my self-consciousness. "At least your parents can't keep track of your every move. It can be such a drag."

Her parting words played over in my mind as I bopped homeward. When would I ever have something that I wanted to keep from my family?

And, come to think of it, what were her secrets?

{ 9 }

Potlucky

I woke up the next morning feeling exhausted. For once I was relieved I'd left my bike at school. The downtown F platform wasn't too crowded, and finding a column to lean against was easy enough. The only problem, I realized a moment too late, was that a subway musician had set up his bucket-chair directly across from my post. He was plucking an instrument that was one very long string attached to a wooden base, and his scraggly white ponytail made him look like a crazy escaped monk. I'm sure that from the right distance his music would have been just the right morning pick-me-up, but from where I stood it just sounded like a whole lot of *waa-waa-waa*-ing.

I closed my eyes and let the dream I'd had the night before play through my mind.

Old jets were flying around the sky, doing fancy loop-de-loops and leaving behind puffs of smoke like in an old war movie. I was flying, too, and as I shot through the sky felt light as a meringue.

It was all in grainy black-and-white—and not like a "maybe" black-and-white. I knew for sure because I had the smarts to look down at my hands. My red nail polish was chipped in exactly the same pattern as it had been last time I'd checked, though now it was a dull gray. I continued to zoom about, trying to get the attention of the planes. They'd come nosing my way, only to pass over or under me. And one by one, they streaked out of sight. The clouds bled together, until I was left in a field of white.

The dream was still so vivid I didn't know if I was supposed to shudder or laugh at the thought of it. I had no idea what it was trying to tell me, but I knew this much: there had been no need for Kiki's talk that night in the Waldorf lobby. You'd have to be in a coma to have dreams like that and not pay attention.

I opened my eyes just as the train was about to pull into the station. The old man continued to play, even though there was no way any of us commuters could hear him over the rumbling.

As I dragged up and down the hallways between classes, I kept my eyes peeled for Becca. But every time I caught sight of a head of long dark hair, it turned out to belong to another person. I was starting to wonder if I was losing my mind and she'd been an invention of my admittedly febrile imagination.

If I had any fun at school that day, it must have been extremely subtle, because I sure didn't notice it. The one lesson I learned: exhaustion and Henry Hudson do not mix. I was too tired to pick up a hand weight in gym class, and when I fell asleep in music appreciation, my last class of the day, our teacher, Mr. Wropp, decided against leaving me in peace.

"Did you find the answer in your dreams?" Mr. Wropp was towering over me, and a bunch of kids were staring at me.

Considering how insane my dreams are, I wouldn't be all that surprised.

I asked Mr. Wropp to repeat the question, raising a laugh from the other kids.

"I have an idea," Mr. Wropp said, his eyes brightening. "You can help your classmates figure out the answer. Why don't you stand up?"

I rubbed my eyes and rose to my feet.

"Repeat after me," Mr. Wropp said. " 'This is my speaking range.' "

Unsure at first, I did as told. A smile grew on my teacher's face.

"Very good. And again?"

"This is my speaking range?"

Mr. Wropp scanned the other kids' faces, exchanging conspiratorial looks with them. Had I misunderstood the directions?

"Oh!" A kid in the back raised his hand, squirming as if his armpit were on fire. "Tenor?"

"Close." Mr. Wropp was perking up. "Alto. You see, even though her voice is deep, it would have to be even deeper to be tenor. Like this." Without bothering to thank me for humiliating myself in front of the whole class, he returned to the front of the room, put on a video of a barbershop quartet, and told us to keep our eyes on the man wearing a polka-dotted bow tie.

Unbelievable.

That afternoon I biked home and found Mom in the kitchen, wearing her blue and white striped French apron and mixing quiche filling.

"*Bonjour!*" she said when she saw me.

"Hello to you, too." I had to bite my tongue to keep myself from reminding her that the words embossed on her passport said *United States of America*.

"Would you like a yogurt?"

"I'll pass, thanks."

I waited until I was sure she wasn't looking and stuffed a jar of jam and half a baguette under my jacket sleeve. There was no time to grab a knife—my finger would have to do the trick.

Out in the living area, Dad and his colleague Crystal de la Montaigne were on the couch, planning some class they were going to teach together. I'm not Crystal's biggest fan. Her specialty is the French Revolution, but every time she sees me all she seems to want to talk about is how hard it is not to let her beauty get in the way of being taken seriously by her students. You could say I have a hard time taking her seriously, too.

Dad and I waved hi, and before Crystal was able to go in for the kill and start telling me for the hundredth time why she wore her huge beige-framed glasses instead of contact lenses, I stole into my room. With the door safely shut, I ate my *très interdit* snack while checking my e-mail. There was a boring note from Cade Scherer, one of the Farmhouse girls I used to be friends with. "We had our Supper Club dinner last night, and the guest was the news editor of *Cosmo*," she wrote, seemingly unaware that she'd just used an oxymoron. "She told us about butt surgeries. Ud have loved it. Come back!"

I wasn't sure how to take that, and I moved on to an e-mail from Louis. He'd written to ask me for the name of the French Moroccan restaurant we'd been to with my parents—no doubt he was planning some fun outing that I wasn't invited to.

"I think it was around 52nd St.," I wrote back. "You can look it up online. Have fun!"

The second I pressed Send, I realized how unhelpful my reply was. Oh well. He'd have to invite me to get anything else.

Next I turned to my homework—I had a worksheet for chemistry, a problem set for math, and I had to read a children's story about a baker who lost her sense of taste for my French class. It was all pretty easy, and when I was done I celebrated by curling up on my fake polar bear rug and rereading part of *And Then There Were None*, one of my favorite Agatha Christie books.

I must have been more tired than I'd realized; when Dad poked his head into my room to tell me I had a phone call, I was fast asleep on the floor—for the second time that week. Was I not getting enough iron or something?

"Hello?" I said, using my fingers to tweeze a fake polar bear hair from my mouth.

"Hey," a mysterious voice said. "It's Becca Shuttleworth, from yesterday?"

"Hi!" I said, and dived across the floor to turn on my iPod dock. The Caravelles' "You Don't Have to Be a Baby to Cry" came on, protecting me from any potentially embarrassing parental background noise.

"Is now a bad time?" Becca asked.

"No, it's a great time. I was just . . . um . . . hanging out. What's up with you?"

"Not much. I wanted to make sure I remembered your number correctly."

"Yup, this is it."

Silence.

It was strange; we'd had so much to talk about the day before, but now I didn't know what to say. It was what I imagined it would feel like if a boy I had a crush on called me out of the blue, except in this case I felt sure that once we'd broken the ice again, we'd have tons to talk about. With guys you never know.

"So where are you?" I asked.

"Wandering around, downtown. My boyfriend and I went to Washington Square Park, and now he's at an appointment."

Actually, I'm not sure if that's where she said he was. She could have said he was in a tree eating poisonous mushrooms and I wouldn't have noticed. She was near Washington Square Park was all I heard. And that was right by me.

"That's where I live," I blurted out, stupid with excitement. "Not, you know, in the park, but right around there."

"I didn't know that." She sounded even-keeled.

"If you want, you can come over for dinner. As long as you don't mind French food."

"Will there be snails?"

"Highly doubtful."

"Bummer. . . . What's the address?"

I was so out of practice at inviting people over, I'd forgotten you're supposed to check with your parents first. As it turned out, Mom and Dad were having one of their potluck salons. It was actually awesome timing—we Voyante kids were normally required to spend an hour at the dinner table, but salon night was the exception.

When Becca showed up, she was greeted by the sight of eleven shoeless French professors, one wannabe French professor, and one little brother, all feasting on Gallic goodies and talking hyperactively. It's Dad's hope that they would focus on intellectual issues at his salons, though the most popular topics are tenure gossip and cheese, two things I am allergic to.

Becca stood in the doorway, her trench coat open to reveal a white button-down shirt tucked into wide-legged gray pants. Her hair, slightly wavier than I'd remembered, streamed down one shoulder. And her posture was perfectly erect. Kiki would have adopted her on the spot.

I straightened up and rushed over to meet her. "I'm so sorry," I said in a low voice. "This is a little awkward, but I forgot this was going on when I invited you. We can go out— you don't object to greasy diners, do you?"

She scowled. "Hell no. I'm a great lover of the cheese fry. Though it does look interesting in here."

She said "interesting" in an inscrutable tone, and I glanced over my shoulder and tried to see the place through her eyes. There were candles stuffed into empty wine bottles. Chili lights strung around Toulouse-Lautrec posters. And over on the windowsill, Mom's minilibrary of astrology books in a stack next to an imitation Art Nouveau lamp. All the professors were engaged in dramatic conversations, except for Douglas Winkler, who sat at the end of the table and appeared to be nodding off. But that wasn't the only reason Douglas didn't really fit in. He's younger than the other professors, and better looking, with soft brown curls and crinkly blue eyes. Douglas is the star of the French department and one of my parents' favorite people. Mom and Dad chalk his sweetness up to his being Midwestern, though I can't help suspecting it has something to do with his feeling guilty for being half my father's age and twice as successful. As for the other professors who were at the table, well, if you don't have anything nice to say . . .

But the scene didn't seem to put Becca off in the slightest. "Wow," she said. "I've never seen so many candles."

"I know, it's a regular séance in here," I grumbled, and wondered if there was any chance we could make our exit without further embarrassment.

I approached my parents to say goodbye, squatting down to their level. "My friend Becca and I are on our way out," I said. Seeing that Becca had come to hover over me, my face went pink. There was no way my parents wouldn't notice that she was still wearing her shoes—a gorgeous pair of black granny boots with stacked heels. Dad looked up at her and I flinched. But instead of saying anything about the "You only need to cover your feet in the street" rule, Dad just waved.

"You must be Becca. I'm Gustave and this is Priscilla."

At this point Mom smiled beatifically and touched the bottom of Becca's trench coat. "That is lovely stitching," she said. "It's hard to find detail like that these days."

Would somebody please tell me what's going on?

And then it hit me: they were too thrilled to see that I had made a new friend at school to do anything other than rejoice. I fantasized about digging up one of Dad's cigarettes and telling Becca to light up. Would they object to that?

I didn't press my luck.

"Okay," I said, "we're outta here. *Bon appétit!*"

As Becca and I made our retreat, Dad called me back over. What now? The last time Mom and Dad had hosted a salon they'd needed my help removing candle wax from Crystal de la Montaigne's hair.

"Your friend seems nice," Dad said in a stage whisper.

Then he slipped me a five-dollar bill. It was barely enough to cover a Coke, but still, it wasn't every day Gustave Voyante parted with spending money.

And who was I to turn down the offer?

"Thanks, *Papa*," I said, and slipped out of the apartment before any candle wax emergency arose.

Becca was waiting by the elevator in the hallway, using a metal stick to enter something into a PDA. Next to her stood Douglas Winkler, a mustard stain on his blazer lapel gleaming in the fluorescent light. I hadn't noticed him get up from the table, but he *had* looked pretty sleepy in there.

"A for effort," I told him. "You almost made it all the way through."

Douglas shook his head ruefully. "It's just been a long day. I was volunteering at the shelter this morning, and I worked all day straight."

"And you still came to the salon?" I squinted my eyes. "I mean, willingly?"

"You shouldn't give your parents such a hard time," Douglas said. "I remember when you used to get dressed up on salon night and dance to Édith Piaf for us."

Oh no. Please stop. Please stop.

Becca stifled a laugh and stuffed her gizmo into her brown leather bag.

I turned to my new friend, eager to change the focus of conversation. "Were you playing solitaire or something?"

"No, Édith." She smirked. "I was dealing with my weird family. My mom just sent me an urgent message asking if I want her to buy me a pair of cashmere sweatpants she saw on sale." She shook her head apologetically.

"I'd give anything for a mother like that," I said. "Mine's always copying things my dad says about American capitalism, and then she buys suitcases full of the most useless things in France so long as they have French words on them."

"Oh?" she looked especially interested. "Like Coco Chanel?"

"Not so much. More like J'*adore l'amour.*"

I glanced over at Douglas, who was watching us with growing interest.

"Is this what girls talk about?" he asked.

"Only when we know other people are listening in," Becca said. "We save the good stuff for later."

The good stuff? I could hardly wait.

"Did either of you press the button already?" I asked.

Douglas nodded and rolled his eyes. "The left elevator's stuck."

"Again?" I groaned.

"Gotta love Washington View," Douglas said. "Now, where are you fashion critics headed?"

"The diner," I told him. "And you?"

"Bed. I have a flight at six in the morning. I've been invited to speak at Miami University on cartoons of the French Revolution." He smacked his lips. "I knew nothing about the subject until this morning."

"And I'm sure you know everything by now," I told him.

"Hardly."

I turned to Becca. "Meet Douglas. He's the rock star of the French department."

"Becca." She thrust out her hand with the self-confidence of a child star. "How do you do?"

When we finally filed into the elevator, Frank Camiello, a history professor who lives on the tenth floor, and his eleven-year-old twins, Simon and Byron, were already on board. I greeted them with a vague smile. I couldn't stand them. The Camiellos were always staging the twins' oboe recitals in the basement Sunrise Room and hounding the other residents about coming to watch.

Mr. Camiello and Douglas exchanged a few words. I watched in horror as Mr. Camiello reached into his pocket for a flyer for his sons' next concert and pressed it into Douglas's palm.

The door dinged open not soon enough, and I couldn't help myself. "Lucky you," I muttered to Douglas once the others had skittered off. I had a bad feeling I'd have to hear some of that recital, but luckily, I wouldn't have to *see* it. Douglas was too nice, though. He smiled and folded the flyer, putting it in his pocket.

"Mind if I walk you guys?" he asked, changing the subject. "I could use some fresh air."

"Sure," I said. I was grateful to have Douglas on hand; I still didn't know exactly where I stood with Becca, and I was nervous about what to say around her. Sometimes self-assured people can be painfully quiet, and I'm not always the best at coming up with scintillating repartee to fill in the blanks.

On the walk over to the diner, Douglas kept the conversation rolling, telling us about the shelter where he'd started volunteering and his new intern.

"He'd read some articles of mine, and I guess he saw a posting for the position on the NYU Web site. His introductory e-mail was so great I offered him the job sight unseen. But when I saw him, it turned out he was really . . . experienced."

"You mean old?" Becca asked. So maybe she was paying attention after all.

Douglas nodded. "At least sixty. And now I feel terrible asking him to do anything. I give him coffee and tell him to make himself at home in my office."

"Sweet deal for him," Becca said.

Things were going so smoothly, before I knew it we were standing outside the diner's entrance.

"All right, ladies," Douglas said. "I'll leave you to yourselves."

"Hey," Becca said, glancing my way. "Why doesn't he join us?" She turned back to Douglas. "Sounds like you could use some young company to even things out with your intern."

I was amazed by her blasé affect. If I ever tried to ask somebody's family friend to join me for dinner, well . . . I wouldn't. I just don't have that kind of moxie. The totally surprising thing was, my family friend accepted. Douglas seemed happy not to have to go straight home.

Becca made a beeline for a window booth and pulled a bulky leather organizer from her bag. It was like a portable museum, its pages stuffed with old letters and postcards and ticket stubs. As she flipped through, a pile of pictures fell onto the table.

"Tell me the name of the animal shelter you work at, will you? My mom's always looking for new volunteer opportunities."

"Sure thing," Douglas said. "But it's a homeless shelter."

"Oh, that's fine, too," Becca said. "She says she'll do anything but Red Cross. She can't handle the sight of blood. I can handle anything . . . except, maybe, volunteering."

Douglas and I exchanged "I can't believe she just said that" looks.

"I'm not a bad person, I swear," Becca went on. "I had a bad experience doing community service at boarding school. I used to walk this old lady's dog and . . ."

"And what?" I pressed.

"You're going to think worse of me."

"Too late," said Douglas. "Out with it."

"It peed all over my boots."

"Isn't that a famous fairy tale?" I asked.

Douglas grinned. "Piss in boots?"

Becca laughed. "Very good. Anyway, before we get completely off topic, what's the name of your shelter? For my mom?"

Becca wrote it down, then tidied up the snapshots that had fallen all over the table. "Pardon my organizational skills." She paused to look at a picture and smiled. "Andy just gave these to me. Aren't they funny?"

The first picture showed a young boy in a suit holding a grumpy-looking infant—presumably baby Becca. In the next picture, a toddler was laughing while her older brother blew raspberries on her stomach. And the third picture showed the two of them on a green lawn. Andy was jumping through a sprinkler while Becca, now five or so, was cutting paper dolls.

"They're all from my grandparents' farm in the English countryside. I used to sit out there for hours with paper and scissors," Becca said, taking the pictures back. "I guess I was easily amused."

I felt a strange jolt in my stomach. The picture looked familiar, but I didn't know why. I stared at it and tried to figure it out. When the waiter came over, he said something to me, but all I heard was a whooshing sound.

Becca had to nudge my leg. "Coke and cheese fries for you, too, my dear?"

I just nodded and tried my best to act as if everything were completely normal in my world. Then I attempted to make that falsity a truth.

I pulled myself together, and by the time our food came, it felt as though we'd known each other for longer than twenty-four hours, and our conversation moved easily from one topic to another. We touched on bad middle school fashion trends,

Becca's love of all things zombie/horror/vampire, and whether ketchup was originally made from mushrooms and anchovies, as Becca insisted it was.

"I don't buy it," I said.

"Trust me," she said sternly. "I know my condiments."

"You know something, Claire?" Douglas asked, pouring a packet of sugar into his tea. "Something's telling me not to mess with her."

Becca ducked under the table. She came up holding a retainer I hadn't even noticed her wearing and balled it up in her napkin. She shrugged apologetically. "Sorry. It's usually less gross than that."

"You girls are funny," Douglas said, shaking his head.

"No offense, but you need a girlfriend," I told him.

"Wow," he said. "What a perceptive insight."

"Let's help him find somebody," Becca blurted out, turning from me to Douglas. "Do you want us to be your life coaches?"

Douglas smiled. "I haven't tried one of those yet."

"Remember when I snuck onto Mom's computer and gave you that great horoscope about waking up in the land of love?" My favorite thing about Mom's weirdo job was playing around with other people's fortunes.

"How could I not?" Douglas said.

"Am I missing something?" Becca asked, and Douglas filled her in on Mom's secret identity.

"She is *not*!" she squealed. "I read the *Planet* every week. Seriously, your mom's Priscilla Pluto—the lady in the turban?"

"Yup. You actually saw that turban tonight. Under everyone's dinner." I waited to see if her face registered what I was saying. It didn't. "We used the tablecloth for the picture."

Becca scrunched her eyes tight and looked as if she'd just

taken a bite of a mud sandwich. "I don't know why that's so disgusting, but it is."

"Hey," I said, "I'm not going to disagree."

The night only got more fun, and we ended up staying in our booth forty-five minutes after Douglas paid the bill. Even Douglas, who should have gone to sleep hours earlier, hung around until the bitter end.

Later on, as I lay in bed staring at the glow-in-the-dark star stickers on my ceiling, something strange happened: I found myself wishing Mom and Dad would have their potluck salons more often.

{ 10 }

Ace in the Hole

Henry Hudson's rebels came in the same flavors as they would at any big school—we had our goths, our graffiti artists, even a sprinkling of spandex-clad girls who, in the right light, resembled backup dancers in a low-budget hip-hop video.

But the afternoon social hour didn't last very long. By five o'clock, the area outside the building was deserted. Once they'd put in their mandatory after-school face time, my fellow students all ran off to the library, club meetings, or advanced placement prep.

Becca and I didn't have such obligations. We agreed that there was no point in studying just for the sake of grade grubbing, and besides, we were doing pretty well for ourselves without even trying. All our tests were multiple choice, which made things easy. Becca had a photographic memory, and as long as I studied for a few minutes beforehand, I could usually work out which of the four options was right.

My intuition failed to serve me in other respects, though. I still had no idea how to get a conversation going with my classmates, and I was perpetually at a loss for the right comeback whenever a BDL would come along and say something obnoxious. There was some solace to be found in the fact that Becca was having integration problems of her own—there was only one kid at school whose name she knew. That would be me.

In any other circumstances, it was doubtful we would have become so close. After all, Becca was tall, aloof, and oddly worldly for fifteen—everything I was not. But we were both stranded on the same island, and every day after school let out, we both wanted to get away as fast as we possibly could.

Becca and her boyfriend had broken up for reasons she wouldn't get into, though she didn't seem too troubled by his disappearance. On the days when she didn't have voice lessons, we'd go on little field trips, alternating who got to come up with ideas. Her picks: seeing the Audrey Hepburn movie *Charade* at Film Forum, going to Belvedere Castle in Central Park, and wandering around Little Tokyo scouting fancy shoelaces. My picks: walking across the Brooklyn Bridge to go to the best chocolate shop in DUMBO, visiting Partners & Crime mystery bookshop, and looking through the racks of astronomically priced dresses at Upper East Side consignment shops.

One Wednesday, I decided we should go to Trudie's, a knickknack store in Herald Square that boasts a real genie in a bottle, but when we showed up, the door was locked and the lights were out. The sign in the window said: GONE FISHING. BACK NEXT WEEK.

She turned to me. "Now what?"

We were used to having all day to plan where we wanted to go. With the pressure on like this, my brain turned to oatmeal.

"Um, do you want to go up to the Waldorf and meet Kiki?" I asked. "I heard they're doing the James Bond press junket."

"Nah. I hate action movies." She fiddled with her white lace headband, and I could tell her mind was racing. "Wanna go see *Night at the Asylum*? I think it's opening today. Lemme check."

She pulled her phone out of her bag and tapped a button.

"Damn it," she said. "Again."

"It's not working?" I asked.

"No, no, I'm just . . ." She looked around at the people surrounding us, then down at her phone again, and frowned. I could tell she didn't want to talk about it.

"What is it?" I said softly, as if talking to a cat that was figuring out whether it should be afraid of me.

"I keep getting these weird text messages."

"Weird how?"

"Somebody just decided to tell me they like my headband. And they called me Alice. Hilarious, right?"

"Like Alice in Wonderland?" I asked. "Why are you upset? It's a compliment—probably from someone at school or something."

"I guess." She shrugged. "But why do these compliments have to come from a number that's unrecognizable. It feels like someone's watching me."

"You just have a shy admirer, that's all." I smiled, an attempt to bring some levity to the situation.

"Or a creepy one." She pressed her lips together. "Anyway, you up for the movie?"

"*Night at the Asylum?*" I shook my head. I hate horror movies. "Hey—we can go watch Louis play tennis. He gets so arrogant on the court, it's almost a horror movie. And you still have to meet each other."

"Some other time. I'm not really down with spectator sports. . . . Oh, here's an idea." One of her eyebrows drew up her forehead. "Let's go shopping at Bendel's."

"I don't even have twenty dollars on me." Not that twenty dollars would have done much good. The one time I'd set foot in Henri Bendel, I'd been with my dad, and he'd gone white as a Kleenex when he realized the pair of socks he wanted to buy my mom cost $45.00, not $4.50.

"We don't have to buy anything." Becca's enthusiasm was building; it was as if the text message moment had been wiped from history. "Trust me, it'll be fun."

"I don't know . . ." I looked over her shoulder and stared at a flock of tourists who were all wearing huge purple LIVE WITH REGIS AND KELLY T-shirts. "Why don't we go see a TV taping?"

"Sure, when you get us tickets. I think the waiting list is like six months." She grabbed me by the arm. "Now, do you want to walk or take the bus?"

When we entered the department store, I couldn't remember why I'd been so reluctant to come. Urns of fresh flowers filled the lobby, and the shoppers moved about with blissful expressions on their faces, as if they'd all just had massages. Something about the subdued lighting and counter people's easy smiles made me feel floaty, too.

Slightly dazed, I let Becca guide me past counter after counter of cosmetics, my eyes darting from one mysterious product to another. There was an inverse relation between price and fluid ounces; the going rate for a Pink Pearl eraser–sized vial of Alphoxa Vitralift was nearly the Voyante family's monthly rent.

Soon we were up to the designer dress floor, which was thronged with unnervingly skinny women, all weighted down with shopping bags. "Those are what we call social X-rays," Becca whispered as she scooped up a few gowns. "My mom once went to a chichi Halloween party dressed as one, but it didn't pan out."

"The ladies found it offensive?"

"No, the skeleton T-shirt and pearls combination was lost on everyone, and she ended up having to hold up a sign. She looked like a cabbie at the airport waiting for a social X-ray. A total bust."

"Sounds it. . . . You wanna get a bite?"

Ignoring my question, Becca blew across the floor and asked a saleswoman with spiky red hair for a fitting room. "Big enough for two, please," she specified in a sweet but assured voice. Almost as if she'd done it a thousand times.

The fitting room was as big as the Hudson auditorium, and outfitted with two black leather chairs. In the corner, a purple and yellow orchid had been propped up on a waist-high glass box filled with glossy pebbles. There was even a framed print of an eggplant on the wall. Was it possible there were people who knew this place existed and didn't make a point of spending their every free second up here?

Barely two seconds after we'd closed the door, the saleswoman rapped on it. "Everything all right in there?" she asked in an aggressive, fake-helpful voice.

"We're fine!" Becca called back. She had already taken off her long navy cashmere sweater and was shimmying into a cream-colored gown with a crystal-studded cowl-neck. "Though there is one thing."

"Yes?" the saleswoman replied.

Becca zipped up her dress and opened the door. "If you have anything to eat, we're famished. Maybe a sandwich tray?"

I glanced at the pile of ten-thousand-dollar gowns heaped on the floor and nearly burst out laughing. As if there were any chance Miss Snooty was going to bring after-school snacks to a messy, half-dressed fifteen-year-old and her slack-jawed friend.

But what did I know?

The saleswoman nodded timidly. "Of course."

"B, what did you just do?" I asked after Becca had shut the door and unzipped her dress.

"It's an old trick I picked up. They'll do it for their favorite customers, but even if you're not their favorite customer and if you ask them to do it, I guess they can't say no. Discrimination or whatever."

"That's funny. I doubt that when our founding fathers were coming up with the Bill of Rights, they had free sandwich at Bendel's privileges in mind."

"Well, equality's equality." She stepped into another dress, with a corset bodice and a bow in the back. "Can you zip me up?" As I pulled on the slider, I suddenly felt a tingle of uneasiness. I couldn't put my finger on why exactly, but something about this afternoon didn't quite stack up. I wasn't going to complain—I was having fun, and I was starving—but still, something was up.

"What do you think?" she asked, sizing herself up in the mirror.

"Honestly? It's a little baggy."

"Yeah, and in all the wrong parts." She cupped her hands over her boobs and sighed, then took the dress off and threw it at me. I tried not to stare at her body. It was tall and creamy, slender without any bones poking out. In other words, flawless. "Your turn."

"Oh, I'm not really in the mood."

"The mood?"

"For you," I said, my voice growing meeker, "to see my butt in its voluminous glory."

"That's too bad. If you don't uncover your ass, I don't know if I'll be in the mood to share my sandwiches with it. And the chicken salad is beyond yummy. I'm convinced it has something to do with an abuse of butter."

The thought set my tummy growling, and a few wheezes and hops later, I was in the dress.

Becca was circling me. "It's epic."

"Thanks a lot," I snapped, glancing in the mirror to see exactly how big the dress made my butt look.

"Not your rear, dum-dum. The dress."

Until then, I'd forgotten about the dress's bow, which was a perfect distraction from my gargantuan backside.

"Wow. It is nice," I said in shock. I twirled around and ogled this polished version of myself in the three-way mirror. It was me, but better. A lot better. "Would it be weird if I sewed a bow on the back of all my clothes?"

"Not if you don't mind looking like Minnie Mouse." Her expression perked up. "Did you hear somebody knocking?"

"I don't think so," I said, but she'd already disappeared into the foyer. And she returned a moment later holding the most sumptuous tray of miniature wrap sandwiches and pastries I'd ever seen outside of France.

"Rub-a-dub-grub," she said, pushing the orchid aside to set the tray on the table. The door sailed closed behind her.

But before it clicked completely shut, it opened again. Standing in the doorway was a tall girl with a glamorously disheveled hairdo and numerous gauzy scarves coiled around her neck. For a second I thought she worked for the store and had come to scold us for abusing the secret VIP sandwich service. Then I noticed the two brown and white striped Bendel bags dangling from her wrists. One of the bags was ordinary sized, and the other was tiny—was it possible somebody this young needed fountain of youth potion?

"Becca!" She stormed into the fitting room, stepping on a pile of dresses that was easily worth ten college educations. "I thought I heard your voice."

I looked over to my friend, hoping for an explanation, but the new girl had already hijacked her attention, holding her by the elbow and firing off meaningless snippets like "Your hair looks so cute!" and "Isn't it mobbed here?" between air kisses.

And just when the room was feeling as cramped as humanly possible, two other girls came charging in. They looked like slightly more sophisticated BDLs, with their hooded sweatshirts, tight black pants, and shoulder-grazing earrings. They were pretty, in an airbrushed way, and they both cut me vague smiles. Now at least I had a shot at getting introduced.

Or so I thought.

"There you two are!" the initial intruder turned to the newcomers. "Becca, you know Regina and Coe, right?"

Anger rose in me as the four carried on, but to be fair, Becca did keep eyeing me and opening her mouth, only to be cut off by more fussing and clacking.

"What is this? Isn't prom season a little while away?" the

first girl asked, and I realized she was addressing me. Or, to be perfectly accurate, my dress.

"This is my friend Claire," Becca finally had a chance to say. "Claire, that's Regina and Coe." She paused before gesturing to the scarf girl. "And that's Rye."

Rye scanned me, then turned to Becca. "She's so cute! Is this the girl you told me about from the volunteer program?"

Becca tossed back a strange, hiccuppy laugh. "No."

"Um, what girl are you talking about?" I asked Becca.

"Nothing." Becca said it in a tone that was supposed to sound casual, and the girls in the background looked away guiltily. "Claire goes to Hudson with me," Becca explained. "And Rye goes out with my brother, Andy."

"I see," I said, straining not to show how unpleasant this little reunion was becoming. Well, I could keep standing there like a clod or I could take the higher ground. "Do you go to Columbia, too?" I asked with a polite smile.

"No," Rye said distractedly. She was rifling through the dresses on the floor and mumbling something that sounded disapproving. "I'm at Bennington."

I'd never heard of the place, a fact that my expression must have given away.

"It's a small liberal arts college in Vermont," one of her friends told me.

"But she lives in the city," Becca said.

"I'm double-majoring in social theory and women's studies via correspondence course."

"Tell her why," Becca urged her, shooting me a devilish smile.

Rye rolled her eyes, as if she'd already been asked to explain this a hundred times in the past hour. "I wanted to go to a small school in the country, but I didn't want to actually have to leave the city. I need to soak up the urban setting. It's more inspiring than a bunch of trees."

A chuckle bubbled up inside me, and it took every muscle in my upper body not to let it escape my mouth. "I've heard of interesting reasons for college choices, but that's a first," I said.

"I'm glad you find my higher education humorous," she drawled.

"Rye," Becca said levelly, "you know it's kind of funny."

She exhaled again, this time through her nose. "No hard feelings."

Becca threw me an apologetic look as Rye frantically kissed her goodbye. "And don't even think about buying anything you're trying on. I just read the most *amazing* essay about how dresses are a tool for oppressing women. I'm totally giving it to you!" And with that, she led her hangers-on away.

Once we were alone again, the room felt bright and cold.

"Um, would you care to explain what that was all about?" I asked Becca.

"The thing about the essay?" Her voice was edged with nervous phoniness. "She's always saying I have to read something."

"That's not what I'm talking about. Don't pretend that wasn't horrible—that entire encounter."

Becca's shoulders slackened. "Okay, it *was* sort of horrible." She laughed with relief. "She wasn't exactly at her best, but I wouldn't take it personally. She's strange."

"Strange how?" I challenged.

"For one thing she's an only child."

"So are lots of people."

"And she's also a member of the Calorie Restriction Society. It's supposed to make you live longer and feel invigorated . . . but sometimes it just makes her act weird."

"Sounds fun," I grumbled.

About as much fun as the Peeling Off Your Fingernails Society.

"Yeah, I hear you," she said. "I'm not planning on turning in my Free Sandwich Appreciation Society card anytime soon." With that, she popped a miniature club sandwich in her mouth. I could tell she was dying to steer the topic away from Rye.

There was a tense silence. "Any good?" I asked, somewhat reluctantly.

She nodded and looked up. "Thank you, founding fathers." She took another bite. "What are you waiting for, C? The chicken salad is on the marble bread."

{ 11 }

Dead Men Walking

Later that night I was back in my room, halfheartedly IM-ing with Louis about his bitchy stepmother while my thoughts wandered miles away. Something about Becca was troubling me. She hadn't done anything that could be classified as outright objectionable—it was Rye who had been the jerk, not Becca. But still. I knew she was holding something back. She'd acted so strange about the fairly innocuous text message, and there'd been nothing normal about how she'd run around Bendel's as if it were her playground. I looked over at Didier and Margaux, who were swimming circles around each other in their tank, and envied them their carefree life and easy friendship.

I let Louis finish recounting getting in trouble for mentioning his stepmother's new hair extensions in front of a neighbor.

"what does she think," he wrote, "that everyone's going to believe her hair magically grew eight inches overnight?"

"i think she's the one who should be in therapy," I wrote back.

"who said she isn't?"

I was hit by a wave of exhaustion and just wanted to crawl into bed. "gotta go help with the dishes. sorry."

It was a lie, but he wouldn't have let me go if I'd told him the truth. It was bedtime.

I was walking barefoot along a path paved with smooth, flat stones. Moonlight shone down on the ground, and I couldn't see much else besides the outline of my feet. My movements as slow and careful as a monk's, I kept going until I reached the end of the path, where I was pulled into a dark room. Candles hung from the ceiling in an old-fashioned candelabra, burning a rich gray fire. A man whose face was barely formed, like an olive with a nose stuck on, turned to me. He was holding a glass box that was full of little suns, moons, and stars that were all twinkling in and out of sight. Mesmerized, I felt myself pulled closer to the warmth of the box. I reached out toward the heat, though my body started to float away. I drifted, focusing on his receding figure as he drew a dark cloth over the box and blew out all the lights.

When I woke up, I felt tired, but not as freaked out as I had after my other black-and-white dreams. I had no idea what—if anything—they meant, or where they were leading me, but I was getting used to them.

I nearly bumped into a car on my bike ride to school, and in English class nobody woke me up until the kids started to file in for the next class and a girl needed her seat.

"Sorry to disturb your nap," she said, giving rise to laughter from a few of her classmates.

I mumbled an apology and gathered my books. I ran down the hall as fast as I could, but I was still seven minutes late for chemistry class. Have I mentioned I'm no natural athlete?

"So you decided to come after all," my chemistry teacher, Mrs. Marcollini, announced in my direction as I entered the classroom.

As much as I hated chemistry, my teacher had always seemed nice enough, and I had no idea what her problem was.

And then I got it.

All the other kids had study sheets and flashcards stored under their seats. Pencils were moving faster than mice skittering across a kitchen floor. Good God. When I'd slept through class on Monday, she must have announced a test. A chemistry test I hadn't studied for at all. A test there was no way I'd pass.

Frank Vitti, the kid who sat in front of me, turned around to shoot me a sympathetic look. I tapped my foot nervously as I waited for Mrs. Marcollini to give me the exam and bubble sheet. The papers landed on my desk with a heavy *whoop*.

I could only figure out the answers to about a third of the questions, and I had to rely on my fabulous hunches for the rest. I don't know why I bothered.

I was screwed.

"Claire," Clem said when I got up to pour myself another Orangina. "Where's this Becca we keep hearing so much about?"

We were up on the Waldorf's Starlight Roof for Kiki's Sunday-night Scrabble game. They'd all been begging me to bring Becca up, but so far the timing hadn't worked out. I turned to my grandmother. "I forgot to tell you. She said she's sorry that she can't make it tonight. Her parents were having some people over and she needed to be there."

Kiki nodded and said, as an aside to Edie, "You can't blame the girl."

"No," Edie twittered. "I'm sure her home makes this place look like a halfway house."

Kiki turned to me. "Tell her that we forgive her absence. But we're dying to meet Her Highness."

I wondered if she'd started her martini hour earlier than usual. "You feeling okay?" I asked.

"Oh dear," Kiki laughed. "It seems our babe has been wandering around the woods with her hood over her eyes."

I tightened my fists and felt them whitening. "What are you guys talking about?"

"You see that red thing at the center of the table?" Edie asked, nodding at a shrink-wrapped miniature bottle of Soul Sauce. "Does that mean anything to you?"

"Um, should I say 'ketchup' or is this a trick question?"

George was rocking back and forth, laughing under his breath.

"Claire," Edie said evenly, "your friend's family owns that. Not that particular bottle, of course, but the Shuttleworth Corporation, which manufactures Soul Sauce."

I gulped. Normally, I'd assume they were just pulling my leg, but I could tell by their expressions they weren't.

"I mean . . . ," I started to say. "I knew they were well-to-do."

"Well-to-do?" Kiki chuckled and rubbed her meaty hands together. "The Shuttleworths are American royalty. A dynasty unto themselves."

"The kings of ketchup," George boomed, and started to hum the Soul Sauce jingle.

"Wait," I said, my mind still spinning. Was that why Becca had said she knew her condiments the night we first went out, with Douglas? And how she knew how to score all the food at Bendel's?

"Are the pieces falling into place?" Kiki asked.

"There's a new Shuttleworth chemistry lab at school, but I didn't—"

"They're a very philanthropic family," Edie interrupted. "Remember where Kiki and I took you to see *Silk Stockings?*"

Of course. At the Shuttleworth Theater. I was such a half-wit.

The rest of them jumped in, adding the names of museums, sports arenas, and colleges that benefited from the Shuttleworths' generosity.

"Um, I just need to sit down for a second." I sank into a lounge chair.

So Becca's family was stonking rich—even richer than her familiarity with Bendel's had led me to suspect. Part of me was mad at her for not having made this clear, but I could see why she might not have wanted to advertise it.

At least now I understood where all those great shoes came from.

Now that I knew about Becca's situation, I felt embarrassed for not having pieced it together sooner. Did the rest of Hudson know they were sharing oxygen with an American princess? It was well within the realm of possibility. You could set yourself on fire and not get a reaction out of my classmates. Unless, of course, it was during an Emergency Training class they were being graded on.

"Hey, guys," I said to my pseudofriends at lunch as casually as possible. "Have any of you ever heard of the Shuttleworths?"

"Nope," Zach chirped, too involved in arranging his lettuce and tomato to look up from his burger. Eleanor cocked her head from side to side, to indicate that she was thinking. When she was done, she scratched her nose and took a long sip of iced tea.

I turned to Ian. He would have to interpret. "Survey says no," he told me.

"And what about you?" I asked him. "Does it ring a bell?"

"Yeah, I think so. Shuffleworths. Isn't it, like, a famous golf club that's racist?"

"Not quite," I said, feeling slightly less ridiculous about my own obliviousness.

"Well," Ian said impatiently, "what is it, then?"

"It's just something I overheard some other kids talking about," I lied, my eyes sweeping over the green and black linoleum floor until they landed on a loose flyer promoting a debate-a-thon. The last thing I wanted to do was blow Becca's cover. So I picked up the decoy and threw it at the table. "I think it's supposed to be some big-deal . . . mock trial competition or something?"

Ian pulled a Tupperware container out of his suitcase. He pried the lid off and threw a carrot stick at me. "Why didn't you just say so in the first place?"

"Yeah," said Zach. "Way to lead up to a letdown."

Eleanor kept her eyes trained on me as she helped herself to one of Ian's carrot wands. She took a bite and shifted her sights to the scuffed-up debate-a-thon flyer, mouthing the words. The edges of her lips curled into a smile. I didn't know exactly what she was thinking, but I could tell she was no fool.

• • •

"The bad news is most of you did poorly," Mrs. Marcollini said, walking up and down rows of desks to hand back our tests. "The good news is this will give you incentive to study properly for the remaining exams."

Upon receiving their grades, students were falling forward, one by one, like dominoes. I was actually looking forward to getting the test back and putting it behind me once and for all. When Mrs. Marcollini came to the last row (V–Z), she stopped at my desk. "And you—quite a performance." She tossed my paper on my desk.

Frank Vitti whipped around. "What'd you get?"

"No idea," I said. "I'm too scared to look."

"Allow me." He plucked my paper off the table. "Holy cow. That's just nuts."

"Thanks for the commentary," I said, snatching my test back, facedown. What business of his was it if I sucked at chemistry?

Mrs. Marcollini was up at the blackboard, talking way too rapidly about "dipole-dipole forces." I waited until I felt sure nobody was looking, and I curled up the corner of my test. I rolled it over bit by bit until a 16% came into view. Ouch. I knew I hadn't aced the test, but this was a new personal record in underachievement.

Not caring about school had been a lot easier when I was doing well at it.

I stuck my test sheet in the back of my notebook and set about copying down the circles and dotted lines Mrs. Marcollini was drawing on the blackboard.

Holding back tears, I copied her Hs and Os as accurately as I could. The words sixteen and percent kept running circles in my brain. God, I was a loser.

It wasn't until I was done drawing that I noticed it: the exam book was upside down. The 16% I'd thought I'd received had been a 91%.

Something seriously weird was going on.

My heart banged against my chest as I balled up the booklet and shoved it in the side pocket of my striped bag.

"Now you're thinking," a girl seated to my right said. She copied me and crumpled her exam in her fist. Then she punched her fist in the air and mouthed something not very nice at Mrs. Marcollini's back.

A few other kids gave me sympathetic looks.

If only they knew.

"Yes!" Becca said as she came out of our bathroom. "I finally got the hang of your toilet handle. You have to hold it to the right, then jiggle it at the end."

"Bravo," I said. "Ever consider plumbing school?"

In truth, I was touched. Becca had spent more afternoons at my place than I could count, enough time to absorb our family's strange rhythms and customs. She knew how to read Dad's erratic moods and what it meant when Henry left the apartment without saying goodbye. She was even aware of the fact that Mom's crêpes were made out of Aunt Jemima pancake mix.

My parents loved Becca, and not only because her existence hinted that I might not be so miserable at Hudson forever. Even if I were the most well-adjusted kid in Washington View Village, Becca would still be a parent's dream: she was inquisitive about my parents' work, she laughed at their not-very-good jokes, and when Mom wanted a captive audience to talk to about her latest ghostwriting project—a memoir-cum-diet-book by last year's Miss Rodeo America—Becca was all too happy to look through a rodeo coffee table book with my mother and feign interest.

It was only natural, then, that with Kiki's revelation and Becca's visits to apartment 8C becoming more frequent, I found myself feeling more curious about meeting her family. And as time wore on, I was becoming certain it would never happen.

Which might explain why when it finally did, it practically sailed over my head.

"So? What's the word?" she asked me. We were in my bedroom, waiting for our toenails to dry and hiding out from Henry, who was going through a Harry Potter phase and violently crashing around the living area on a broomstick.

Becca and I were flipping through a stack of ancient *Life* magazines I had found abandoned on a stoop in the West Village.

"What do you think?" she said, her tone mildly annoyed.

"Weird," I said, hoping that was all that was needed.

I'd been too focused on a pictorial about the Kennedys' 1961 trip to Canada to pay attention to what she'd been talking about.

"So is that a yes?" She looked at me intently.

"Repeat the question?"

"God, C, you are such a space cadet. As I was saying, my grandparents are taking us to dinner for my aunt Jocelyn's birthday next Thursday, and they said I could bring a friend. So, once again, do you want to come?"

"Wait." I put my magazine down. "You're inviting *me* to meet your family? To what do I owe this honor?"

"Um, to being my friend? And to the fact that you keep dropping pathetic hints."

My ears felt hot. "That's not—"

"Save it. Besides, it's cute." Still gripping her magazine, she stretched her arms in the air. "It's going to be at this whacked-out place called the Portrait Club. You'll either love it or hate it."

I smiled, but I masked my excitement well, I think. Thanks to Kiki and her friends, I already knew about this centuries-old institution on East Forty-fourth Street, and I'd heard all about the annual pig roasts and the private room where former presidents used to entertain their movie-star girlfriends.

"It will probably be boring, but I shouldn't tell you that because I want you to come and keep me entertained," Becca said. "As long as you go into the place with the right sense of humor, you'll find it entertaining. It's one of those private clubs where everyone looks like a dead white man waiting to happen."

I refrained from telling Becca I was already well aware of the club and kept a lid on the sparks of excitement that were going off in my chest. I had to admit, it was funny that my first club experience would be at the Portrait Club. After all, when most New York girls my age go to their first club, they end up on some third-rate dance floor filled with other under-age kids moving around spastically to electronic bleeps and drumbeats. Then, at the end, somebody throws up.

Tantalizing, right?

"Earth to Claire." Becca rolled up her magazine and came at my head with it. "You in?"

"I think so." I rocked forward and stood up. "Let me just check my calendar."

"Oh, will you quit it? I already told everyone you're coming."

{ 12 }

Dr. Quack

I was biking along a bland suburban stretch, pedaling as fast as I could. The houses were cardboard-cutout plain, with identical rosebushes in full bloom in front. I desperately wanted to get back into the city, but every time I reached a corner and moved onto a new street, it was no different, with the same single line of trees along the curb and silver flowers to the right of every doorstep.

A low murmur turned into a loud rumbling. I looked over my shoulder to see a postal truck blow around the corner and come at me. I didn't want to be run over by some slap-happy driver, so I shifted to the right, turning my handlebars toward the edge of the sidewalk. Instead, my bike levitated and started floating over the vehicle. I was too shocked to keep pedaling, but my bike kept going. This flying thing was pretty fabulous!

The truck disappeared under a canopy of gray leaves, and when it reemerged there was a black and white plaid duffel bag poking through the passenger window. Somebody must have tossed it in the air, because it flew up, straight at me. The bag grazed my front tire before plummeting and landing at the foot of a tree. I turned around to get a last look, but the leaves showering down got in the way.

Flying didn't feel so fun anymore.

"Come on, Tinker Bell," Coach Blendack yelled at me. "You can do it!"

He was cramming his top two favorite conversational tactics into the space of three words: (1) he screamed, and (2) in what must have been some sick attempt to highlight how interchangeable we Hudson students all seemed to him, he called every girl Tinker Bell and every guy buddy.

We called Coach Blendack Bullwinkle—though not to his face. He looked like a moose, with a bulky physique and tufts of hair poking from behind each ear. A former biology teacher rumored to have been moved to the athletics department after a nervous breakdown, Coach Blendack gave us what he called weight-lifting tests every Monday morning. He'd walk around the gym and watch everybody do two sets of bicep curls. It was part of his plan to elevate physical education's fallen reputation or something. During these weekly affairs he was fond of saying, "Anything you fail to do here can and will be used against your grade point average."

Predictably, it worked; a few kids even brought notebooks to PE. Sometimes I kept myself entertained thinking what a Hudson kid wouldn't do for a higher grade point average. Hold your breath all day? No problem. Eat a brown paper bag? Pass the salt and pepper, please.

"Let's go, Tinker Bell!" Coach Blendack's spit sprayed across my nose.

I could feel the shine collecting on my forehead and the stench settling on my skin as I steadied my knees, crooked my right elbow, and raised my arm to my waist. It wouldn't go any farther. How was it that I was so hopeless at this beefcake business?

It certainly didn't help matters that I'd had another black-and-white dream the night before. By this point I understood there was a direct link between my crazy dreams and my bouts of dire exhaustion, and this day was no exception. Just thinking about riding my bike and floating above suburbia brought on a new wave of fatigue. The weight dropped to my side.

"I'm sorry," I said to Coach Blendack.

"Don't be sorry!" he roared. "Be strong!"

"I'm just—I'm just too tired."

"Like the last time," he huffed. "Let me remind you, Twinkie, tired is a state of mind. It should not be your defining characteristic!"

And idiocy shouldn't be yours, I thought.

Beth Blanks, a bookworm who was in my homeroom, snuck over to me once Coach Blendack had moved on to the next victim.

"It happens to the best of us," she said knowingly.

"What does? Him?" I pointed at our teacher's ample bottom.

"Too much studying. Did you see Lucinda Dobbs?"

Lucinda was one of the few Hudson students who didn't need to be identified by last name. She belonged to the group of seniors who stood in the same spot outside school every day. They were called the Queen Bees, after their attitudes or average bra size, depending on whom you asked. Lucinda was the one with red hair. Everyone knew that—even me.

"What about her?" I asked.

"She pulled an all-nighter for civics and then she walked into a lamppost on her way to school," Beth said. "There's a green bruise on her forehead. It won't be long before everybody has one."

It wasn't until I walked into homeroom, still sweaty from the previous period, that I understood the implications of what she was saying. My old friend Sheila was sitting by a Bunsen burner, brushing her bangs off her forehead to display her new injury.

Talk about being a fashion victim.

That night Henry was visiting his friend Dov, so it was just the three of us at dinner. Mom made ratatouille and chicken with forty garlic cloves, a French specialty. She must have wanted information out of me—she started out by asking me a million questions about how I was feeling. When she finally realized I had nothing of interest to share with her, she and Dad got to talking about Dad's latest paper submission, and I doused my potatoes in Soul Sauce and let my mind wander back to what Kiki and her Waldorf family had told me about Becca. Now that I knew Becca's billion-dollar secret, I felt protective of her. There were plenty of worse things to be than a ketchup princess, but still, it must have been pretty weird to be bonkers-rich.

"Hello, Claire." Dad was waving his napkin in my face like a bullfighter. "Are you listening?"

I snapped back to attention. "Now I am."

Mom clasped her hands and leaned over my way, at an angle that suggested we were about to have what she and Dad called a Serious Conversation. The funny thing—if you can call it funny—about our Serious Conversations was that they are anything but conversations. Mom and Dad would prepare little spiels that they would take turns delivering, one overlapping the other, a tactic they'd devised to prevent any interruptions from yours truly. The last time we'd had one of these was in the aftermath of my Henry Hudson acceptance.

My parents cleared their throats and exchanged awkward glances before Mom got started. "Your gym teacher called today. He said you've been exhausted and he wanted to know if you've been sleeping enough," Mom reached out and rubbed Dad's thigh. I looked away.

Dad cut in, "We think it must be hormonal."

Hearing my dad say the word *hormonal* was more disgusting than . . . well, I'd rather not think about more disgusting alternatives.

"We're sure this can be solved," Mom said, "what with all the medical advances of today."

"I don't understand," I whimpered, still not looking at them. "Since when does being fifteen years old and showing up for school feeling a little tired constitute a full-blown medical crisis?"

"Nobody said anything about a *crisis*," Mom said. "We're just concerned."

Oh no. *Concerned*. My least favorite word in the English language. Why didn't she just come out with it and say "major trouble"?

"We called an expert," Mom said.

"An expert." I leaned back and looked up at the ceiling. "You mean you called a decrepit old neighbor who can't remember his own name half the time?"

"That only happened once," Mom said. "Where's your compassion?"

"We've all noticed it," Dad said. "You haven't been yourself. Something's changed."

"Maybe it has to do with the fact that I spend most of my waking hours at the lamest school in America?" I ventured. My necklace started to make my skin itch and I moved the clasp to the back of my neck.

"Don't look so worried." Mom twirled a wisp of hair around her finger. "You're not in trouble. Dr. Rothbart called in a prescription for some very light sleeping pills for you. They'll be ready at Duane Reade on Sixth Avenue."

"Noctolux," Dad said. "The Web site says it enables you to have REM sleep and leaves you feeling energized." He widened his eyes to illustrate his point in case I didn't get it with actual words.

I couldn't take any more of their hassling me, so I got up to clear the table.

The phone rang when I was rinsing the plates. By the time I came back into the dining area, Dad was frowning like a catfish.

"Dov's mother," he told Mom after he hung up. "She said somebody was supposed to pick up Henry at five."

"Damn it!" Mom said into her hands. "With my deadline and this whole medical condition, it completely slipped my mind."

The word condition sent me into a tailspin, and it took all my determination not to throw a hissy fit. As I knew from experience, that would only make matters worse.

With nothing left on the table to clear, I picked up a copy of Paris Match and pretended to find a photo spread of the Prince of Monaco's latest romantic getaway totally riveting. Anything to keep from making eye contact with my parents and being told I had to go out and pick up my little brother.

"Oh, poupée?" Dad said in his best syrupy voice. "Your mother and I have so much work to do."

And before I could come up with a good excuse, Mom was accepting Dad's implied question for me.

"What a great idea. While you're out, you can pick up the prescription." She flashed me her hazy smile.

A smile so mesmerizing that, as far as I knew, nobody had ever been able to say no to it.

Who was I to break tradition?

It was a fine, warm night, and the air smelled of fallen leaves and hot dog steam rising from vending carts.

When I got to Dov's place, a town house not far from us, I saw Henry waiting by the window. He had his raincoat on, with the hood tied tightly around his face.

"He must be happy to see you," Dov's mom told me when she opened the door. "I didn't know we'd have him for so long." She sounded a little uncomfortable. "Dov's already gone up to his father's for the night. I told Henry he could play on my computer, but he just wanted to wait for you."

"What took you so long?" he called out as he stomped down the hallway toward me.

"Don't ask me," I said, happy to see the only seminormal member of our family. "You can take it up with our parents. And by the way, it's not raining."

Dov's mom laughed. "He's been wearing that since Dov left. I told him I think it looks cute."

Henry didn't much feel like talking. He pouted as we walked down Carmine Street, kicking a bottle cap along the way.

"It's not my fault Mom and Dad forgot," I said. "Don't take it out on me."

Henry made a puffing sound and kicked again.

"If you want to sulk, that's fine, but then we'll go straight home. Or . . . you can buck up and we can take a long walk."

It works every time. While most eight-year-old boys dreamed of growing wings or playing professional football, Henry clings to another fantasy: to walk and walk and walk. He shed his morose self on the corner of Carmine and Bedford streets and perked up as we snaked our way through the West Village. With his hood now hanging down his back, Henry told me about the idea he and Dov had come up with to build a mass transit system for time travel.

I was starting to have fun with my weird little brother, and I almost walked right by the drugstore without remembering I had to stop in.

I wasn't dying to pick up the prescription, but I knew it would get my parents off my case. "Just stay here," I said as I parked Henry up front by the Halloween costumes. He lunged for a hairy ape head and pulled it over his face.

"Claire!" His voice sounded muffled through the mouth slit. "Have I told you the gorilla ice cream joke yet?"

"No, and I can't wait," I told him. "Why don't you practice it in your head? I'll be back in three seconds."

Ten minutes later, the line hadn't moved and I leaned back to look down the aisle and make sure Henry hadn't been kidnapped yet. My little sixty-five-pound gorilla brother was still there.

Ahead of me, some angry woman in a red shift dress and a skinny white scarf was monopolizing the pharmacist, yelling about an allergic reaction she'd had to a pill. I had to wonder if she'd been such a crazy person before she took the pill or if this was the reaction. My eyes crawled over her and I found myself transfixed by her watch, which was huge and had the sun, the moon, and some stars on the ends of the hands.

The woman waiting in front of me, who'd been heaving in irritation the whole time, could no longer contain herself.

"Excuse me!" she yelled up to the counter. "I have a dinner date next month, and I'd like to make it."

At last, the culprit stuck her iPod buds into her ears and turned around to leave. As she stalked past, our eyes met, and I realized it was somebody I knew—Rye from the changing room at Bendel's.

I waved hello and she looked at me as if trying to figure out who I was. I saw a flash of recognition register, but she marched past me without a word anyway.

I'm not going to say it didn't sting, but drugstores can do that to people. I wasn't dying to tell her about my sleeping pills from Dr. Quack, and maybe she was buying treatment for some embarrassing intestinal condition brought on by her starvation program. Or, even more likely, for the personality disorder I'd have bet good money she was born with.

I didn't give Rye any more thought until a little after ten, after everybody else had gone to sleep. All the lights were out, and the only noise was coming from the dishwasher. I'd just nearly gagged on my first dose of Noctolux, and was trying to erase the memory. I'd put on a reality show Becca and Douglas had both told me they were fans of, but it was boring with nobody to joke around with. And so I ended up under the covers, thinking the day over. Images of Dov's mom and the gorilla mask and my new bottle of blue pills danced in my head. And then a picture of Rye arguing with the pharmacist came to the front of my mind.

Suddenly, I felt much more awake. I realized that the glowing sun, moon, and stars on the hands of her watch were almost the same as the ones I'd seen in my dream the other night—the weird black-and-white one with that funny-looking grim reaper guy.

Freaky.

{ 13 }

Digging Up Act Two

The Portrait Club was impossible to miss. It occupied a grand building right off Fifth Avenue. The club's flag, which featured the profile of a man with a George Washington hairdo, was visible from a block away.

Inside, portraits of every conceivable size and style covered the first floor's burgundy walls. It was a bit eerie, I thought, the way the members were mounted on the walls like trophy fish.

I made my way into the sitting room, which was dark and cozy, with businessmen sitting in armchairs and puffing on cigars. Anywhere else they would have been called fat, but here the word was surely *prosperous*. Not wanting to distract their smoky reverie, I walked across the floor, heading toward the DINING ROOM sign as quietly as I could.

When I was nearly there, a man in a red suit with brass buttons stopped me in my tracks.

"Can I help you, miss?"

"I'm fine," I told him. But he repeated his question, and I realized he wasn't interested in *helping* me as much as he was in making sure some stray hadn't blown in off the street.

"I'm here to meet some friends," I said. "The Shuttleworths."

His eyes grew wide and he gulped. "Oh, right this way."

He guided me up a short flight of stairs into the restaurant. Waiters were tiptoeing around, pushing cheese trolleys and removing domed lids from plates. It was noisier than below, though the acoustics of the room were such that I couldn't make out what any of the diners was actually saying. Talk of golfing with Congressmen and skirting environmental protection laws, surely.

All the way in the back were Becca and what I assumed was the Shuttleworth clan. Everyone was dressed to the teeth, and I was relieved that I hadn't worn anything too funky. I handed the man my coat and smoothed my cocktail dress—a violet organza Christian Dior number Kiki had recently donated to my cause.

"Come here," Becca shouted, pushing out the empty seat next to her. "Did that man insist on walking you over here?"

If I'd been the club staffer, I would have been offended, but he merely smiled as he helped me into my seat and sidestepped away.

"He was just trying to be helpful," I said, glancing over at a guy who must have been her older brother. He looked about our age, and if he wasn't Hollywood gorgeous, he was definitely appealing, with his light brown crew cut and rose-bud mouth. Lest anyone think he was too perfect, there was a little V-shaped scar by the corner of his eye. My eyes darted away guiltily.

"Helpful, my foot," Becca said loudly. Her hair was up in a loose bun and she was wearing a white wool dress with navy tuxedo-style ruffles. "This place is crazy. They didn't let women become members until, like, two years ago, and they still have all these rules like women aren't allowed to use the main staircase or walk across the lobby unaccompanied."

"Oh my God, that is so sexist," Rye said in a loud whisper. She was so thin I'd only just noticed her. She seemed to have yet to notice me.

"You're free to leave," the man I took for Becca's dad reminded her, and I could see the woman sitting next to him stifle a laugh.

"You must be Claire," this beautiful mom-aged person said warmly, turning my way. "I'm Becca's mom, Deirdre." I could see the resemblance between Becca and her mother. Deirdre was a brunette, and she'd accessorized her simple navy dress with the most amazing violet gemstone earrings. "And this is my husband, D. K. Shuttleworth."

"Good to meetcha," he said, standing to reach over and clamp my hand so hard I wanted to jump up. He had bushy eyebrows and Becca's huge brown eyes. He was wearing a blue monogrammed blazer, knee-length red shorts, and moc-casins. It was an interesting look.

After we'd all ordered, Becca went to the bathroom and I got to talking to her parents. My initial nervousness quickly evaporated. There was a sweetness underneath their formality, and I couldn't stop laughing when Mr. Shuttleworth told me a dopey joke about Beethoven in his grave (the punch line: "He's decomposing").

"Oh, he's a regular Woody Allen." Becca's mother rolled her eyes. "Now, you're from France, is that right?"

"My dad is," I said. "We go in the summer."

"Do you know what a lucky thing you are?" she exclaimed. "Now, where in France do you go, exactly?"

"We start out in Paris, then we drive around and visit other friends and relatives in the countryside."

Her experience of the country was probably a little different than mine—I doubted she'd ever visited a public pool or witnessed a rooster running around a backyard—but I had no trouble talking to her about the long lines at the Louvre or how the consistency of a French baguette is impossible to replicate in America.

"Wait." I remembered something. "Where's the birthday girl? Aunt Joyce?"

"D.K.'s sister Jocelyn," Becca's mom corrected me. "She couldn't make it."

Becca's dad rubbed his temple and took a zealous glug of ice water.

"She's going through a bit of a thing," Becca's mom said.

"Oh," I said awkwardly, not wanting to seem overly nosy.

"A 'her husband just left her for his dental hygienist' thing," she shared. "I don't think this was the first thing her husband had. Just the first one he was caught having."

"Aha." I nodded crisply. "I'm sorry to hear it."

"Oh, we're not," she said, smiling wearily. "It's for the best."

"Then I guess I'm not sorry to hear it?"

"She catches on fast," Becca's dad said.

"I screen my friends carefully," Becca bragged as she wedged herself back in next to me.

I enjoyed the appetizer course—and not on account of my crab cake, which tasted like a broiled hockey puck. It was entertaining to listen to the family talk about their upcoming weekend in the Bahamas as nonchalantly as if they were planning an outing to the movies, and then they did that thing I'd only read about in Kiki's etiquette books where people change seats between courses to maximize the number of conversational partners.

Next, I sat with Becca's grandparents, D.R. and Dixie. I could tell Becca's grandmother was eager to size me up. "So, Claire," she started in a Southern accent as deep as the sea, "what do your parents do here in New York?"

"My mom's a writer," I said, not wanting to get into the weirdo particulars of her career. "And my father's a French professor."

"Is that right?" She raised her eyebrows in what seemed like appreciation. "Well, you and Rye must have a lot to talk about. Her father's in foreign capital at one of the big banks."

Her husband nudged her. "Dixie, she said *French professor*, not *French investor*."

She paid him no mind and smiled across the table at Rye and Andy. "Aren't they a darling couple? And did you hear how they met?"

"No." But I was dying to.

"They were at school together, and Andy was always chasing Rye around but she wouldn't acknowledge him. Then this summer, she showed up on his doorstep and said she'd changed her mind."

"Completely out of the blue," D.R. said. "She's quite something, that one."

"I can relate," Dixie added. "When D.R. first asked me out, I thought he was a playboy."

"She made me jump through some serious hoops." He chuckled. "The good ones will do that to you." He glanced over at Rye and nodded approvingly.

During dessert I ended up sitting between Becca's dad, who was taking care of some business on his BlackBerry, and Andy, who was too occupied shoveling his pecan pie into his mouth to introduce himself to me. All I could do was sit in my chair and pretend not to notice that Rye was at the other end of the table, eyeing me witheringly.

"Don't worry about her," Andy finally said. "She's nice on the inside, I promise."

"Thanks," I said, spearing a piece of plum tart. "But isn't the point of being nice that it's on the outside?"

"You sound like my old etiquette school teacher."

I gave him a double take. "You went to etiquette school?"

"Is it that hard to tell? Thanks."

Before I could apologize, he told me not to worry about it and nodded over at his parents. "They're brilliant at finding ways to waste money on their son."

"It was that good?" I smiled.

"The only thing I remember is that you're supposed to walk around with your umbrella pointing down."

"Did you skip the 'no elbows on the table' lesson?"

"Apparently." A smile crept across his face, and he walked his elbows off the table. I was overcome with a strange urge to run my hand over the top of his brown fuzzy head and had to focus all my attention on my dessert.

He put his fork down. "I'm Andy, by the way."

"Claire." My face went hot.

"Right." He gave me a strange look and went back to polishing off his pie.

"You'd think they could find a piano player who knows

at least a few songs besides 'Imagination,' " he said a few moments later. I hadn't paid much attention to the music, but suddenly I realized that he was right—the guy at the Steinway *had* been playing the same song all night. "Why don't you go and put in a request?"

"I doubt I'd be of any use," I said. "The only songs I know by name are by girl groups."

"Don't think they're all that into girl anythings around here. Except girls." His eyes scanned the room. I saw his point—practically everyone else in the room was an old man. "I used to know all the old standards. Too bad my memory is subpathetic."

"Speaking of your memory." Rye pulled a chair up between us and started to massage the back of Andy's neck with her spidery fingers. "Did you recall I have a paper due for my women's studies seminar?" While she and Andy exchanged quiet words, I stared at her inky mane and wondered how long it would take my hair to grow into a shampoo ad like hers.

"If you just wait ten minutes—" I overheard Andy say.

"Sure," came Rye's perky response, "as long as you make the clocks go back an hour."

"Fine." Andy pushed his chair out from the table. "Let's get you out of here."

The pair stood up, exchanging unenthusiastic looks. I couldn't shake the feeling that there was something wrong about them as a couple. As far as I could tell, they had nothing in common—apart from the fact that they were equally hot. "Rye has to go write a paper," Andy told the table. "I'm going to help her get a cab."

While everyone else said their goodbyes, I sat there playing with my napkin, worrying that Andy wasn't coming back and that Rye had whisked him off to whatever black mushroom cloud she came from.

Becca and her dad were talking to an elderly man who had wobbled over to the table, so I didn't try to butt in. At last Andy returned and twitched back into his seat, but we didn't exactly pick up where we'd left off. He was instantly consumed in a bout of under-the-table text messaging, a million worlds away from me.

Finally, when being ignored by him was becoming unbearable, I mustered the courage to ask him about Columbia. "Have you joined any clubs at school or anything?"

Great opening gambit, Claire.

He laughed. "I'm not much of an organized activities kind of guy. I take a lot of long walks. Does that count?"

"Let me clarify," Becca broke in. "By 'long walks' he doesn't mean sixty-minute power walks. This guy will go till all hours."

"I'm not a total antisocial weirdo, I just like exploring the city." Andy defended himself.

"My little brother's like that," I told him, "and I know it's not the same thing, but I like to ride my bike to far parts of the city."

"Far? Where?" I couldn't tell if he was skeptical or just curious.

"Everywhere. . . . My parents have all these old New York City guides. In Queens I've gone as far as just before La-Guardia airport. . . . the Botanical Garden in the Bronx . . . this really cool public garden in Riverdale called—"

"Wave Hill? I've been up there, too. Ever been to the cactus house?"

"That place rocks!" I burst out. "Did you see the hot-pink cactus?"

"No, I missed the most obvious thing in the room." He stuck out his tongue playfully.

I felt my blood turn a hundred degrees hotter, and I had to look away and think about something less exciting. Slugs. Shoelaces. Vinyl siding.

None of it worked.

I liked this guy. And apart from the facts that he was (a) my best friend's brother, (b) already taken, and (c) a zillion levels out of my league, he was perfect for me.

After dinner, Becca's parents and grandparents went home, and Becca suggested that she and Andy and I go upstairs. "There's always a book party on Thursday nights. Sometimes they're fun."

I couldn't say that was exactly what I was in the mood for— the few times I'd let my parents drag me to their friends' book launches I'd found myself in some fluorescent-lit university office watching academics eat cheese and crackers with their mouths open—but I had a feeling this night might be different.

And was it ever. The library was all dark wood paneling and rolling ladders and books dating back to the American Revolution. The bookends were classic stone busts— presumably of deceased Portrait Club members. Piles of the book that was being celebrated were stacked next to the globe on the table in the center of the room.

As for the living members in the room, well, Becca's description of "dead white men waiting to happen" wasn't completely off the mark.

Andy led us through the crowd to another window seat. I ended up in the middle, and Andy turned to face me.

"You having fun?" he asked.

"Of course. It's great up here." I made sure to look at both of my hosts.

"It's too bad the roof is closed," Andy said. "You can see everything from up there. . . ."

"It's true," Becca jumped in. "You'd go nuts, C. There's some very good peeping opportunities. Last time we were up there we were looking right in on some dinner party where all the guests had to come dressed up like trashy celebrities."

"Those *were* trashy celebrities," Andy said. "VJ Salmonella lives in that apartment."

"He means DJ Umbrella," Becca said to me, rolling her eyes.

It was doubtful that Andy noticed, but his leg was pressing against mine. It made me a little nervous, and I scooted back.

My spine rammed into something pointy and I spun around, expecting to see a piece of hardware—a coat hook or window latch.

"What the . . . ?" I cried. It was the exact same duffel bag from my dream, with the black-and-white plaid and everything.

"That's called a bag," Andy said. "I believe it's an item that's associated with gym-going homo sapiens."

"You don't understand," I said, "I had a dream with . . . Never mind." It dawned on me that telling them about the levitating bike and my flying was probably not the smoothest move. Same went for Kiki's spiel about my dreams leading me somewhere. "Well, it's a long story, but there was a duffel bag that looked exactly like this one, with the plaid and everything."

"Spooky." Andy's voice was deep—almost the male equivalent of mine—and I couldn't tell if he was making fun of me.

"There must be a present for you inside," Becca said. "Go on, take a look."

"No," I protested.

"Live on the edge a little." She raised one of her eyebrows deviously. Then, when I still wasn't budging, she reached over and took the bag from me. As discreetly as she could, she unfastened the zipper and pulled out a worn copy of a book called *Take Two: How to Manipulate a Man with a Winning Second Impression*. Next, she unearthed a pink and silver scarf that we both instantly recognized. It was Rye's.

"No way!" Andy didn't seem to be too troubled by our discovery—he was shaking lightly with mini-fits of laughter.

"Rye does not own that!" Becca squealed. "I can't be seen holding it. You take it!" Becca tossed the book, hot potato style, into my lap.

Before I could thumb through and read any of it aloud in the mocking tone it surely deserved, its rightful owner was standing over me.

"Looking for something?" Andy inquired teasingly.

Rye let out a nervous squeak and snatched the bag away from Becca, bringing the book to her chest. "I was studying up here before dinner and forgot my book bag."

I felt absolutely mortified. "I'm so sorry, I had no idea."

"What's with the self-help crap?" Andy asked his girlfriend, clearly holding back laughter. "I thought you only read feminist theory."

"That's what it's for." Her cheeks crimsoning, she murmured something about a feminist theory research paper.

"What are you talking about?" said Andy.

She took a deep, impatient breath and explained, "I'm deconstructing contemporary how-to manuals for women and comparing them with Victorian guides for young ladies. Kind of silly, I know." She paused, our cue to assure her it was anything but silly.

Andy took the bait. "That's cool," he said, scooting away from me and reaching out to pull his girlfriend onto his lap. He wrapped his arms around her and mumbled into her hair. "Just don't get any lame ideas from that book. You know more about manipulating men than any self-help guru."

And then everyone giggled. Well, everyone but me.

{ 14 }

Divine Intervention

"**E**nter at your own risk," Henry said as I walked through the front door. He was slumped on the couch, sipping out of a Mont-Saint-Michel souvenir mug and watching some show about turtles.

"What's the matter? Am I in trouble or something?"

He looked confused. "When have you ever been in trouble, Claire?"

Our parents don't do trouble. They can be nags about things like homework (they're pro), snacking (con), and wasting money (violently con), but they're pretty lax about the drugs, sex, and rock and roll stuff—at least, so far they are.

"So what, then?" I slipped out of my shoes and padded into the apartment, trying to puzzle out what my brother was talking about. All I could see was a typical postdinner crime scene at the table: a hardening casserole, balled-up napkins, and a huge pile of unpaid bills standing in as the centerpiece.

"Here we go," Henry said, rolling his eyes toward our parents' bedroom.

The door cracked open and out thumped Mom, clutching a huge stack of paper and an enormous bottle of Evian. She looked as much like a model as usual, only this time for a runway show with an "electrocuted tragedy" look.

Mom placed her stuff on the table and started walking in circles, talking to herself. "Earmark the proposal . . . rodeo index . . . file the column . . ."

"She's been like this all night," Henry whispered under the narrator, who was explaining that turtles used to have teeth.

"Wish me luck," I said, and got up to pull out a chair for her. "What's up, Mom?" I asked cautiously. She collapsed on the seat almost immediately and pressed her thumb over her right nostril, breathing in through the left side. With her eyes still closed, she covered up the left nostril and breathed out through the right side.

"I'm just overwhelmed," she said when she was done with her breathing exercise. I'm used to seeing her get melodramatic about her professional life, but this time there was an unfamiliar edge to her voice. "I can't keep up."

"Keep what up?"

"Everything."

"And what part of everything in particular?"

It went on like this for a little while. Finally, I got her to explain. She'd been trying to help Dad with his Zola research, and meanwhile, the Miss Rodeo America book was taking longer than she'd hoped, and her astrology column was due the next day at noon. "Every time I finish anything, I'm already late with the next thing," she said. "It's my third extension, and they said if I don't get something in, they're finding a new astrologist."

"You're not in such bad shape," I told her, trying to be positive. "You just need some sleep and you can bang out the column in the morning."

"I can't." She sniffed. "I have to go to the Miss Rodeo publisher's first thing tomorrow. They said they have an office for me to work in."

"That's a good thing, isn't it?" I said. "You always complain about working from home."

She looked at me as if I had a discarded pistachio shell for a brain. "It's not a good thing. It's so they can watch over me and make sure I'm not doing other things with my time."

"Like writing an astrology column?" I asked unhelpfully. Henry fired a look my way, but luckily, Mom was too upset to notice.

"I'm going to lose both my jobs, and then what?" she said.

I guided Mom's fingers back up to her nose and oversaw her breathing. When it calmed down some, I offered to write a draft of her column. "It won't be perfect," I said, "but it'll be something. You can fix it in the morning."

She thought long and hard. "Well, it can't hurt to try."

I helped her get to her feet and I walked her into her room.

"After some rest, everything will feel completely different," I told her. "The world makes no sense when you're not sleeping right."

Don't I know it.

She crawled under the covers and dug a book out from under the bed.

"Not tonight, Mom." I removed the book from her weak grasp and turned off the lights. "Just get some rest. You can do all the work in the world tomorrow."

When I went back out into the living area, Henry came over and put a napkin on my head. "It's a miniturban," he told me. "It'll get you in character."

I didn't mind staying up and channeling Priscilla Pluto. This way, at least, I didn't have time to read the chapter in my global studies textbook about Central American farming practices. I didn't have to think of a fake-happy response to Louis's last e-mail, in which he'd informed me that he'd met a girl in the waiting room at his shrink's office. Robyn with a Y—the name alone made me want to gag. As did the thought of another nasty Noctolux pill.

Before starting to type, I gazed out the window. A group of teenagers were huddled under the statue, drinking out of brown paper bags. The moon was full, and a V of birds blazed across the sky. I drew in a deep breath and got going on the column.

By the time I went to bed, there wasn't a single other light on in our complex. I'd outlasted everybody, and I still wasn't ready to fall asleep.

"I hope last night wasn't too weird for you," Becca said as we walked through the Hudson lobby. We had to make our way around a lanky kid who was passed out under the fire extinguisher, a chemistry textbook open over his face in lieu of a sleep mask. "Thank you so much for coming to the stuffiest club in America."

"I didn't think it was that out of control. It was kind of funky, with all the pictures and statues."

"And the dress code? And the requirement that at least eighty percent of the members be senior citizens?"

"Okay, maybe not funky. But it was . . . unique. And I loved meeting your family. They're surprisingly nice." Becca cut me a sidelong look. "I mean—I knew they'd be nice, but they're pretty low-key." I scrambled for something to add that would make it less obvious that I had any particular reason to expect them to be uptight. I still hadn't fessed up that I knew about the Soul Sauce connection. "You know," I said, "considering they're members of the so-called stuffiest club in America."

"They're just people." She shrugged. "And it's my grandparents who belong to the club, not my parents."

"Of course, of course," I responded quickly. I was wide awake and jittery, no doubt thanks to the huge Noctolux pill I'd forced down my throat in the wee hours of the night before.

"Well," Becca said, "my family really liked you, too."

I pictured Andy playing with his pecan pie, and a jolt of adrenaline burned through me.

"They did?" My voice cracked, and I felt as though I had three Noctolux pills stuck in my throat.

"I wouldn't sound so surprised if I were you." She looked around to make sure there were other kids within earshot, then raised her voice. "It's not like I told them about that sick thing you do to puppies with Scotch tape and string."

I snorted. "You need help. Have you ever considered laying off the creepy movies?"

When we got outside, the air was thick with humidity and the sun was blinding.

"Congratulations, Claire!" It took me a second to realize it wasn't Becca speaking. It was one of the BDLs, who were standing in their usual post next to the entrance. "You made a friend here!" Sheila squealed sarcastically. "I'm really proud of you."

Becca tossed me a confused look.

"I knew it was just a matter of time," Ariel added.

"I like how one of you is short and fair and the other is tall and dark." Curly blond Lauren was appraising us as if she were a judge on a reality show. "You're a modern-day Betty and Veronica."

"Except," Sheila turned to her friend, "wasn't Betty cool?"

I was mortified, but Becca seemed unscathed. A subtle grin rose to her face, and she took her time giving them the once-over.

"Very good," she said. "And if you keep practicing your act, you might actually be intimidating one day. But if I can make one suggestion—avoid dressing identically. It makes you look like you all work at Starbucks."

Sheila's eyes were popping out, and at least two of her friends were fingering their hoop earrings as if considering whether to take Becca's advice and remove them.

Becca poked me. "Ready, Veronica?"

"I think *you're* supposed to be Veron—" I said, but I was laughing too hard to finish my sentence.

At dinner that night, Mom seemed considerably more relaxed, and when Dad was clearing the table, she pulled me aside. "Nice job," she said softly. "I barely had to change anything. It's funny, you wouldn't know it from how little you talk, but you have a way with words."

"Scorpio," I told her, "you will damn your daughter with faint praise."

"Oh, you know what I mean!" She wrapped her arms around me from behind and buried her face in my ponytail.

Saturday night Louis invited me to go to the movies with him and Robyn with a Y, but I was feeling a little sick, so I stayed in and wrestled over the remote control with Henry. He wanted to watch the World's Strongest Man competition and I wanted to see *Mystery!* on PBS—it was a Hercule Poirot double feature. We ended up changing channels every ten minutes, which was fair because that way we didn't understand what was going on in either show.

I was still feeling sniffly the next morning, and apart from a quick run to the West Fourth Street magazine stand for a fresh pile of November issues, I didn't end up leaving the apartment until it was time to head to Kiki's for my Sunday-night visit.

The second I stepped into the Waldorf's lobby, every morsel of stress and confusion left my body. You would have to be Ebenezer Scrooge to be there and not feel as if all was right with the world. People were pacing around and talking on their cell phones while honeymooners held hands and floated about, overstuffed on sleep and love. The enormous Art Deco clock rang its quarter-hourly chime.

I had to pull myself away, and walked over to the elevators.

Kiki's gray eye came to the peephole before she unlatched the lock.

"Am I too early?"

"No, you're nice and punctual! I'm practically ready."

She had on a robe and her hair was in rollers.

"Sure looks that way."

"Oh poppycock." She engulfed me in a big hug and reeled back to readjust my cameo necklace.

"Have you been wearing it regularly?" she asked.

"Always, except for baths and showers."

"Good." She ushered me into the main room and shuffled back into her bedroom. "Now, keep your shirt on. I'll be back in a flash."

"I'm in no rush." I free-fell onto one of the damask couches and inhaled deeply. The best perk at the Waldorf is the twice-daily maid service. The cleaners wear French maid outfits—the nonsexy kind—and they keep the apartment smelling like marzipan and lemon zest. Which reminded me.

I slipped into the bathroom and helped myself to a shrink-wrapped oval of almond soap. I was on my way back to the couch when I stopped and looked out of the corner of my eye. Sometimes when I walk past mirrors, I try to trick myself into seeing what I really look like. This entails making a conscious effort not to look in the mirror and forcing myself to be surprised by my own reflection. Of course, surprising yourself on purpose is, by definition, impossible, and in this exercise I always come out looking like the same old me: blond and ducklike. As was the case this time. Sighing, I leaned in closer to the mirror and tried to force my face into Rye's sour expression, with her puckered lips and quick, critical eyes.

"For pity's sake!" Kiki cried from the doorway. "What on earth is going on in here?"

Her hair was set and she was dressed, hugging her Deluxe Scrabble board to her chest.

"Just, you know, practicing a new self-defense technique I read about in *Seventeen*," I said feebly. "People are more likely to leave you alone if you look like you have a medical condition."

"I'll say," she said with a sniff, and strutted out the door, indicating for me to follow.

While Kiki lives in the forty-two-story-tall Waldorf Towers, the Starlight Roof is part of the regular hotel, which is only twenty-seven stories high. On the elevator ride down to the lobby, which connects the towers to the main hotel, she inspected me and smiled. "You're looking well."

"Thanks," I said. "Or I guess I should say thanks to Noctolux."

Kiki's brow twitched. "Thanks to *whom*?"

"I told you I was falling asleep at school, right? My gym teacher called Mom and Dad, and they got me on this blue pill."

"Is that right?"

"It's a pain to swallow but you might like it—even when I only get five hours of sleep, I feel fine the next day." I'd always taken Kiki for an advocate of sleeping pills—her medicine cabinet was jammed with them. But oddly, she looked worried, and her eyes were filming over.

"And let me guess. In the week since you started taking this pill, you've stopped having your interesting dreams."

Until now, I hadn't even thought about it.

"Yeah, I think so."

We watched the elevator numbers tick down. Twenty. Nineteen. Eighteen. My ears felt as if they were about to pop.

"So am I to take it I messed up? . . . I didn't realize there was a connection."

Kiki laughed. "Really, you never cease to surprise me. Let me guess, you didn't see the connection here, either: once you started wearing a black and white cameo, you began to have black-and-white dreams."

I pulled out the necklace to examine it upside down. How had I been so clueless? Only now did it click: the black and white cameo perfectly matched my black-and-white dreams.

"And then you start taking sleep medication and you cease to have the dreams."

"Another connection," I said quietly.

"Bingo. Now, Claire," she said, suddenly serious. "Promise me you'll stay clear of sleep aids." Kiki's words came like a jab. "Toss them out. Unless, that is, you're not interested in reaching your potential."

"Okay, but what is this potential you keep referring to?"

"How are you ever going to learn if I spell everything out for you?" Kiki swallowed audibly. "I'll say this: it would be a shame to give up now. If you play your cards right, you stand a very good chance of becoming a girl of extraordinary talent."

The doors opened and Kiki strode out, not bothering to look over her shoulder to make sure I was following her.

I wanted to hound her more, but she'd already turned the page.

"So, darling," she said in her party voice, indicating we were to put the previous topic behind us. "Aren't you looking forward to tonight's game? I've been hankering all day for some good conversation."

{ 15 }

Mode of Expression

"**H**uggy seven!" somebody shrieked. I spun around and watched Sheila's friend Ariel grab a skinny guy from behind and hold him tightly in her arms. He looked as if he was torn between hating her and enjoying it.

"Huggy Bear," Sheila and co.'s new favorite after-school pastime, entailed tackling members of the Hudson student body and smothering them with hugs.

All of the BDLs were wearing baby-sized Knicks jerseys with their usual black yoga pants. If only there were a way to get Louis's father to use his position as the team's general manager to intervene.

Sheila tossed her hair back, and I wished I could flush

her and the rest of the BDLs down the toilet with my Noctolux pills.

Sheila caught my eye and let her jaw hang, mimicking my gaping stare.

"What's up, Claire?" she pressed. "Do you want a hug or something?"

"No thanks." I shook my head. Sheila's eyes narrowed into knife slits.

"I think she wants a hug and is afraid to ask for it," Sheila told her friends.

"No," I repeated, coming back to my senses. "I'm just fascinated how some people get off on mixing affection and aggression. Call me boring."

Sheila looked confused and turned away.

"Where do those girls get their inspiration?" Becca asked after I'd shambled over to her. She was standing across the street, near the Queen Bee posse.

"We used to play a game like that at birthday parties," I said, watching the skinny kid disentangle himself from his flirty perpetrator. "But that was, like, ten years ago. And cooties played a big role in it."

Becca snickered and pulled her bag higher onto the shoulder of her ochre washed-silk dress. "My voice lesson's in half an hour. Walk with me to the train?" In typical Becca fashion, she asked me this when we were already walking. And in typical Claire fashion, I left my bike behind.

It was one of those sweet-smelling autumn days that make me reconsider calling summer my favorite season. There was a charge in the air, and the leaves were starting to curl like ribbons.

"C'mon, slowpoke," she said, tugging my arm. "I was crazy late last week, and I know I'm going to get booted out."

There wasn't a chance in hell Becca would ever get kicked out of the Young Friends of Lincoln Center program. Unlike the other kids she studied with, she hadn't been invited to train because of her prodigious musical abilities. She'd gotten in through the golden side door. The Shuttleworths were patrons of the Metropolitan Opera, and the family name was etched into the marble donor wall. Plus, Becca had studied piano since she was little, so she knew the difference between a trombone and a treble clef.

"Hey, there was something I wanted to ask you," Becca said. We were approaching the French bistro we had come to dub Chez Illiterate. Indeed, the blackboard in the window pronounced today's special to be "braised lamp chops."

"Looks illuminating." Becca snickered. "Anyway, lemme run this by you. My family's supposed to go skiing next weekend and Rye had to pull out at the last minute. She has some school project that she says is going to be too time-consuming."

"And?" I was dying for her to get to the point.

"And, well, if you wanted to use her tick—"

"Are you messing with me?" I exclaimed. "You're inviting me on a family vacation?"

"It's only two nights. More like a family field trip."

"Sounds like a vacation to me."

"There will definitely be some boring family stuff, but I'm hoping most of the time we can hang out just the two of us."

"You don't have to talk me into it," I told her. "I'm in."

A smile spread across her face.

"I do have one question, though," I said. "Where in the world are you taking me?"

"Aspen." She fixed her eyes on me and waited to see if I

recognized the name. I guess she could tell I didn't. "It's in Colorado. That's a state in America."

I blushed. "Thanks, I think I've heard of it. My parents will be pleased to know you're not taking me to some war zone."

"Better luck next friend. My parents don't really do war zones."

Giggling slightly, I added, "Please make sure to send Rye my thanks."

"Yeah, we're lucky she was the one to drop out, and not somebody in the family." She pulled her MetroCard out of her wallet.

"Because she's not your favorite person on earth?" I asked hopefully.

"No," she sounded impatient. "Because she's the reason we're flying commercial."

"What are you talking about?" Was there any other way to fly, unless you planned to sneak onto a FedEx plane or something?

"My dad is obsessed with all of his planes, but he's squeamish about letting non–family members on them."

"*All* of his planes? How many are we talking about, here?"

"I think there are about twelve." She sounded nonchalant. "But there's this one, the Dassault Falcon 7X, that's his true love." She thrust out her hand and pointed to her ring. "He had it special made."

"The ring?"

"Yes." She looked slightly embarrassed. "And the plane. He keeps it in London, just so nothing bad will happen to it."

I scrunched up my nose. What about London was immune to "bad"?

"But," I started quietly, "wouldn't he want it here so he can, you know, use it?"

Becca's face clouded over and she twirled her hair. "Yeah, I don't know. He's crazy with his ideas. He's convinced his planes are safer there. You can ask him."

"I think I'll pass."

"Well . . ." Becca looked past my shoulder, as if the words she was searching for were floating in the air behind me. "I'm really glad you can keep Rye's seat warm."

"No biggie," I said, trying to make it sound as if I were doing them a favor instead of the other way around.

I was playing pickup basketball on the West Fourth Street courts with Rye, of all people. But the fact that she was there wasn't the weirdest part. You should have seen me going crazy out there on the court—my body was suddenly a million times smarter and faster and, yes, taller than it actually is. In normal life, I've never been able to see the point of competitive athletics, but now I was starting to see why people cared. I felt as if I had been put on this earth for no reason other than all this pivoting and dribbling and looking down on my opponent. And I wasn't even breaking a sweat. Then I cut across the court and pulled off a slam dunk that was so forceful it bounced off the court's concrete and over the fence. The air filled with whoops, and a few fans rushed out to hoist me into the air. I wouldn't say Rye looked ecstatic.

On Tuesday morning, I woke up feeling short and groggy, but I pressed on. Inspired by my dream, I threw on the sportiest thing in my closet: a bright yellow cap-sleeved dress with a line of blue buttons along the front.

When I went to the kitchen to get some juice, Mom was watching the French news on the Internet in the living room.

"Hey, Mom, remember when you said you owe me one for doing your column?"

Mom looked up at me and yawned.

"I'm calling in that favor. Any chance you can make a batch of your special lemon crêpes?"

"You're never hungry in the morning."

"It's not for me. It's Silent Eleanor's birthday."

"Who's that?"

"She's a Hudson friend. We sit together at lunch."

"Another friend at school?" She leapt up from behind her laptop. "And on top of a weekend away with Becca? *Fantastique!*"

"I'm going to refrain from reminding you that you were born in this country."

"And I'll refrain from reminding you that it's a *free* country."

We squeezed into the kitchen, and I helped her by measuring pancake mix and breaking eggs. Mom was in charge of the frying pan and spatula. The crêpes were coming out paper thin and slightly golden. All smooth sailing until she turned around to pick up her water bottle and ended up with her nose in my collarbone.

Mom pitched forward, and before I knew what was happening, her batter-covered fingers were coming at my neck like ten sludge monsters emerging from the bottom of the sea. My heart started pounding and my fight-or-flight instinct kicked in.

"My mother used to have a necklace just like it. It's not the same one, is it?"

"Not so close!" I flinched. I knocked over the bowl of remaining mix and it sluiced all over the floor.

Mom just looked confused.

"Sorry," I said. "I just didn't want to get my dress messy."

"Of course not."

She switched her stare from my dress to the expanding pool of batter. I could tell I'd let her down.

"I'm sorry," I repeated.

"It's okay. I think there are more paper towels under the sink."

Luckily, she'd already made five crêpes—more than enough to feed my lunchtime posse. I thanked her by cleaning up the mess I'd made and letting her go back to watch whatever important news was happening in the motherland, knocking her away had been a strange reaction that I couldn't stop thinking about as I wiped Aunt Jemima off the floor. Math would have to go on without me that day.

When Eleanor saw me take the lid off my Tupperware container to reveal a short stack of crêpes with a birthday candle, she waved me away with her hands.

"There's no hiding," I said. "Ian told me. Happy birthday."

Zach presented her with a thermos of fresh-squeezed orange juice, and Ian gave her a comic he'd made. "It's based on the classic Little Lulu," he explained. His version starred Little Eleanor, an all-black-wearing daredevil who befriends a crow and convinces him to peck at Henry Hudson High with his beak until the building crumbles.

Eleanor was beaming with every page, and there was a slight bounce to my step when I strode over to English. For once, I was ready to face Mr. Bunting. A tall man with a little stub of a nose, Mr. Bunting was the only English teacher in the eastern United States who (a) hated books and (b) fell asleep and woke up at least a couple of times during every class.

When I got to class, Mr. Bunting was in his seat, reading the newspaper and turning the pages in a loud, energetic fashion. This was a method favored by many Hudson teachers to avoid having to make conversation with the students.

When the first bell rang, he stood up and, moving in the stiff manner of a robot, he approached the blackboard to write: "The Short Story."

"Now that the poetry unit is over," he announced, "we are going to focus on a new mode of expression."

He said the word *expression* so unexpressively I couldn't hold in my laughter. Shooting me a dark glare, he brought his long fingers to his forehead, as if I were personally causing his headache.

He started walking up and down the aisles, passing out a new book: *Fictional Impressions*.

I flipped to the introduction. It was written in 1953 and said that the ten stories in the book were the ten best stories ever written. Not ten "of the best." The ten best.

Who knew God guest edited crappy textbooks?

"Miss Voyante," Mr. Bunting said. "Is something amusing?"

My classmates were all staring at me, as were the U.S. presidents bordering the top of the walls. "Well, I don't know, I just think it's funny that the book says these are the ten best stories. I mean, how can anyone say that?" My voice sounded small, and I felt even smaller. The room had gone completely silent, and Ian sent me a stealthy thumbs-up from his seat.

Mr. Bunting flipped through the book. "Jack London. Ernest Hemingway. Nikolay Gogol. I'm sorry that's not good enough for you, Miss Voyante." He glared at me and then proceeded to circle the room, his beige dress sneakers squeaking on the linoleum until he reached my desk. "How about this? If a story's value is so subjective, why don't you create your own stories? We can compare them to the ones in the collection and see if it really is all relative." I slunk into my chair as he clarified the assignment for us—we were going to work in pairs, and then we'd present next Thursday. "You can partner up after class. In the meantime, we have a lesson to learn." He returned to the blackboard and wrote: "Noun. Verb. Adjective."

The halls were vibrating with more than the usual amount of end-of-the-day excitement as I made my way to my locker. Kids were standing around in tight clumps, all chattering and studying what appeared to be the same green piece of paper.

I wondered what groundbreaking change in school policy the paper detailed—maybe they were going to start allowing us to use calculators during tests or rounding our grade point averages to the nearest whole number. But within a few more seconds, I realized I hadn't given my fellow Hudsonites enough credit. They were getting worked up about an up-coming social event—and it wasn't a citywide bagpipe competition.

"A party?" I overheard a girl say, utterly dumbfounded. "And it's not for anyone's birthday?"

"I hope my parents will let me go," another chimed in.

"You can't tell them, dumbass. You'll ruin it for all of us."

I slowed down some near a guy who, despite a four-inch-high flattop, still stood shorter than me. Peering over his shoulder, I confirmed that the Hudson student body was about to have its first big party. At least, the first big party I'd ever heard of.

And from what I could tell, the school itself had nothing to do with it. The invites didn't have the Hudson insignia, and the layout was actually cool—a mash-up of bubbly hand-writing and slightly blurry pictures of different people set at different angles. The only one I instantly recognized was Lisa Simpson.

The short kid must have felt me breathing behind him.

"Sorry," I said when he whipped around. I started to bar-rel away, but he reached out to stop me.

From behind a pair of frameless glasses, his eyes were al-ternately narrowing and widening.

"Wait—are you . . . ?" He looked back down at the invite and focused on me again. His friends were doing the same thing, until one of them, a kid in a SPACEMEN DO IT BETTER T-shirt, turned to the rest and said, "Close approximation, but ultimately negative."

I had no idea what he was talking about, but as I made the rest of the short walk to my locker, I couldn't help noticing that other kids were looking at me, too. And I wasn't being paranoid. Nobody at Hudson knows how to pretend to be looking somewhere near you if they actually want to get a look at you. They'll just look straight at your eyeballs.

"Claire!" somebody shouted from behind. I knew from its tone and assertiveness that it had to belong to one of my favorite girls.

The BDLs were coming at me in lockstep, wearing matching white tank tops and leers. Brown-haired Lauren was holding a basketball. I had no idea what this meant, but it kind of freaked me out.

"Like anyone would think of having a party without you!" curly blond Lauren crowed.

"Let's just hope she stays this time," Ariel cackled.

"We decided to have a little shindig this weekend," Janice said when they'd all caught up with me. She was carrying the stack of green papers. "You should definitely come."

"Superdefinitely," seconded brown-haired Lauren, tossing the basketball to Sheila. What on earth was I supposed to make of this? "You're practically essential."

"I'll bet," I rasped, trying to pack as much sting as possible into my reply. Sadly, I don't think it was a smashing success.

"A bed?" Sheila asked me. "Is that what you said?"

"Yes," I said, sarcasm oozing through my voice. "And a nightstand."

"What?" she snapped.

"Never mind," I said, suddenly acutely aware of how many other kids were staring at us and thinking that I was the one who was out of her mind.

"Go on," Sheila instructed Janice. "Give her one."

Janice did as told.

Trying to look as if I didn't care, my eyes grazed over the words and I must have absorbed only half of them—"Theme Party!" and "Freaks and Geeks" and "BYOBB—BRING YOUR OWN BUNSEN BURNER."

"Much as I love doing science experiments at social gatherings," I said, "I'll be out of town this weekend."

"No!" Sheila cried with fake disappointment. She bounced the ball to Ariel.

"Well, she'll still be there in spirit," Ariel pointed out as she caught the pass.

"Superdefinitely," I growled.

Sheila made a cutesy-poo smile and motioned to her friends that their work was done. "If your plans fall through, drop by!"

Once they'd sloped off, I was able to study the rest of the invite. Interspersed with the lettering was a collage of legendary dorks: Lisa Simpson as well as Napoleon Dynamite and that weird monobrow guy from *Star Trek*. And, in the bottom right corner, there was a picture of a certain young lady performing with the Weirdo Beardos at her seventh-grade talent show. It didn't really matter that the girl was hiding behind a long multicolored cloak, stick-on Rasputin beard, and massive xylophone. She had the same blond hair and scrunched-up confused duck expression as somebody who now attended Henry Hudson. And judging by the way my classmates were leaning in to get a better look at me, this resemblance did not seem to be lost on any of them.

"It *is* her," I heard somebody whisper. "You *so* owe me two dollars."

My blood was boiling.

So what if I had shoe boxes filled with embarrassing pictures of Sheila posing in a padded leotard and wielding a stone-encrusted sword? She'd already beat me to the punch.

I pedaled freakishly fast uptown, taking out some of my frustration on my bike. Kiki was lending me some of her ski clothes for my Aspen adventure. And thank goodness. After being forced to revisit my Weirdo Beardos phase, I was ready for something slightly more Audrey Hepburn–worthy.

Somebody had already locked a bike to the one available pole near the hotel, so Ray, one of the nicer bellhops, helped me carry my Schwinn up the hotel's stairs and into the baggage room. The lobby was overrun with Secret Service men, as only happens when the President stays at the hotel. The presidential suite is on the top floor, and anybody who stays there has to sign a form agreeing to change rooms if the head of state comes to town. Supposedly there's an underground tunnel connecting the hotel to Grand Central Terminal that President Kennedy and his aides used, but I haven't been able to find it on any of my searches.

"So," I said to Ray. "Have you seen him?"

"Who?" Ray didn't blink. The Waldorf prides itself on its discretion, but sometimes the staffers take it too far.

I didn't bother to reply and only gave him a thin thank-you when I left.

"*There* you are," Clem said as he let me into Kiki's apartment. "I've been helping your grandmother pick out an outfit for tomorrow night. She's having dinner with some beau from her past."

"Don't believe a word Clem tells you!" Kiki cried from

the other room. "Sergio is a dear old friend, and pure as a lamb!"

"I'd like to meet *that* lamb," Clem whispered, sitting down on one of the damask couches. He had on a navy blazer, a bright orange silk scarf, and a huge silver skull ring. He looked awesome. "Oh Claire, if you'd got here ten minutes earlier you'd have witnessed the Sultan of Brunei throwing a hissy fit down in the lobby. It was splendid."

"What happened?"

"The hotel needed his room, for obvious reasons"—he looked at me pointedly—"and the Sultan had to be moved to a smaller room. You know he owns the New York Palace Hotel, don't you? But he has it in his head he has to stay here." Clem made the international symbol for crazy with a finger by his ear. "I told Keeks one of us should just offer to put him up. Wouldn't that be a hoot?"

"I don't see why you didn't." I ducked into the bathroom to fix my hair and pilfer my 157th bar of almond soap.

When I came out, Kiki and Joe, the hotel general manager, were dragging a black and brown checkered trunk into the apartment. Joe let Kiki use the hotel's storage facilities in exchange for her friendship. I wanted to tell Kiki about the basketball dream and my run-in with the BDLs, but something told me she'd prefer that I wait until we were alone.

"Curses!" Kiki cried. "Are you sure nobody's loaded any dead bodies in here?"

"Let me get that," I said, taking the trunk handle from her. Joe and I pulled the trunk across the floor until she told us to stop.

She crouched down to flip open the lid, and a musty smell drifted through the air. "There should be a few goodies in this time capsule," she said, and started to yank out select pieces.

Clem and I watched in disbelief as swatches of silk and

oversized zippers and sparkly buttons flew through the air. I practically had to wipe the drool from my chin when she handed me her selection: a black hooded cashmere dress, huge black Balenciaga sunglasses, and a white strapless dress with a heart-shaped neckline.

"It's all rather impractical for skiing," she said, "but you won't actually be going near the snow, will you?"

Kiki knew I couldn't ski. The Shuttleworths, on the other hand, had yet to learn about my disability.

"I might make a snowman or something," I said.

"Then take this," she said, and tossed me a belted blue coat with white mink trim. It was the Rolls-Royce of coats: so luxurious it practically taunted the world to climb inside. I wished I didn't find fur so repulsive.

"The only thing is . . . ," I started.

"Oh, relax," she said. "It's faux. Now, give it a whirl."

I stuck around for dinner with Clem and Kiki—creamed chicken hash and Cobb salads from room service (my idea, again). At Kiki's insistence, we prepared for my trip with the Shuttleworths and reviewed some of her favorite rules.

"Knife and fork?" Kiki took a sip of her martini.

"Easy," I said. "Cross them between bites."

"Arrive at the table with . . . ?"

"A few interesting stories to contribute."

"That one's very important," Clem chimed in. "And don't think they can't be made up."

"Embellished," Kiki corrected him. " 'Made up' sounds so tawdry. But a little imagination can be a girl's best friend."

"Don't I know it," I muttered under my breath.

"The cameo necklace?" Kiki asked.

I had to think about this one. "Don't take it off unless I'm showering?"

"Right-o." She smiled. "And getting engaged on a whim?"

"Um, don't do it?"

"Correct—unless the man is a Shuttleworth."

"What!" I nearly spit out my food. "I'm only fifteen!"

"Oh, lighten up," Kiki said. The phone was ringing, and she pushed herself out of her chair to answer it. Kiki's phone doubles as an intercom for deliveries and visitors; otherwise she would ignore it during meals.

"Claire." She shot me a strange look. "For you."

Turned out the strange look was justified. It was Mom, who hardly ever calls me at Kiki's.

"Claire, we have to talk," she said. To an outsider, her voice might have sounded normal: soft and breathy, but I could detect a tremor. "I was sneaking in the last sign on the astrology column at the ghostwriting office and my boss caught me."

"That sounds okay," I said, trying to sound sunny to distract Kiki and Clem from the true nature of the call.

"Hardly. My boss went berserk. I was already so far behind on the book, I was ordered to hand over the project to somebody else."

Turning my back on the diners, I whispered, "You mean you were fired?"

"Yes and no," she said. "Well, yes, from the Miss Rodeo job. But listen," she said, and proceeded to explain that Tom Blakeson, her friend and editor at the *Planet*, had come to the rescue. He'd asked her to come down to Tampa for two weeks to work on the special "Stars We Love" issue.

"I'm sorry to bum-rush you like this, but everything's falling into place so fast and I just wanted to tell you before you heard it from someone else," she said. "Cheri-Lee's offered to pop by and lend a hand when you're in Aspen. And the rest of the time, you can help out around home, right?

Nothing crazy, just make sure everyone washes and eats something green once in a while. Okay?"

"What can I say?"

"You're a good kid." She sounded sincere, and I felt better for hearing her say it. "We should probably go over some stuff before you leave."

"I'll be there in a little over an hour." And to throw Kiki and Clem, who were straining to listen in, I groaned, "I can't believe you're making me go to another Professors Who Paint show."

"Again?" Kiki asked after I'd hung up. "Those ninnies don't even wait for the paint to dry, do they?"

{ 16 }

The Worst Kind of Magic

Mom and I both had Friday flights, and we both waited until early Friday morning to pack. Watching Mom get ready for Florida was a master class in economy. She filled her Day-Glo suitcase with four days' worth of clothes and a travel-sized box of laundry detergent—even though she was raised by Kiki, she hates wasting money on hotel laundry services. My packing method for my two-night trip was a bit more festive: I brought enough to allow for three daily changes, plus an emergency clothing supply to last through the unlikely but possible event of a thirty-day hostage situation.

That's not to say I was completely on the ball when I got ready. I forgot to deal with my chipped toenails, and more importantly, I never got around to telling Becca that I don't know how to ski. I kept meaning to, but after listening to her rhapsodize about the space-age gondolas or the thrill of careening down Aspen Mountain at a million miles an hour, it began to feel too late, and I tried to convince myself that it would be less jarring for everyone if I waited until we got there to tell Becca.

Once we touched down late Friday night, I couldn't get any alone time with my friend, and I didn't want to announce my handicap to the entire Shuttleworth clan. There were seven of us—Becca, Andy, the Shuttleworth parents and grandparents, and yours truly. At the airport, we stuck together in a tight cluster, only to fan out when a fleet of town cars picked us up and ferried us to the hotel.

We were staying at an enormous two-winged guesthouse at the base of Aspen Mountain, with stone walls and red shutters. I felt dizzy when we got there—and not just from altitude sickness. The lobby was extraordinary. A few guests crowded around a fireplace; others were taking catnaps on oversized leather couches. The windows overlooked a steaming hot outdoor pool, just beyond which stood the snowy mountain.

"I'll be right back." Becca ran off.

"Where are you—" I started, but something heavy landed on my shoulder.

"I'm so tired." Andy was resting his face on my collar. "If I fell asleep here, would you mind?"

"Um . . . be my guest." I stood stock-still, praying that he wouldn't be able to detect my galloping heart.

"Andy!" His mother scolded him for "bothering our nice guest" and pried him away from me before Becca returned from wherever she'd run off to.

Everyone seemed delighted with the hotel except Becca's dad. He'd been in a bad mood since we'd left New York, and he'd spent the entire plane ride tapping the side of his shoe, his mouth set in a frown.

"How about dinner already?" he asked, his first words all day. "I'm tired of waiting around."

Becca's grandmother Dixie looked slightly shocked, then decided to smooth over her son's prickly mood with her Southern charm. "Well, you know I'm always up for a good prime rib," she purred.

The hotel's welcome ritual was as beautifully choreographed as a Christmastime ballet. As soon as one dapper hotel employee had relieved us of our bags, another swooped in bearing a tray of espresso cups filled with hot chocolate. Normally I like a proper-sized cup, especially when it's filled with anything chocolatey, but after I took a sip I understood why the portions were so small. With a consistency somewhere between liquid and solid, there was no way anybody could make their way through more than a few ounces of this stuff. It was one of the strangest and most delicious things I'd ever tasted, second only to the caramelized curried pecans at the Walforf's Bull and Bear bar.

"Nutritious stuff," Andy said before drinking his allotment like a shot.

"Yeah, it's got plenty of chocolate and . . . sugar."

"You're forgetting lard," Andy reminded me.

"Ew!" Becca cried, elbowing her brother in the ribs. "He's just messing with you."

I didn't care. I wanted to wipe up the remnants inside the cup with my finger, and could use the discouragement.

"Shall we?" Andy asked.

I looked up and realized the rest of his family had started walking to the restaurant.

"I guess we don't have much choice." I smiled.

"Booty warming," he said as we trailed the others.

"I think my hot chocolate got stuck somewhere around my lungs," I said, blushing. My booty was something I liked to cover up, not discuss.

He laughed at me. "I wasn't talking about your digestive tract." He pointed to the sign at the concierge desk. It offered hot stone massages, gourmet dog meals, and, last but not least, boot warming services.

Whoops.

The restaurant was an oasis of beige and gray tones undoubtedly designed to please older patrons. If I ever had a restaurant of my own, I'd hire Clem to deck it out with hot pink walls and disco blobs.

The only empty seat was next to Andy, which meant that I barely registered the beautiful scenery and five-star dishes. Still, in my befogged state, I couldn't help detecting something awkward in the air. Or maybe Becca's dad was just profoundly grumpy. He seemed to bounce into a better mood when the waiters brought out his rib-eye steak, even if he only ate a little bit.

At the end of dinner, after all the grown-ups had their dessert wine and a waiter in a knee-grazing jacket brought out a box of handmade truffles, Becca's parents decided to call it a night. "It's been a very long day, and we're not as hip and happening as you," Becca's dad said to us. "I'm going to go upstairs and check in with my old friend Larry. He comes on in ten minutes."

"Would that be Mr. King?" I asked.

"None other." He winked.

I pictured Kiki sipping tea in bed as she waited for her suspender-wearing boyfriend to come on TV already.

"Now I'll tell you what we 'hip and happening' kids are doing," Becca announced once her parents had disappeared. She pointed at the lobby's glass wall. Beneath the darkening sky, the swimming pool stretched out under a cloud of steam.

"Isn't it freezing?" I asked. If I could have made a list of all the things I'd rather not do in front of Andy, wearing a bathing suit would have been right up there, along with freaking out to "Peanut Duck" with Henry and helping my dad trim his mustache.

"Don't worry," Andy said. "We did it last time. The heat's turned up a million degrees, so you don't even notice how cold it is."

Before I could tell them I didn't have a bathing suit, Becca was distributing towels and disposable bathing suits in vacuum-packed cases. "Gotta love the concierge desk," she said.

We all got changed in the lobby bathrooms, and before I knew it, I was the only one still indoors, with a towel wrapped around me. The other two had left their clothes in a heap by the door and jumped into the pool. I couldn't see anyone's faces—just shapes moving around the steam.

I dropped my towel on top of the pile and ran shivering toward the pool, the ground frosty against my bare feet. The water was warm, and I darted about like a happy little tadpole. The steam by the water's edge was too thick to see through, and the only way to tell whether somebody was nearby was when the water surged or rippled.

Something grazed against my shin, and I didn't think much of it. I just kept going. Or I tried—I didn't get very far. In fact, I didn't go anywhere. I was floating on my stomach when I realized somebody was holding my ankles from behind. I looked over my shoulder and saw Andy's silhouette, his prickly head atop his lean body. I looked around for Becca but couldn't see anything.

"I think your hands got tangled up in my legs." I was trying to sound matter-of-fact, as if it were perfectly normal that he was holding me like a wheelbarrow, my huge butt about three inches from his face.

"I'm sorry," he said, and pushed my feet toward the pool floor. Then he took hold of my shoulders and turned me around so we were facing each other. I stepped closer and reached out to take his hand. Every cell in my body felt hot, even warmer than the water, and I looked up at the moon and wondered how it could be as cold as I'd heard it was if it was burning that brightly.

I heard some splashing, then pitter-pattering that grew quieter.

"Becca went back inside," he whispered, pulling my fingers, one by one.

"How can you tell?" I looked toward the hotel. "I can't see anything."

"What did you think that sound was? A duck walking around the side of the pool? Here," he said gently, and before I knew it his face was so close to mine I could feel his breath on me. Apart from the fact that I was wearing a hideous disposable bathing suit, this was everything a kiss was supposed to be—slightly scary, and more than a little fluttery. And we hadn't even started kissing yet. Drifting closer, I wondered if it was humanly possible for things to get more exciting.

As it turned out, things did get more exciting, but not in the way I'd hoped. Suddenly Becca was poolside, yelling at us from a patch of fog. "That celebrity magician guy, Daniel What's-his-face, he's doing a show in the lobby! Hurry up!"

Andy's shoulders tensed, and the space between us suddenly felt emptied of the turbocharged energy that had been there just seconds ago. "We should probably go in before we get into any more trouble," Andy murmured, and before I knew what was happening, he had sunk underneath the surface and was shooting over to his sister.

That night the magician performed a whole slew of tricks, but none as astonishing as the first: he'd made Andy disappear.

{ 17 }

Snowcaps and Setbacks

Still in our bathing suits, Becca and I hung around to watch the magician stick a needle through his arm and make his socks change color before heading up to our room.

The room was infinitely better than the magic show. It was absurdly luxurious, with a theater-sized television set and two hot tubs—one in the bathroom and one in the ballroom-sized bedroom, abutting the window. Of course I'd seen fancy hotel rooms before, but never had I had one of my own. If a war was going to break out in the West anytime soon, I wished it would happen this weekend. Camping out would be a dream come true.

We let our towels drop to the floor and put the hotel robes

on over our wet suits. Becca went to get washed up and I lay on top of the duvet, replaying my nonkiss over and over.

I felt like squealing—and at some point I must have.

"What's that?" Becca called from the bathroom.

"The TV!" I quickly grabbed the remote control and flipped through the channels. A police drama. An ad for a psychic with a 900 number. A Hallmark special on "Dads We Love." Which got me thinking.

"Hey," I called out, turning the TV off. "Is everything okay with your dad?"

I heard Becca spit out her toothpaste. "Long story."

She came back into the bedroom wearing a pair of tortoiseshell glasses that I'd never seen before. Sometimes I forgot how short a while we'd actually been friends.

She flung herself on the bed. "If I tell it to you, you have to promise not to share it with anybody. Can I trust you?"

Um, can you trust somebody who almost kissed your brother in the pool ten minutes ago and isn't telling you about it?

"Of course." I could feel the guilt sloshing in my stomach.

"I'm serious."

"So am I."

Becca stuck her fingers under her glasses and rubbed her eyes. "Earlier today somebody tried to steal the key." She looked at me, waiting for something to register. "Wait, you have no idea what that means, do you?" She kicked off her fuzzy boots and shook her head. "Oh God. This is gonna be a long night."

We stayed up talking until two in the morning. Well, we stayed up and she talked. There was a lot of ground to cover—four centuries' worth. Back in the 1640s, the Shuttleworth family left England and settled in Virginia, where they set up a tomato farm. And that was only the beginning of things.

Becca explained that her ancestors did quite nicely for themselves every year. But in 1739 they had a bumper crop, earning far more than they ever expected. Rather than sit on the extra money or blow it on a bunch of petticoats or whatever it was people wasted their money on in the eighteenth century, Becca's savvy ancestor Arthur purchased an extra acre of land, four horses, and something that would prove to be the biggest payoff: a recipe from the neighboring Soyle family, who sold their delicious Soyle Sauce ketchup, which they called "Saul Sauce," at a few general stores.

"It must have seemed logical to go into the ketchup business," Becca said, "being a tomato farmer and all." She went on with the history lesson, telling me how Arthur Shuttleworth and Edward Soyle settled on the sum of four hundred pounds for the recipe.

"Nothing to sneeze at back then," Becca told me.

"I'm sure," I said, remembering how the kids in the Little House on the Prairie books would buy a pair of overalls for a dime.

"It was a good deal for the Soyles," Becca said, "but they started to get the idea that they'd been screwed. And while my family grew the business, the Soyles hit a streak of bad luck."

"What do you mean by bad luck?" I asked.

"Everything, really." She tented her hands together. "Scrapes with the law, bankruptcies, failed business plans. They've been trying for hundreds of years. They started a candlestick company, a hotel, a chain of restaurants, a department store. All failed. No one remembered the original recipe, and they tried to start a gourmet ketchup company, but nobody wanted to buy a fifteen-dollar roasted organic tomato compote for their hot dogs, so that went belly-up. Then they tried to package generic ketchup in single-serving foil packets, but it turned out people like to squeeze the bottles themselves. Their lost luggage Web site flopped, and now they just had another big disaster, a company that designed video games for dogs."

"I'm actually surprised that didn't work. People can be so weird with their pets . . . So now what? The Soyles are off in Siberia, licking their wounds?"

"If only." She flipped onto her back and stared up at the ceiling. "They're right across the Hudson River, in Bayonne, New Jersey. They have a new project, a chain of retro steakhouses, with topless waitresses. It's called Rumps and Humps."

"Classy."

"The classiest. They also manufacture tube socks. I'm sure you've seen the factory. The one with the huge smog cloud over it."

"Um, aren't there a few that fit that description?"

"Yeah, but last year Soyle Socks was handed more labor violations than any other company in New Jersey."

"Sucks to be them." The clock said it was nearly one o'clock. I got up to close the curtains.

"It's crazy, but I really think they're cursed," Becca said quietly. "One of their sons is in jail for armed robbery, and last year a grandchild got in a nasty car accident. He can't walk."

A chill shot up my spine. I spent a moment looking out at the dark mountain before pulling the curtain shut.

"I wouldn't feel too sorry for them," she said when I'd made my way back to the bed. "They think we're thieves, and Lazarus—he's the president of Soyle Socks—is constantly scheming to get the recipe back. And then there's Otto—that's Lazarus's son. He's the devil in white-rapper clothing. He and his thug friends used to wait for Andy outside school and mug him."

"Mug him?" I repeated, wagging my head in disbelief. "I can't believe this is all about ketchup."

Becca looked as if she was getting impatient. With what, I had no idea. "You've probably never stopped to think about this, but ketchup is a big deal. You should hear my dad get started on the subject. He calls it the great universal food. At least, now it is. When ketchup was first invented, in the 1600s, it was made of mushroom and anchovies."

"I think you mentioned that before," I told her. "Sounds delicious."

"I know. But then they figured out how to use ripe tomatoes and everything changed for the more delicious. They came up with a sauce that's not too sweet, and not too spicy. Everyone likes it. In America we eat it with our potatoes, Japanese people eat it with rice, and in Poland they eat it with pizza." There was a broken-record element to her speech, and I suspected she'd heard her dad's spiel more than a few times. "The Soyles have been trying to come up with their own versions, with different spices and flavors, but here's the thing: people just like their ketchup . . . ketchuppy."

"Makes sense," I said, readjusting the pillow under my neck. "That's how I like mine."

"Well, Soul Sauce has been around so long, that's what people think ketchuppy tastes like. And of course my family is obsessed with keeping the magic formula private. They act like it's the nectar of the gods."

"Well, based on what you're saying, it sort of is."

She shrugged. "At this point, it's hard to keep perspective. My parents especially. They used to lock the recipe away in the company headquarters in New York, but people kept breaking into the building, so we had to move it to a bank safe. The key to the safe was just moved to a secret location that's not even in the country. Anything to keep Lazarus away."

"Do you actually think they'd ever get the recipe?"

"That's the least of anybody's worries." Her eyes clouded over. "They've done other stuff. My uncle William was kidnapped for a week when he was seven. Nobody officially knows who was behind it, but still . . . And my dad's totally paranoid that we're not safe in the family planes." She looked over at me to make sure I was following.

"Is that why we had to slum it and fly first class instead of on one of the Shuttleworth shuttles?"

Becca rolled her eyes and nodded. "At this point we have to run background checks on practically everybody who comes near us."

I considered this for a moment.

"Does that mean——?"

She nodded. "You passed yours with flying colors."

They'd run a *background check* on me? "That's supremely weird," I said, taking out my barrettes and bobby pins. I wondered what kind of dirt they'd uncovered. Had there been a classified file they passed around at dinner one night? Did all the Shuttleworths know about my love of trashy magazines and my complete and utter lack of a romantic history?

Never before had my entire existence felt so embarrassing.

"C, have I ever seen your hair down? It's awesome. Is it naturally that . . ."

"Big? Yup . . ." I had to take my chance at turning the conversation away from my yellow 'fro. "So have *you* ever run into Soyle trouble?"

She fiddled with her pillow and breathed in hard. "Last year at boarding school there was this creepy man who'd show up in town and follow me around. My parents pulled me out of school."

My mouth fell open. "So you didn't get the boot for sneaking out like you told me?"

She shook her head guiltily. "I hardly knew you."

"But you haven't seen him since?"

"No, not him in particular," she said distantly. "But somebody's watching me. You remember that creepy text I got the other day? The one about the headband?"

"Where they called you Alice?"

"Yup." She cast her eyes down. "There have been more of those. A few more."

I felt a little queasy. "And you think the Soyles found somebody at Hudson to play on their team?"

"I wouldn't put it past them. I'm just hoping that if that's the case, the point was to find somebody to keep me on edge and that's all."

"Have you told your parents?"

She shook her head. "I'm not going to unless something actually happens." She made a pistol with her fingers and pointed it at her head.

"Becca!"

"I'm just kidding. They wouldn't do that. But seriously, I just hope I don't get so freaked out that I have to switch schools again."

My stomach started to turn inside out, but then I thought of something uplifting.

"Hey. Are all your messages to do with what you're wearing?"

She considered my question. "Pretty much."

"Well, then it's Sheila! It's got to be—that's what she does, make's fun of people with her nasty little messages and phone calls."

She looked lost in thought. "You think?"

"Of course. I bet you anything she's just messing around."

"Or maybe they got her working for them." She looked at me quizzically.

I pshawed. "Please. If she were really out to get you, wouldn't she be less obvious about it at school? That girl picks on us all the time."

"Maybe." Becca didn't sound convinced. "Or . . . it's possible they've got it all figured out. Why would I suspect that she had anything to do with them if I wrote her off as a garden-variety bully?"

"Look, I know her pretty well, and she's not the slickest cat. If I were one of the Soyles and I needed a mole, I think she's the last person I'd give the job to." I studied her face and beamed her a comforting look. "There's no need to worry about Sheila. She's just a recovering sword and sorcery addict. That's all."

"Yeah?" She inhaled deeply and wrapped her arms around herself. "Okay, I feel a little better."

"But how does this whole story tie into what happened today? With the key that you mentioned?"

"Somebody broke into my grandparents' farm last night."

"The one in England? Is that where you guys keep the key?"

"I'm not supposed to say." She smiled coyly. "So yeah, that about sums it up." She reached above the headboard to turn out the light. "Welcome to my life. Now let's pray we don't go home with any broken bones."

We might have been at a ski lodge, but I had a feeling she wasn't referring to any sports-related injuries.

{ 18 }

An Unfortunate Plus One

Becca and I woke up around ten the next morning. She went into the bathroom without saying anything, and I could tell she felt a little uncomfortable about how much she'd told me the night before. We got ready in near silence.

Down in the restaurant I spotted Andy sitting with his back against the wall, his arms outstretched to hold up the biggest newspaper I'd ever seen. He flashed me a smile over the top of his paper and, feeling pleased as could be, I followed Becca over to the buffet table.

I don't buy it when people say they can't eat when they're in love. I loaded up on everything in front of me—muffins, mini and English, not to mention eggs and bacon and perfectly spherical scoops of melon—before prancing back to the seat across from Andy.

"Hey," I said in a tone I hoped conveyed that we shared a secret, but not that I was desperately in love with him. "How's the paper?"

"You know, the usual." Andy swallowed hard and looked slightly panicked. I was kind of flattered to see he was thinking about what had happened in the pool.

"Any good news?" I pressed.

Andy opened his mouth, but before he could answer, a familiar voice came out from behind the foreign page. "Very good news."

I couldn't believe it. The paper folded back to reveal Rye, wearing a pom-pom hat and sitting next to my almost-kissing partner.

"You look like you just saw the grim reaper." Rye laughed. "My undereye circles must be awful."

I forced a chuckle. "No, no, I just—" I was speechless.

"Hey, babe." Rye smiled affably at Becca. "I love that shirt. Is it Calypso?"

Becca looked down to check what she was wearing—a long gray top with white embroidery around the neck. "No . . . I think my mom got it from some catalog . . . Where'd you come from, anyway?"

"I got a last-minute ticket on Expedia. I am so exhausted; my flight got in at one-thirty last night."

"I thought you had a big school project." Becca took her time as she buttered her sesame bagel.

"It took less time than expected," Rye said, avoiding making eye contact with me. "I'm almost done with it."

"She's going to finish it here," Andy said. He glanced at me, then looked away.

How could he! I put my hands on my thighs and dug my bitten-off nails in as far as they would go.

"I see," Becca said, then took a bite. "Well, that's good, then. Right?"

"Right!" they both chirped. But Andy was struggling to fold the paper, and I detected a few beads of sweat on his upper lip.

"So you guys psyched to hit the slopes?" I asked.

"I am," Andy said. "Rye can't come out."

"I'm nearly done with this paper." She adjusted her hair.

"More 'How-to-Snag-a-Man' self-help manuals?" I intended it as a joke, but it came out sounding bitter.

Rye shook her head, as if in dismay at my stupidity. "It's actually on women's rights in western Africa. And it's due first thing Monday morning. Totally stressful. I need a good massage." She turned to Andy and I had to look away.

Once their make-out session was over, Andy's cheeks were magenta and he opened the paper to hide behind it.

A little while later, after he had deposited Rye in the hotel's business center, Andy came clopping back into the dining room. He was sporting a puffy white cap and a bright red parka. I couldn't help thinking that he looked like a walking bottle of Soul Sauce—albeit a very attractive one.

As he came our way, we locked eyes for ten of the slowest seconds I'd experienced in my life. Was he trying to tell me something? I didn't blink until he stuck out his tongue at me.

"What do you say we hit the slopes before the snow melts?" He gently tugged his sister up by her ponytail. I followed a few steps behind, trying to think of the best way to break the news to the pair about my inability to ski. If I didn't speak up fast, I'd end up communicating it via my full-body cast.

"Um," I said when we reached the door, "I can't go out with you guys today."

"Like you can tomorrow?" Andy asked through a grin. "So you can't ski, big deal."

I was completely shocked, and slightly relieved.

"When you tried on my skis at the airport yesterday, you stepped into the bindings backward," he explained.

"I did?" I gulped.

"Afraid so." He patted me on the shoulder, his hand lingering for a pleasing extra few seconds. "Priceless stuff."

"Don't worry about it," Becca said. "The best part of skiing has nothing to do with skis. Why don't you meet us for hot chocolate at Ernie's? At four?"

My confusion must have showed.

"Just take the gondola to the top of the mountain," Andy said. "Cell phones don't work that high, but it's the only restaurant up there. And if you get there on time, I'll show you how to put skis on the right way." His tone was calming, and I felt easy all over.

I'd been eyeing the lobby's huge couches ever since we got there, and as soon as my friends were out of sight, I curled up on one of them. Its leather was soft and brown, like an old baseball glove. I felt lulled by the grandfather clock's ticking, and I slept straight through the rest of the morning.

When I woke up I was discombobulated. I needed some fresh air, so I pulled myself off of my new favorite couch and exited the hotel for the first time since I got there.

Downtown Aspen was like a Disney version of the Wild West, with rows of perfectly maintained brown buildings tucked into the base of a mountain range. I didn't get the sense I was going to run into any cowboys or Indians, though; behind the restaurant windows sat lovey-dovey young couples and groups of wealthy older women catching up over white wine.

I was a little hungry, but most of the places I passed were too expensive for somebody with eleven dollars and change in her pocket. About five blocks from the hotel I found a diner. There were even a few normal cars along with the BMWs and Range Rovers parked out in front.

I sat at the counter and ordered a Western omelet. It seemed like the right thing to get, being in Colorado and all. Almost immediately the waitress brought my plate. But when she came closer I didn't see my lunch; instead, I realized I was looking at the fruit salad of my dreams. And no, by that I don't mean the perfect fruit salad—I'm talking about the ridiculous fruit sculpture I'd dreamed about making once upon a time. There were even the same heart-shaped strawberries, except now they were red instead of muddy gray.

Oblivious to my stare, the waitress walked straight past me and to the back of the restaurant, and directly to—of all people—Andy's girlfriend, who was reading an issue of Cosmo, the one women's magazine I never pick up at the newsstand. Was it possible they'd started running articles on the plight of women in western Africa? I'd have to check it out the next time I got a chance.

She must have eaten only three bites of fruit before balling up her napkin and throwing it on her plate. And then, as soon as the waitress carted it away, she went outside to make a phone call, dialing the number and screaming "Baby!" into the phone before the door swung shut. It was hard to tell for sure, what with the clinking of plates and the jukebox going at full-blast, but I was pretty sure I heard her say it in a vaguely English accent.

My heart was beating even faster than it had when I'd first

seen her that morning. In as nonchalant a manner as I could muster, I swiveled around to face the window and keep an eye on her.

Making sure to pull on my sweater hood and push my sunglasses down onto my nose, I watched her lean against a lamppost and cuddle the phone, smiling dreamily whenever the other person was talking. At one point, she brought her index finger to her mouth and ran it over her lips; then she squished her face up to make several kisses before getting off. My head was spinning—Andy had told me that his cell phone didn't work from the top of the mountain. I guessed it was possible she had caught him at the exact moment he hit the bottom, but that seemed a little unlikely.

I couldn't believe my dreams were pointing me to Rye. And, more specifically—and even more unbelievably—to the fact that she was two-timing Andy. How could she?

The door swung open, and Rye shot back into the diner.

Fast as I could, I whipped around and faced the way I should have been facing.

Please please don't let her see me.

My omelet had been delivered, and as bewildered as I was by what I had just seen, I dug in. There's nothing like omlettey goodness to ease a girl's mind. Other than chocolate, that is.

Aspen was wasted on me. I was so disturbed by the Rye sighting, I barely noticed the majestic view on the gondola ride up the mountain. And when Andy kicked me under the table, my first reflex was to apologize. I didn't catch on that he'd been flirting with me until a few minutes later, when I realized he was telling me about some documentary about New York that he loved, and he made a point of noting that my neighborhood used to be full of thugs and fallen women. "Some things never change," Becca said. In jest, I hope.

After hot chocolate, Becca and Andy returned to the slopes, and I spent the remainder of the afternoon in our hotel room, tweezing my eyebrows according to *Elle*'s instructions for heart-shaped faces while taking in part of a cable marathon of *The Twilight Zone*. When the episode ended, I called Dad and left a message letting him know that I was still alive. Then I left a message for Louis saying hi and flaunting the fact that for once I was the one on the schmancy vacation. Finally, I rushed through my French and global studies assignments.

We had dinner that night at the Hamlet, the hotel's supposedly "fancy" restaurant (as if the place we'd eaten in the night before was Applebee's). Rye was in Andy's room, still working on her paper. Everyone else was at the table and in a great mood, especially Becca's parents, who had gotten over the previous day's troubles by spoiling themselves rotten. Her dad had just come out of a two-hour hot stone massage session, and her mom had treated herself to a pedicure as well as a solar-powered pepper grinder from one of the luxury stores in town.

"Ever heard the term *shopaholic*?" Andy whispered to me. "Mom once went to a shrink about it and at the end of a few sessions he told her that she shouldn't come back—he said it was clear shopping gave her a 'sense of empowerment' that therapy could never provide her."

"He sounds normal. Not like any of the shrinks I know."

He looked at me with interest. "You know a lot of shrinks?"

"Just from my building," I said quickly, not wanting him to get the wrong idea. "All the psychology professors also have private practices, and at the holiday party the Freudians and Jungians stand on opposite sides of the room and refuse to mingle."

"Are you serious?" He scratched his thigh. "That's friggin' hilarious. Next time I go to a party and don't feel like schmoozing I'm going to say I'm a Freudian."

"Jungian," I corrected him. "The Freudians are friendlier."

"Seriously," he said. "I'm dying to come check out this nutty-professor complex."

"Fishing for invitations?" Rye piped up, bearing down on us and taking a seat on Andy's other side.

"There you are," Becca's mom said. "Do you want to order something?"

Rye shook her head. "I had some fruit in the hotel room, thanks."

What a liar. I turned away and spent the remainder of the evening talking to Becca's grandfather about his memories of Hudson, his alma mater, back when it was an all-boys school. I tried to pay attention to his stories about the mandatory electrical engineering classes and not think about the fact that I'd seen Rye eating fruit *not* in her hotel room and blowing kisses into her phone earlier in the day. Now she and Andy were barely an inch apart, doing Lord knew what under the table.

But I couldn't keep ignoring Rye when she reached over to tap me on the shoulder. "Hey, Carrie, you weren't at the diner today, were you?"

"Me?" My knees were knocking together. I was so nervous it didn't even occur to me to remind her that Carrie isn't my name. "Um . . . yeah . . . why? Were you there?"

"Barely. I spent most of the time outside talking to my dog, Pickle. He waited until I went out of town to come down with a bug. He puked all over my dad." She frowned.

Call me self-sabotaging, but a huge wave of relief rolled over me. There had never been a second when I was particularly delighted that Andy was going out with her, but I would have been even less delighted to know she was running around on him. It would have been the wrongest thing on earth.

So she'd been phone-kissing her dog—not the weirdest thing I'd ever heard of. A lot of people were grossly intimate with their dogs—I once saw a woman in Washington Square Park use a straw to blow water into her poodle's mouth.

As for the whole fruity dream connection? It had to be wishful coincidence. Or, as Kiki would say, piffle.

A smile broke out on my face.

"I know," Rye said, smiling back. "Gross."

Then, as if I were no longer sitting there, she abruptly turned to Andy to tell him about the diner she had "discovered." "It was so cute," she said. "Everything was out of the 1950s. They had a jukebox full of country music, and those old place mats with scalloped edges. We should go there tomorrow, for an après-ski snack."

"Sounds good." Andy nodded.

I wanted to gag.

"And how was your afternoon, dear?" Dixie asked me after a fortifying sip of wine.

"It was fun," I told her. Trying to ignore the lovebirds next to me I detailed my every move—except the part about misinterpreting a dream and hiding behind my sunglasses and hood to spy on Rye as she flirted with her canine lover. I wrapped up with, "And then I took a bubble bath and watched four and a half episodes of *The Twilight Zone*."

"Did you say *The Twilight Zone*?" Rye screeched. I nearly fainted—from the sound of her voice and the simple fact that never in my life would I have pegged her as a Rod Serling fan. "I think I've seen every one," she said, and went on to profess a preference for the episodes not involving robots or outer space—which did narrow things down. "My all-time favorite one is about the woman in the hospital who keeps getting plastic surgery so she can look like everybody else—"

"But then it turns out she's a babe," I jumped in, "and everyone else has pig faces!"

"Sounds like some of my friends and neighbors," Becca's mother said. "I'm not sure, but I think I'd rather look my age than try to see through two tiny little slits."

"Not with the slit talk again," Becca's dad said. "How many times do I have to tell you that you're beautiful the way you are?" He rubbed his wife's back and kissed her on the lips.

"God, you guys are so corny!" Becca covered her face with her hands. "What are we going to do about them?" Through her fingers, she looked over at Andy for support, but he was too wrapped up in his hot girlfriend to notice his little sister.

Dejected, Becca brought her hands down to her lap and pouted.

I knew the feeling.

{ 19 }

Red-Light District

What is it with planes? They have roughly the same effect on me that double espresso has on others. Rye had taken an earlier flight back home, and I was the sole member of our party who wasn't tired out from a half-day spent skiing. The only other person on our flight back who wasn't napping was Becca's mom, and even she looked dozy as she circled items in the in-flight shopping magazine. Becca was snoring in the seat next to me, our shared *Teen Vogue* clamped between her ear and the tray table's plastic surface.

After I finished *Death Comes at the End*, an Agatha Christie book I'd found at the hotel gift shop, I was left with nothing to do but crack open my English textbook, *Fictional Impressions*.

In addition to the stories we were supposed to write, Mr. Bunting had told us to read what the book identified as the ninth-best story in history: "A Perfect Day for Bananafish" by J. D. Salinger. I was shocked by how good it was. Possibly even worthy of top-five status.

Our landing was choppy enough to rouse my fellow travelers. While we waited for the pilot's go-ahead to disembark, Becca's dad scrolled through his new BlackBerry messages. "Excellent," he said, and whistled; then I overheard him whisper to his father, "About time."

"Good, then," said Becca's grandfather. "I've always liked my steak well done."

It didn't take Hercule Poirot to figure this one out. They were talking about the Soyle family. Probably some payback for the attempted break-in on Thursday night. Could it be related to the Soyles' topless steakhouse venture Becca had told me about?

"Here, boy." Becca's dad passed the BlackBerry to Andy, who was standing up two rows ahead of me. Somehow we caught each other's eye. I smiled softly. He smiled back, turning my insides to mush.

As we walked through the airport, Becca and I trailed behind everyone else, giving them a chance to talk among themselves.

"What's everyone so excited about?" I asked Becca.

"Same old story," she replied sullenly. "Another retaliation."

"For the English farm break-in the other night?"

"Yup." She sniffed. "It turns out more happened than just an intruder. My cousin Frank and some of his boarding school friends had snuck out for the night and they were partying there. Frank's in the hospital. Somebody beat him up pretty bad."

Whoa. In my household, a scratch on Henry's knee constituted a thrilling emergency.

"Is he all right?" I asked.

"Oh, I'm sure he's fine. I don't even know if he needed to go to the hospital. He's always been such a little prince. It's just a black eye."

"Still, that's awful." I tried to touch Becca's shoulder, but she pulled away.

"That's okay," she mumbled, then looked down at her feet. "But here's the really messed-up part: there was a small fire at the steakhouse last night. Nothing too serious, but I guess twenty thousand dollars' worth of meat was doused in fire extinguisher fluid."

"And so soon after the incident in England. What a coincidence." I widened my eyes, pretending to be shocked.

"Yeah right. If there's one principle you'll learn from my family, it's that one bad thing tends to lead to another. And another." A fearful expression crossed Becca's face and then, as if she thought better of it, she focused ahead and strutted forward.

When we stepped outside, it was freezing, and all the airport employees were wearing face masks. "Bundle up, gang," Becca's dad ordered. "You too, Claire."

I couldn't have been happier to comply. My parents were always too busy teasing me about wearing Kiki's hand-me-downs to think to tell me to dress warmly enough.

Becca's dad had us wait by the taxi line while he walked up and down the platform, searching for the cars that he'd ordered to pick us up.

"There they are. Hurry up," he snapped at us, and we all scurried over to the two black town cars with SHUTTLEWORTH signs in the windshields. The grown-ups slipped into the first car in the lineup, and as Becca's mom was pulling the door closed, I yelled out an insufficient thank-you for the weekend. "I had a wond—!" I called out as the door slammed shut.

"Where to?" our driver asked us.

"Good question," Becca said, looking at her brother. "Should we drop you off at your dorm first?"

"No, go to Mom and Dad's first," Andy said. "I have to get Claire that DVD I was talking about, before I forget."

"Oh yeah," I said. "That's so nice of you."

Now was probably not the time to tell him I didn't have the foggiest idea what he meant.

We all scooted into the car and Becca told the driver the address.

"Those are the worst fingernails I've ever seen," Andy pointed out as the car pulled away from the airport. "Are they tasty?"

He reached for my wrist and I flinched. I was terrified Becca was going to suspect something was up between her brother and her best friend. If she did, though, she deserved an Academy Award for her own cover-up job. Becca was acting as natural as an organic peanut, frowning as she checked her cell phone messages.

"So, that was a pretty good trip, wouldn't you say?" she said when she was off the phone. We were crossing the Queensboro Bridge, and the city was lit up like a birthday cake.

"I wouldn't go that far," Andy answered. "It was too short."

"Mmm-hmm," Becca said, sounding distracted.

"And what about you?" Andy elbowed me. "Were you ready to come home? I know you're not an Olympic skier, but don't you wish we had one last night to hang out, to swim some more in the outdoor pool?"

Did I hear that right?

"I'm okay!" I said nervously. "I can use the pool at the NYU gym." Considering how obsessed Andy was supposed to be with Rye, he did an awfully good job of forgetting about her when she wasn't around. Maybe this had to do with the learning disabilities Becca had mentioned—could attention deficit disorder make you forget you're going out with someone except when they're standing in front of you?

I looked out the window, desperate for something else to talk about. "Don't you guys just love the Empire State Building?" I said, like an imbecile. "Look at how all the lights are orange."

"For Thanksgiving," Becca said. "They coordinate the colors with the holidays." Andy was now wiggling his fingers against my hip. What was with him? Wasn't this intimate ground for two people who hadn't even kissed to be treading? And what was with me for liking it so much? I asked Becca whether she had received any interesting messages on her phone. It was all I could do to keep from laughing or screaming.

"You mean in addition to the fifteen hang-ups?" She cast me a wary look. I tried to respond, but she picked up in her typical unruffled tone and kept going. "Just a few friends from boarding school. Everyone's getting ready for Thanksgiving weekend. My friend Gillian invited me to go to her house in New Jersey and my friend Kim wants to organize a house party with me at our place."

"What are you going to do?" I asked her.

"Probably not the party." Fine. She didn't feel like talking about her threats. "We had one last year," she went on, "and my parents invited a hundred Shuttleworths and turned it into a family reunion."

"I remember that," Andy said. "All your friends went to

the East Side Lounge and you were stuck playing cards with some long-lost cousins."

"Emphasis on *lost*," Becca said. "I had no idea who half those people were."

We pulled off the FDR Drive and were riding through the Upper East Side, the neighborhood the Shuttleworths call home, along with every other socialite and captain of industry. When the town car rolled up outside their building, an oversized limestone town house just off Fifth Avenue, Andy jumped out. "I'll be right back." He sounded a little nervous.

"Bye, C," Becca said to me. "See you in hell tomorrow."

I hugged her tight, partly wishing I didn't have to let her go. I was worried, and not only because I didn't like the sound of the hang-ups. If what I thought was about to happen actually did happen—that is to say, if Andy and I kissed, for real—things would definitely get more complicated.

"Are you going to take it or are you just going to sit there?"

Andy's words startled me. I'd been spacing out, watching an old man in slippers and a silk bathrobe pick up after his dog, and now Andy was back, holding a box out to me.

"Ric Burns's *New York* documentary," he said. "It's possible there's a better way to spend sixteen hours than watching this, but I have no idea what it would be."

"Thanks," I said. I was scared to make eye contact with him, and instead examined the DVD cover. It featured a picture of a group of baby-faced construction workers sitting on top of a beam suspended over the city, decked out in newsboy caps. "I can't believe how long it took them to invent the hard hat," I said, finally looking up at him. His eyelashes were casting shadows on his cheeks and there was a faint curl to his mouth.

"Maybe people's heads were harder back then." He

reached into the car to knock the crown of my head. "They've definitely become squishier."

Everything inside me went limp.

"That would explain it," I said, trying to sound wise and sardonic. "So, I guess I'll see you later?"

"I'll drop you off." He crawled in and shut the door behind him. I smiled uncomfortably. From the car I could see Becca's room, her Hermès orange walls and A HISTORY OF THE WORLD IN SHOES poster. The closet door had been flung open, and I imagined her putting away her sweaters while she talked on the phone to one of her old friends.

The car started up and I folded my hands in my lap, trying to calm myself down by imagining Andy was somebody else, somebody I could act normal around.

"It's not like I'm in any rush to go back to my dorm," Andy went on. "They have three of us bunking in one room."

"Not that you're ever there," I told him. "Your roommates must love you."

"For the record, I go to all my classes."

"Me too. Unfortunately."

He sighed. "Yeah, I heard Hudson sucks."

"Maximally."

The car glided through Central Park. Silence fell between us, and then he sidled right on over next to me.

"Hi," I heard myself say. I must have sounded scared, because he backed away and apologized.

"You must think I'm a creep."

That was the last thing I was thinking.

"No," I told him. "I had a feeling you were N.S.I.T."

He looked confused.

"It's an old saying of Kiki's. Not Safe in Taxis."

He nodded appreciatively. "I like that."

"Me too." I looked at him, straight on. "I mean," I paused, "I like that you're N.S.I.T." I was suddenly feeling bold.

"You're funny. Not all girls are, you know."

He didn't have to say names. We both knew he was talking about Rye.

We were heading west when the car stopped at a red light. Our driver waited for a group of girls who were around our age to scurry over the crosswalk. They all reminded me of Rye, with their skinny limbs and striped scarves, and it struck me as funny that for once I was the girl in a car with a boy.

Andy turned to me, his face bathed in the traffic light's red glow. "You okay?"

I nodded. Never better.

"Good." He rubbed his palms over his knees. "Me too."

I turned away and let my eyes shut, trying to steady my nerves. He was about to kiss me. What was I doing facing away? I couldn't hide forever. I took a deep breath and opened my eyes. When I turned around again, I was prepared to see Andy staring adoringly at me, mustering the courage to do the one thing he'd been too scared to go ahead with until now. I was not expecting to see him leaning forward and panicking while one of the girls outside gawked at us with a cockeyed expression.

"No way." Andy reached clumsily for the door handle.

How could I not have noticed that the girls didn't just look like Rye—one of the girls *was* Rye? "I can't believe this." His voice cracked pathetically.

The car started up again, and Andy lurched toward the driver.

"Excuse me! Can you please stop the car? I need to jump out, but she's still going to the Village."

His hand on the door handle, he looked back at me. "I

really can't believe this." The door creaked open, and I didn't watch as he climbed out of the car and slammed the door.

My eyes blurred over, and even if I'd turned back to look, I wouldn't have been able to see a thing.

I took the building elevator up with Eamon Dagwick, a Celtic studies professor who was still mad at me for my detective days and never greeted me with more than a sniffle. Thanks to the state of my personal affairs, I could manage a sniffle back.

When I stepped off and was assaulted by my hallway's psychedelic kaleidoscope of orange, yellow, pink, and green, I felt a new rush of tears coming on. I slid down the wall by our door and prayed that the hallway would just stay still and empty, and nobody would come by to see me in this sorry state. The more tears streaked down my face, the emptier I felt inside.

The crying finally slowed, and I opened my compact and wiped myself off. Horrible didn't even begin to describe the way I looked. My eyes were salmon colored and my nose had inflated to roughly twice its original size.

Still, I had no choice but to stagger through the door. The apartment was as messy as I'd ever seen it, with unfolded blankets and newspaper pages strewn about.

"Hey," Henry said. He was on the couch, with huge rings under his eyes and looking exceptionally dirty. Dad was next to him, eating food from a McDonald's bag. The two were staring at an episode of E! True Hollywood Story.

Wasn't my brother the kid who didn't watch TV unless it was a cartoon or science program? And was my dad not the same man who called fast food poison?

"Um, what's going on?" I asked.

"*Ma poupée.*" Dad got up to pull me in for a tight hug. He didn't seem to notice that I looked as pink and bloated as a puffer fish. "Thanks for your message yesterday. Was the rest of your trip good?"

"Good enough," I said, still harping on Andy. "Is everything okay here?"

Dad let go. "It's been a long day."

"How was Athens?" Henry asked absentmindedly.

"Aspen. Fine." I sat on the easy chair near them. "What happened here?"

"Nothing." Cheri-Lee flitted out of the kitchen, answering before Henry could. "Nothing, thank God, nothing." She made a *pssst* noise and motioned for me to join her back in the kitchen.

Even Cheri-Lee seemed different; she wasn't smiling, and her glasses were all smudged.

"I've been over since last night, when your dad called me. We had a bit of a stressful evening," she said. "Henry went out on one of his walks and found Douglas camping out in Washington Square Park."

"Since when did Douglas take up camping?"

"It was a fund-raising exercise he was doing for his homeless shelter." Cheri-Lee shook her head and rolled her eyes. "So Henry decided to join them." She paused. "And stay out past eleven. I know your mother always makes Henry come home by eight, and he's only allowed to walk as far as the corner, but I guess his eight-year-old mind assumed with her being gone, those rules no longer applied."

Actually, I thought, *he's been known to nip out later than that.* But I didn't need to get into it with Cheri-Lee.

"Why didn't Douglas do anything?" I asked.

"You can take that up with him. He claims he told Henry

to go home, but said he was trying to get into the role, and since homeless people don't have phones . . ."

I poured myself a glass of orange juice. "Why are smart people so stupid?"

"Mind-boggling, isn't it? Listen, I'm going to help out all I can this week, but I need you to pitch in. I'm speaking at a poetry conference next weekend, and I'm weeks overdue in judging a contest for Poetry magazine. I'll need you around as much as you can stand."

I peered into the main room, where the duo was staring, as if in a trance, at the overmascaraed actress on TV. "Of course," I told her. Considering I'd just skipped off to a five-star getaway and left them high and dry, it was the least I could do.

"Marv," she said, sounding like her old self. "And while we're both here, I'll help you tidy up a little."

I followed her out of the kitchen, and we began to clear the living area of all the pizza boxes, paper napkins, and newspapers. I was amazed at how much better the place looked after just five minutes.

"I'm going to go home, but I'll pop in tomorrow morning to check up on all of you." She picked up the trash bag and headed toward the door. "I'll take this to the garbage chute."

And then I saw something.

"Oh, wait," I said. "Before you tie it . . ."

I grabbed a back issue of the Planet that was by the foot of the coatrack and crammed it in the bag. I'm usually good about recycling, but given the recent turn of events, I felt strongly that the magazine's Young Love Heats Up headline belonged with all the greasy napkins and snot-covered Kleenexes.

{ 20 }

Shakespeare in Sheep's Clothing

Not to get all sentimental or anything, but even though Mom had barely been gone four days, I was beginning to see her in a new light. You could even say I was starting to appreciate her. Kiki had always made it sound as though my mother's household management skills consisted of nothing more than making *croque-monsieurs* and decorating the walls with Le Bon Marché ads, but now I was starting to have my doubts. Could it have been a coincidence that as soon as Mom left, our household began to fall apart at the seams? On Monday, my first full day back, Dad slept through his morning class, Henry showed up for school lunchless, and when I got home that afternoon, there was a card in our mailbox from the

Department of Sanitation notifying us that a random garbage check had turned up a magazine with our address label—and we owed a fifty-dollar fine for failing to recycle.

This must have been for the "Young Love" issue of the *Planet* I'd thrown out. I was terrified Dad was going to kill me, but he took the news in stride, and even put his anti-American spin on it. "What is this, a totalitarian state? They want to tell me how to throw out my trash, fine. Then I would like to tell them how to spend my tax money. More gardens, less guns."

"You are so right, *Papa*," I told him.

I'd been home for less than half an hour when Becca called to invite me on a walk. "I'm in your neighborhood," she said. "Orthodontist appointment. I got a new retainer. Wanna see?"

"You know how to put an irresistible offer out there."

It wasn't one of our best times hanging out together. The sense that I should be home with my family was weighing on me, and after she showed me her new retainer, Becca fell into an unusually quiet mood, continually looking down at her feet. There was a small chance she was admiring her mustard tights and deep blue shorts combo, but it was far more likely that something was bothering her.

On Bethune Street, we passed a store called Boyfriend's Closet. The windows were filled with female mannequins wearing rolled-up chinos and oversized button-down shirts— clothing that was supposedly on loan from a boyfriend.

"It's a good thing there are so many single women in New York," I said. "Otherwise they'd be out of business."

"Hmm." Becca barely glanced in the window's direction.

What was going on? Was there any chance Andy had read my mind in the car and told her about what a loser I'd been, sitting there and wanting more than anything for him to kiss me?

"B, if you were mad at me, you wouldn't have asked me to come out on a walk, would you?" I asked.

Her shoulders rolled forward and she sighed. "Considering the fact that you're my only friend in the city, I probably would have." She jabbed me in the rib. "But no, I'm not mad at you. I'm just a little annoyed."

"Huh? Did I say something?"

"It's not you. Look . . . when I was leaving the orthodontist's office I got this weird text message." Becca's fingers did a little tap dance on the gizmo and she passed it to me. I zeroed in on the text.

WHAT HAPPENED TO THE REST OF YOUR PANTS?

"I think you were right about Sheila," she told me. "It's her. And she has to be the one doing their dirty work."

"Actually, I'm not so sure," I said.

"Who else could it be?" Her mouth hung slightly open.

"No, no, it's practically got Sheila's fingerprints all over it. But I remain convinced that she's just harassing you for the sake of it. I bet it has nothing to do with the Soyles."

Her lips were quivering. "I don't see how that's possible."

"No offense, but what makes you that different from everybody else? My money says Sheila's just being a jerk and the Soyles aren't even thinking about you."

"Maybe." Her tone was anything but satisfied. "Wouldn't that be nice?"

When I got home, all I wanted to do was go to my room and lie down and listen to the Shirelles. But Henry was looking at me with puppy dog eyes, so I joined him on the floor and helped him build a spaceship out of cotton balls, Q-tips, and glue. My selflessness evaporated when Dad remembered to give me a message. "A young man called."

"Who!"

Dad frowned and tilted his head the way he does when he's trying to remember something. "Liam?"

I was racking my brain for Liams. "You mean Ian?"

Dad nodded. "*C'est ça.*"

Crap. I'd totally forgotten that we were supposed to meet up at the diner after school to go over our English story-writing project.

"Time out," I told my brother as I lurched over to my backpack, glue bottle still in hand. I ran to the phone like a mad person and punched in the number scribbled on the back of my English notebook, waiting impatiently while it rang.

"I'm so sorry I stood you up. I totally forgot," I said once Ian was on the line. "Any chance you can come by my apartment later? You'll get to meet my cool fish." Dad was watching me, clearly amused. He never got my fish fixation. "And my very cool father," I added.

That night we ordered broccoli pizza and ate picnic style—or, as Dad called it, *au picnic*—on the living room floor. Apart from Henry's minor Coke spill, the meal went without a hitch, and afterward Dad suggested we all stay put. "Let's make an independent work circle. Your mother and I used to do them all the time when we lived on Hester Street."

Reenacting Mom and Dad's former days in a quasi-commune (they'd lived with two other couples) sounded kind of weird, but soon enough we were absorbed in our projects: Dad was revising a chapter in his book, Henry was using tongue depressors and markers to invent a new language called Glow-Ki, and—though exhausted from my Noctolux ban—I was pretending to study math while actually fantasizing about Andy showing up at the door on bended knee.

I was the size of an elephant, and my black and white polka-dotted maternity dress was flapping every which way. It wasn't pretty. Being pregnant wasn't all that physically uncomfortable, but walking down Madison Avenue was a bitch—you try putting one foot in front of the other when you can't even see your feet.

As if being a mom-to-be wasn't weird enough, I was the only actual person on the sidewalk—everybody else walking around me was a plastic mannequin. I slowly crossed the street and a doorman stepped out from under an awning and tipped his hat to me. At first I thought he was saluting me for being the biggest lump he'd ever seen. Then he gestured to the sidewalk. A baby was sitting on a picnic blanket, smiling and cooing and reaching out to be picked up.

I must have dozed off, because when I woke up, Ian was sitting on the floor, flipping through his sketchbook for my family.

"Hi, sleepyhead," Henry teased me as I rubbed my eyes and made my way up to a seated position.

"That looks just like Sheila," Dad was saying to Ian.

"How do you know Sheila?" Ian looked confused.

"She lives here," Henry said. "Our parents all used to be friends, but not anymore. Well, they're still friends with her mom, but her father left the family for a German grad student."

Dad looked like he was about to choke. "Henry! That's private."

"Your secret's safe with me," Ian assured him. He still hadn't looked at me—he probably thought I was a freak. First I stand him up, then I invite him over and fall asleep.

"What's going on?" I asked. Henry passed me the book. There she was, my least favorite redhead, standing at the top of our school's steps and looking as big-shouldered and bossy as ever. Sheila was holding a tangle of leashes that were attached to about a dozen guys from school, Ian included. It was pretty awesome.

"I thought you only drew superheroes," I said skeptically.

"I'm a man of many talents."

"Apparently." I eyed him admiringly.

We moved ourselves to the polar bear rug in my room and tried to brainstorm a story idea for our English assignment. But we couldn't agree on a genre, let alone a plot; I wanted to write a mystery and Ian wanted to do a—surprise!—superhero story.

"Why did we have to do them in pairs anyway?" I asked.

"Isn't it obvious?" He smirked. "This way Mr. Bunting only has half as many stories to grade." He opened his sketchbook and began to add shading to the Sheila drawing.

"So what exactly led you to draw this?" I asked.

"If I tell you what happened, you're going to say I'm an idiot."

"There are worse things to be called."

He squinted and told me about his latest humiliation. On Saturday a girl who introduced herself as Maxine had called him and asked him to meet her at Sammy's Noodle Shop.

This setup was starting to sound familiar.

"Did she say her locker was near yours?"

"She said she had lunch the same period as me."

"And let me guess. You went?"

He turned red. "So did, like, five other guys. And then some girl in a wig showed up and took pictures."

"God," I said, burying my face in my hands. "You *are* an

idiot. Now might be a good time to introduce you to my fish. You should take a lesson from Didier. Whenever Margaux acts coy and teases him, he becomes very angry and attacks her."

Ian pressed his face against the tank. "You're saying I should *attack* Sheila? She's twice my size."

"Not physically. But you don't have to take it lying down. When she's mean to me, I stand up for myself."

"No you don't."

"Well, I try." I picked a Waldorf notepad up off the floor and started to doodle, spelling out Sheila's name, then rearranging the letters as if a clue might be hiding in there. I picked it apart, looking for little words contained within. *Shed. Rad. Lash. Drivel.* And then something clicked.

"Ack! Ian, will you look at this?"

Ian glanced at my paper. "*Evil radish?* I don't get it—do you have something against vegetables or something?"

"Look closer." A smile tugged at my mouth. "It's Sheila's name jumbled up. So now you know what we have to write our story about, right?"

"Um, an evil radish?"

"Bingo."

Ian looked at me as if I were crazy.

"And you know what else? Our writing project should be a comic. Seriously, Mr. Bunting never said it can't be illustrated, did he?" I batted my eyelashes. "Oh, c'mon, it will be *so* good. . . . Please?"

"I've never drawn a radish before. I guess I could try." Ian flashed me a weak smile.

"Chalk it up to a learning experience."

The next morning I crawled out of bed feeling dog tired. After a quick shower, I threw on an easy outfit of black lace tights and a blue turtleneck dress. I barely had time to dry off and still felt a little damp under my clothes. I hoped I wouldn't arrive at school smelling like mildew.

When I came out of my room, Dad was at the table, reading the paper and administering his morning shot of espresso—he is adamantly opposed to carrying around a paper coffee cup like all the other professors did; it's too American for his tastes or something. My brother was seated across from him, building a fortress out of his Eggos and wearing the same GREETINGS, EARTHLING T-shirt he'd had on the previous day. And in the background, Cheri-Lee was noisily fiddling with something in the kitchen.

I kissed Dad good morning and went into the kitchen to down a glass of Orangina.

"Don't mind me," Cheri-Lee said, brushing against me as she opened the fridge. "I just popped in with some of last night's leftovers. It's Caesar salad with dried cranberries and roasted peach slivers."

"You shouldn't have," I told her.

And I meant it. The slimy greens looked positively disgusting.

"Nothing as impressive as what your mother would make, just simple healthy food," she said.

"Thanks." I smiled. "Did Dad offer you some coffee?"

"Oh no!" she said with a wave of her Gumby bracelet. "I woke up feeling inspired to write for the first time in years. I'd better buckle down before the feeling eludes me."

"By all means, buckle away."

"Are you poking fun at me? I can tell you are." Cheri-Lee grinned and started to skitter across the apartment, then turned back around. "Oh! How could I forget? I'm going to a crafts expo in Brooklyn later this afternoon. Last time they had these fabulous knickknacks made out of antique typewriter keys, and there was a girl who sewed used kitchen sponges into skirts. Sheila said it's not her thing, but how can you say that about a place where there's something for everyone?"

For once, Sheila and I were in agreement.

"Would you like to come along?" she asked.

"I'd love to," I told her, "but I'm supposed to meet Kiki this afternoon."

"No hard feelings, then." Cheri-Lee made a strange gobbling noise as she headed for the door.

"Are you going through a layering phase or is this an invitation for another strange message?" I asked Becca. Her outfit was only slightly less outrageous than her Shakespearean getup from the day before: she was wearing a paisley minidress over a pair of cropped leggings and, for good measure, gold boots.

"I'm just trying to get away with whatever I can before I have to enter the Witness Protection Program." She said it like it was a joke, but her eyes weren't laughing at all.

"Oh, look," she said, her gaze fixed across the street. "Here comes my favorite."

Eleanor was making her way down the school steps, listening to a pair of purple headphones. She didn't bother to look at any of the kids clogging her path—she just sailed around them, as if she were the only person in the entire Lower East Side. She was my guru.

"I love that girl," I murmured.

"And I bet she has no idea how cool she is," Becca agreed.

"Wanna get out of here?"

"Can't," she said, still studying the school steps. "I'm doing an experiment. I got another text today."

"What did it say?"

"Nothing."

"Tell me," I urged her.

"I just did. It said nothing. No letters, no characters. Just black space. Fade to black. The most classic threat in—"

She stopped short. The BDLs were streaming out of the building, all wearing matching polka-dotted tunics over their yoga pants. Sheila had taken the look one step further, with a yoga mat bag.

"Roll out the red carpets," I groaned.

"Or red yoga mats, as it were." Becca pulled out her phone on the sly. "Now, keep your eyes on them, will you?"

"Why?"

"Just do it."

Facing away, she punched a message into her PDA. "Now we wait."

"Aren't you crafty?" I complimented her.

"Did you see any of them reach for their phone?" she asked.

"You're also impatient. Give it a chance to go through."

She counted to ten so fast I couldn't hear the spaces between the words. "Anything yet?"

"Nope. They're all just standing around by the bottom of the stairs, asking guys to pose for pictures with them. Looks like Ariel got a new digital camera."

"Oh, the MySpace fun that awaits," Becca wisecracked. "Well, back to the experiment drawing board."

When Becca turned back around, the quintet was encircling a bushy-haired guy who was in my music appreciation class. "Why would they choose the day they all wear maternity dresses to take pictures?" Becca mused.

Maternity clothes? And with polka dots, too?

Just like what I'd been wearing in my pregnancy dream!

As I was having my lightning bolt déjà vu moment, Sheila

pulled her phone out of her pocket. She checked something and then spent an entire minute pressing keys. Unless she was playing tic-tac-toe on her screen, she was sending somebody a message. And considering her mom was prehistoric about all things technological and all her friends were standing two feet away from her, the only person I could possibly imagine her contacting was one of the Soyles.

Maybe Becca's suspicions weren't so off the mark after all?

I turned to Becca so we could bug our eyes out at each other, but she was telling one of the Queen Bees where she'd bought her gold boots and hadn't noticed a thing.

I was practically shaking. As I was about to interrupt Becca to tell her what I'd seen, something stopped me. I paused to take stock of the situation and ask myself what I had really seen: just a girl playing on her cell phone. For all I knew, she'd been checking her horoscope or downloading a ring tone. This wasn't exactly evidence that would hold up in court.

That photo session finished, the girls set their sights on a group of vaguely goth guys standing on our side of the street.

Becca's phone gave a little buzz, and before I knew it she was talking to a member of her family, assuring them that she hadn't forgotten about some fancy dinner that night. My eyes lowered, I tuned out my friend and strained to listen as the BDLs bum-rushed their next victims.

Well, most of the BDLs. Sheila was peeling off from the posse.

"Where do you think you're going?" Janice asked her.

"I have this thing I have to go to," Sheila warbled. "It's . . . with my mother. I'll call you guys later."

I could tell by Janice's look that she was skeptical. So was I. Hadn't Cheri-Lee said she was going to a craft fair and Sheila wasn't joining her? And since when was she in the habit of lying to her best friends? My head started to spin. Call me crazy, but I had to see what she'd stuffed up her polka-dotted sleeve.

As Becca gabbed away on the phone, I twisted her wrist around to get a look at her watch.

"Four already?" I mouthed dramatically. "I gotta run!"

And before Becca could get off the phone and ask me what could possibly be of such overwhelming importance, I was loping down the street, with Sheila's brassy bob as my beacon.

A little ways down the subway platform from me, Sheila was sitting on a bench reading a magazine. My palms coated in clammy sweat, I had to keep wiping them on the front of my dress.

When the train pulled into the station, I pretended to study a map and waited for Sheila to board, then clambered onto a neighboring car just as the doors were closing. There was a spot near the window, which made keeping an eye on her pretty easy.

At West Fourth Street, our usual stop, Sheila stood up. I determined with a zing of disappointment that she must be going to meet her mother after all. I was following her for nothing.

But then the doors opened and Sheila did a silly-me double take and grabbed a pole. And she remained standing there until the train pulled into the Thirty-fourth Street stop.

This was getting interesting.

I snatched a *Daily News* from an empty bank of seats and held it in front of my face as I disembarked and followed her up to the street. She was buzzing ahead quickly, too quickly not to be nervous about something. She had to be heading to a top-secret assignation. And unless she was conducting a secret love affair, who else could it be with but the Soyles?

I hung behind by half a block or so and trailed her up Sixth Avenue, with the newspaper held up to my face. I should have thought to cut eyeholes in it—I had a pretty close call when she stopped to admire a street vendor's table of jewelry and I nearly tripped over her. Luckily, she was too busy admiring a pair of hoop earrings to notice.

At last, she turned onto a desolate side street. The afternoon sunlight slanted onto the sidewalk's heaps of old boxes and mattresses, and Sheila and I were the only people around. I found a spot on a stoop and watched through the ironwork as Sheila charged down the block. She looked behind her one last time before disappearing behind a red steel door.

I sat there long enough to see a couple of other people enter by the same door: a drippy middle-aged guy who could have easily passed for an accountant and a heavyset woman with long dreadlocks. They were both carrying musical instrument cases. Did the Soyles have their own orchestra or something?

When I was sure long enough had passed, I approached the building. All my fantasies came to a crashing halt when I saw the piece of paper taped to the door:

N. Y. S. & S. S.
8F, PRESS HARD
BUZZER SEMI-BROKEN

It was a meeting of the New York Sword and Sorcery Society. No doubt about it. That was why Sheila didn't want anybody to know where she was going. And she must have been using her yoga mat bag to hide her sword.

I hadn't got to the bottom of anything. At least nothing more than Sheila's not-so-secret dorkiness.

{ 21 }

Punch-drunk Powwow

The Russian Tea Room is an over-the-top New York establishment that is the dining equivalent of a sequined Versace dress. Everything, from the bright red awning to the massive crystal bear in the center of the dining room, is larger than life. Kiki loves it. As for me, well, I'm still coming around.

Kiki had called me the night before to invite me to join her and Edie for a drink, although it was more an instruction than an invitation. "There is no way I will sit on my hands and wait until Sunday night to hear about your weekend with the Shuttleworths," she'd thundered.

When I showed up, Edie was running behind schedule, so it was just Kiki and me in a back corner.

"When Edie and I were still working in the theater we'd come here, and so many producers would send us drinks, we didn't know what to do with them all," she told me, her eyes twinkling at the memory. "One night Speedy Fitchburg—his name probably means nothing to you, but he was a real big cheese—he invited us to join him in his private dining room upstairs. And he had members of the Moscow circus up there with him! We spent the night feasting on champagne and blini and trying to learn how to walk on our hands." She sighed ruefully. "Why don't people do things like that anymore?"

I was so tired my head hurt, but I didn't want to let it show. The last time I'd yawned at a restaurant with Kiki, she'd made a big production of calling the waiter over and requesting a spare pillow.

"Now, how was your trip?"

Fighting the urge to rub my eyes or slump, I gave Kiki a recap of my forty-eight hours—the first night in heaven, the conversation about the Soyles, and then the final chapter of Rye-and-Andy-induced hell.

"And I see you're feeling dozy," Kiki said.

I gave myself a double pinch under the table. "It's that obvious?"

"You know, when I was your age I was also exhausted all the time."

"Yeah," I said, "but that's because you were running around being fabulous or whatever. The thing that's tiring me out is those black-and-white dreams."

"I know how it goes." She smiled. "Don't forget I had my own little situation when I was younger. The fascinating thing is most people can wear that necklace and nothing will happen. But if you already possess a special gift, the cameo will amplify it."

"And my special gift is being tired?"

"No, darling. Your gift was always snooping around and concocting mysteries out of thin air. Now you can actually be useful."

"Useful how?"

"From my experience," she said, "one uses the necklace to help people you care about, to keep trouble at bay. You're poised to make a difference."

What the hell? How long had I been wearing this necklace and only now Kiki was revealing there was a user's guide?

I looked around the room, taking in the glittery walls, crimson ceilings, and exotic Fabergé egg–ornamented trees. The restaurant vibrated with other people's tinkling conversations, and it seemed inconceivable that Kiki's revelation hadn't caused the rest of the world to stop.

She placed her hand over mine. "When I was younger, I used to have a very strong sense about what other people were thinking. But it was always fluff and nonsense—I'd know that a man on the bus was wondering about the composition of saltwater taffy or a girl was worrying over the dry state of her elbows. And then when I started wearing the necklace, everything changed. I was still able to read other people's thoughts, but . . ."

"But what?" I was desperate for her to go on.

"Well, I could filter out the pointless bits. The first time it happened, I was able to tell that our cranky neighbor Mr. Ringen was hiding something. Turned out he had something in the bottom of his pool."

"He was hiding a body!"

"No, no. His mother's will. He'd hidden it there temporarily and then forgotten to move it. Turned out his brother was supposed to inherit the house, and it wasn't long before we had a very charming—and handsome!—new neighbor."

I felt hot and downed the rest of my water in one gulp.

What did this mean for me? I knew my dreams had a way of seeing into the future, but were they actually telling me something? The ones that immediately came to mind—the flying duffel bag and the fruit and pregnancy dreams—had pointed me to a cheesy self-help book, a make-out session with a dog, and a sword and sorcery meeting, respectively. Was there a greater point I was missing out on?

"As a child," she went on, "my grandmother had a way of seeing pictures in everything. She'd see faces in the clouds or horses in her toast."

I nodded with familiarity. Henry once thought he saw King Arthur in his grilled cheese sandwich and insisted on keeping it in a Ziploc bag in the refrigerator until it started to grow mold. But something about Kiki's tone made it clear there was nothing silly about this story.

"And then what?" I asked. "She started to see pictures that led her to find things in the bottom of pools?"

"In a matter of speaking." She raised her glass at me. "She solved people's troubles. As can you."

I felt my lips trembling. "But why didn't you tell me any of this before?"

"Well, this isn't your typical cocktail chitchat, is it? It doesn't just come up."

"I mean when you gave me the necklace," I said, my tone calibrated between a groan and a plea.

"I told you to pay attention to your dreams, didn't I? I told you they'd lead you somewhere. It would have been boring, completely spilling the beans. Besides, I thought you could use some practice piecing things together."

I still needed more practice on that front. Staring into the distance, I tried to put together as much as I could, but all my dreams dangled unconnected, like toys from an avant-garde baby mobile.

"There's a lot of good you can do. You could change people's lives." She smiled patiently. "And that includes *saving* people's lives."

I felt my cheeks turn red.

"Dear," Kiki said, slightly shaking her head. "Your tonsils are lovely, but—"

"Sorry," I said, closing my mouth. "I'm just a little overwhelmed."

"Well, I won't hold it against you."

An idea lit up inside me like a flame. "Wait—is this also why I've been doing so well on all my tests at school, even the ones I'm totally unprepared for? It's amplifying my hunches?"

"Nicely done." Kiki glanced around the room. At first I assumed she wanted to make sure that nobody was listening, but she signaled to the waiter that she'd like another martini and continued, "I urge you not to let on what you're capable of—*especially* not to good friends who you want to be seeing more of. Best not to make too many ripples, you hear?" She checked my face to make sure I understood before continuing. "Not every dream you have will be worth a million dollars, or even a copper penny, but it won't hurt to chase the clues and see what you come up with. It won't be a waste of time. At the very least, a little adventure is good for the complexion."

"Why didn't you give the necklace to Mom?"

"These talents seem to skip a generation," Kiki said. "Just like the talent for cooking that made its way to my mother and your mother."

"Are you saying Mom's cooking is some kind of superpower?"

"I look at it as a consolation prize. I suppose it's only fair that she would get *something* to sink her teeth into other than that odd father of yours." Kiki went on, "Now, my grandmother used it to help the Sacramento police out on cases that had to do with people she knew—nothing too scandalous, missing dogs and tennis bracelets. I got started keeping tabs on my friends' husbands—incredible, all the dirt I dug up. Unfortunately, I found some things out about my own husband. And that was not fun." She took another sip. "In your case, I take it you're on to something with the Shuttleworths."

Of course I was.

"Might there be some more trouble lurking around the corner?" She tilted her head suggestively.

Before I could ask her what I should do next, Edie was bearing down on us.

"There you two are!"she cooed. She was all decked out in a red minidress and lipstick to match. She took a seat. "Kiki, is that who I think it is over in the corner booth?"

Kiki strained to get a better look. "Well, son of a gun! I thought he'd said the big goodnight ages ago."

"You thought wrong," her friend told her. While the two gossiped about their sighting, I sat there, feeling absolutely stunned.

Kiki waited until Edie got up to go to the bathroom to tell me more about the cameo.

"It's quite simple. The only words of advice I have are to keep the necklace dry and polish it every once in a while. I also found it helped to look right into the cameo once a day or so, but I have no direct proof."

"Okay," I said, trying to commit these tricks to memory. "Anything else?"

"I do believe it helps to sleep on your back, which you may as well do anyway. An old bust-preservation technique."

"So I've heard. Mom's a big fan of that trick."

Kiki frowned at the mention of her daughter. "And of

course, you won't tell anybody about any of this. Not your parents, and especially not the people who you'll be helping. If you decide you don't like what I told you, well, all you need to do is remove the necklace and you're off the hook." Kiki drained her glass. "And if you decide to keep wearing it, I wouldn't feel so overwhelmed. Think of the adventures. Oh my!"

It took me a second to realize she was addressing a waiter who'd just arrived with a flute of champagne. "Compliments of Mr. Lefkowitz," he said, bowing.

"My granddaughter will be having it." Kiki pushed the glass my way.

The waiter mumbled something about serving minors.

"Oh, darling, it's fine," Kiki told him. "She's French."

"Merci." I smiled at Kiki and took the daintiest sip I could manage. I felt lightheaded, but I don't think the drink had anything to do with it.

{ 22 }

Looking for Mr. Goodbar

Even though the champagne buzz wore off well before I got home, I still woke up with what could only be described as a hangover. I felt fragile and shaky, and everything around me seemed to have gone into soft focus.

When I met up with Becca that afternoon, she told me she had to go uptown for a Young Friends of Lincoln Center recital.

"You sure you don't want to come see New York's emerging crop of harpsichordists and flutists perform for five hours?" she asked playfully.

"Sounds dreamy," I told her. "But I think I have to go, um . . ."

Untangle all the dreams I've been having and make sure you end up in one piece.

She lowered her chin and smiled coyly. "When you want to get out of something just say you have to wash your hair."

"I'll come to the next one," I said, trying to keep my gratefulness inaudible. "Promise."

It was a cool afternoon, with a harsh edge to the air. I walked down Delancey Street until I came to the East River. I'd expected to find a spot where I could think alone, but it turned out the waterfront was swarming with other confused souls.

I sat down on a bench and got started on the pack of sugary grape gum I'd bought on my walk over. Meditation did not come easy at first. An oily smell was coming off the water, and the guy seated a few benches to my right was playing an extended version of "U Can't Touch This" on the harmonica.

But after a little while, I barely noticed my surroundings. I had no idea how long I'd been sitting there, but it was time enough for me to have chomped the flavor out of all five pieces of my gum and gotten completely lost in thought. There was no need to be so intimidated by Kiki's news. Now I had every reason in the world to believe that Becca's texts were leading up to something far worse than just plain harrassment. If I stayed sharp and figured out what my dreams were telling me, I could identify Becca's stalker and keep her out of harm's way. Or at the very least, I could prevent her from being yanked out of Hudson.

My motives weren't entirely selfless. This had as much to do with my own survival as with hers.

• • •

When I got home, Dad leapt up from his desk to welcome me. "Let me take your coat, *poupée*," he said, and kissed me on the forehead. "How was your day?"

"Um, fine?" I said, wondering what on earth was going on. The last time Dad had gotten up from his computer when he was working to talk to me was—well, I couldn't think of any time that had happened.

"You missed a magnificent dinner. I cooked *pommes frites* and salmon that was as fresh as Didier and Margaux."

"Dad!"

"You look so cute when you're outrageous," he cooed.

"Outraged," I corrected him.

Dad laughed and kept standing there, swaying from side to side and beaming. "I am also happy as a lamb for another reason," he said, and I didn't even bother to remind him *clam* was the word he'd meant to say. "I was invited to present a talk at the Sorbonne."

"You were?" I squealed. "In Paris?" The last time Dad had been invited to speak anywhere, it had required taking a bus to Stamford, Connecticut. The bus had gotten stuck at a Roy Rogers parking lot in Westchester and the lecture was never rescheduled.

He was touching his mustache, as if to make sure it was still there. I kissed him on each cheek and told him how proud I was. "I can be your date if you need one."

"Only spouses can come. Rules are rules."

"Since when were French people so conservative about marriage?" I sighed and left him with his books and went into the kitchen to grab some food. As appetizing as Dad had made the fish sound, I opted for a slice of leftover broccoli pizza and some cold French fries.

Ten minutes later, I was in my room, overstuffed and

facedown on top of my comforter. I told myself I would start my homework when it said 9:15 on my alarm clock. But the designated time came and went, as did 9:20, and I still couldn't make myself budge. Lying there, I began to imagine that my mattress was rippling like a raft at sea, and I was sure I was drifting off to sleep. But the rippling soon gave way to jerking, and I felt somebody's fist push into the mattress. I had to look under my bed, where I found my little brother.

"Boo!" Henry said, getting up and stretching out his arms like a zombie.

His pockets were bulging, and I saw a familiar shade of yellow poking out by his belt loop.

I grabbed my Mr. Goodbar out of his pocket. "This isn't exactly a help-yourself buffet."

"C'mon, you have so much candy under there!"

"Shh!" I didn't want Dad to hear.

"But I already started it," Henry said, pulling the chocolate bar away. "You'll get germs."

"You're my little brother." I snatched it back. "Our germs are already well acquainted."

Henry dropped his arms and his face assumed a worried expression. "Hey, what's going on with Didier? Why's he making those weird bubbles?"

"What do you mean?" I twisted around to face my tank. Just as I was determining my fish looked perfectly content, Henry the con artist seized the candy from me.

"You little troll!"

Henry was laughing as we tussled over the candy. And then came the loudest whistle I'd ever heard.

Dad was standing all of three feet away, holding the phone. He removed two fingers from his mouth and gave a satisfied nod. "I repeat, there is someone on the phone for you, Claire." He handed me the cordless and snatched the Mr. Goodbar from his son. And then he took a bite. "*Pas mal,*" he said. Henry looked as if his eyes were about to roll out of his head. Served him right.

"Hello?" I said.

"Sounds like I interrupted some very interesting family ritual."

"Andy?" I squawked, shooing everybody away.

"If I say yes, are you going to hang up on me?"

I knew I should be furious, but I'd be lying if I said it didn't occur to me that maybe, just maybe, he was calling to offer me an explanation. I inhaled deeply and waited.

"So what's up?" I asked, trying to sound as if I weren't losing my cool. It worked, and the words rolled off my tongue like cigarette smoke in an old movie. I have to say, as much as I might bitch and moan about sounding like a 900-number worker, I can always count on my voice to make me sound blasé, even in moments of extreme discomfort.

"First, I wanted to apologize about ditching you the other night. I can't imagine how awkward it must have been for you."

"You seemed to be the one feeling awkward," I said quietly.

"I had to get out and talk to Rye. If you knew how jealous she can get, you'd understand . . ."

I stuffed my Eiffel Tower pillow in my mouth and waited for him to get to the point. But after a short silence, I began to wonder whether there was a point, and took the pillow out. The drool had darkened the Seine River from aqua to navy. "Is that it, then?"

"No." He sounded jumpy. "Listen, I know I'm going to sound like a jerk when I say what I'm about to, but I'm in a tight spot here."

"And what's that?"

I drew a deep breath and looked out the window. A plane was moving through the sky, and the bushes in the courtyard looked like no more than shadows. From the plane, all of us—me, Andy, Rye—must be barely passing specks. If only it felt that way to me.

"Here's the thing. She's going to be staying with my parents for the next week, until Thanksgiving break is over. Her parents are renovating their house and their water will be turned off." He took a long breath, and exhaled noisily. "I know you don't come over and visit Becca all that often, but in case you're going to . . . if you could hold off, I think that would be for the best. She sort of has . . . issues with you."

"You're *banishing* me from your house?"

"I'm just doing what I think will make the situation easier for everyone, you included." Now he sounded unfazed, professional, even. I couldn't believe it—it was as if he were an entirely different person.

"Well, that's considerate of you," I huffed, but he must have taken my words at face value, because he thanked me.

"I knew you'd be cool," he said.

I let the pillow drop to the floor and shook my head in disbelief. What was the point of saying anything else? I had my pride, and I wasn't in the business of bullying people into liking me.

He went on, the relief in his voice unmistakable. "I'll probably see you soon, after the wedding."

"You guys are *engaged*?"

I wasn't sure if this was tragic or funny.

"Not quite," he laughed. "Our cousin Emma is. Sorry, I thought Becca would have told you. We're all going to London on Thanksgiving weekend for her wedding. Rye wasn't originally planning on coming, but she's never been to England before, and she says she's dying to see some art show by this guy who makes eighty-foot-tall mannequins with baby heads. She's been working so hard at school, she deserves a break."

I'll *say*.

"It's supposed to be a great town," I offered feebly.

"Well, you know, I'm partial to New York, but I guess it's not bad."

"Sure," I said in a withered voice. "I just . . . Becca didn't . . . This is the first I've heard of her going to London."

"She's not. She has to stay behind for some voice rehearsals."

"By herself?"

"Well, with the housekeeper."

And that's when the idea of Andy deciding to jet off to Europe with his pseudofeminist girlfriend ceased to trouble me—for all I cared, he could get I ♥ RYE tattooed on his forehead.

Becca was going to be in the country alone. Alone and unprotected. Which meant I should probably get a move on things.

{ 23 }

Tired of Waiting

On Thursday, I woke up feeling as deflated as a punctured beach ball. Nothing had come to me that night, just a bizarre dream about sharing the elevator up to Kiki's with a haughty ostrich who kept glaring down its beak at me until I exclaimed, "We both know who's the ostrich here!" In my dream life, this had felt like the wittiest remark of all time, but now I was left with a dissatisfying aftertaste. More dissatisfying, though, was that the dream was in color.

I sat on the window ledge to sprinkle in Didier and Margaux's breakfast and collect my bummed-out thoughts. What would it take to get a clue around here?

Margaux was playing hard to get, circling the plastic

chateau on the bottom of the tank. Didier, blessedly, rose to the surface and wiggled his little orange and white tail at me.

I threw my cadged Waldorf bathrobe over my pajamas and headed for the shower. I took off my necklace and pulled the curtain shut. Standing under the stream of warm water, I stopped thinking about Becca, and my outlook started to improve—but not for long. Midway through lathering on Mom's Institut de Beauté Derrière Minimiseur, I slipped on one of Henry's bath toys.

"*La vache!*" I hollered, tumbling down.

Most of the time I can hold off from blurting out stupid French expressions, but when you find yourself butt-up on the bathtub floor, it's hard to remember to keep your cool. When I got out of the bathroom, prepared to yell at Henry for nearly killing me, I found him at the breakfast table, dressed in a green argyle sweater and eating leftover spaghetti and meatballs. A clump of hair shot up, Einstein-like, from the crown of his head.

"Nice look. Do you have a Young Republicans Club meeting today?"

"I'm practicing for school picture day. It's tomorrow." He said this without any irony, and I felt a smile tug at my mouth.

I leaned in to kiss him on the forehead and fish the cordless phone out from under a bundle of Dad's notes. "We can practice some more outfits tonight, and Mom will be back tomorrow morning to help us out," I told him. Phone in hand, I walked over to the reading nook and dialed Kiki's number.

"Yes?" she asked after five rings, stretching the word into as many syllables. I pictured her sitting up in bed, pulling her baby blue silk eye mask up by her hairline and squinting at the cable box to see the time.

After a minute of small talk, I couldn't contain myself any more. "I'm all blocked up," I blurted out.

"Darling, there's a reason God put prunes on this earth."

"I'm talking about the dreams!"

"Oh. Your generation has to stop being so *vague* about everything. Now, what's the matter, dear?"

"I'm trying to tell you. . . ." I looked over my shoulder to make sure nobody was eavesdropping, then went ahead and told her about how the cameo had stopped working. "I did everything you told me to do—I polish the necklace, I keep it dry, I look into it every day. What else am I supposed to do—sing love songs to it?" I was so exasperated I could have ripped my hair out. "The Shuttleworths are going to London and they're leaving Becca behind by herself. The whole thing makes me feel supremely nervous. I need answers, and fast."

"Oh, Claire, there's nothing attractive about getting hysterical. If something is supposed to come to you, it will."

"But what if it comes too late?"

She made a light clicking sound with her tongue. "What if, what if, what if? You need to get out of your head."

"Unfortunately, I'm sort of stuck to it."

"And unfortunately, you're sort of literal, too!" I could hear her throwing her arms in the air. "How's this for a thought? Why don't you call Louis and take a trip to the Metropolitan Museum? Go and have a good time, get your mind off your troubles. Clem and I just saw a marvelous show on Art Deco Paris."

"Art Deco Paris," I repeated dryly.

I was reminded of my first day at summer camp, when all the counselors were ordering us to make friends with each other and have fun. Why didn't people ever understand that what sounded so logical—and easy—was anything but?

"Yes, my lemon drop. You mustn't worry overmuch."

"That's not exactly an option at this point," I said. "Becca's family is leaving in a week."

Kiki sighed. "You don't have much wiggle room, do you?"

"To put it lightly."

"Well . . . I do have one little suggestion. It worked for my grandmother, but I'm telling you, was useless when I tried it."

"I'll try it. What is it?"

"Look in the mirror."

"Okay," I said, walking over to the mirrored Renault poster. It looked like a new freckle was coming up on my right cheek. "I see a girl in her bathrobe. Now what?"

"No, darling, not now. Bring a mirror into bed with you at night, and look at the cameo before you fall asleep."

"Really?" I looked at my necklace in the mirror, half expecting a jolt of inspiration. "I'm doing it now. What should I be feel—"

"Before bed, dear. Not now."

Just as I was returning the phone to the cradle, Dad sloped out of his room.

"Was that Mom?" he asked me.

"Kiki. Why?"

A corner of his mouth twitched. "Mom was going to tell you herself," he said softly.

"Supposed to tell me what?"

"They've extended her job. She'll be in Florida until the Tuesday after Thanksgiving weekend."

"What?" My heart started to race and I glanced over at Henry, who was mixing pizza-flavored Combos into his cold spaghetti. How was I going to get to the bottom of this very important mystery if I had to stick around doing Mom's job and look after Henry? "She's not going to be here until *after* Thanksgiving? She can't just *do* that."

"I'm disappointed, too. Now she can't come with me to the conference in Paris." Dad frowned. "We'll have Thanksgiving the next week. And you can help me cook a welcome-home supper for your mother, *ma petite puce*."

"I am not a little flea!" I huffed. I was so incensed— couldn't he tell I had better things to do than hang out in the apartment cooking welcome-home suppers and reminding my little brother to brush his teeth?

"Whoops!" Henry cried. "They make these grape juice boxes so wobbly."

Dad cut me a look. "Can you help him clean that up?"

Well, there was my answer.

I showed up for school a little early, and there was no shortage of kids hanging around outside the building. Some were bent over their notebooks, cramming for tests. Sheila and her gang were wearing matching pink tutus and laughing like a bunch of drunk sorority girls.

"Okay, who's going to get him?" Sheila shrieked, pointing at a guy who was approaching school. Everything about him was scrawny except for one thing: he had a nose that I could picture his grandmother constantly assuring him he'd "grow into one day."

"Hey, baby," Sheila greeted her victim.

He turned to look behind him. "Me?" He grinned like crazy.

"You don't have to sound so scared." She waited until he'd come nearer. "Do you know what day it is today?"

"Um, your birthday?"

"Try again," she said, strategically playing with her sweatshirt to expose an inch of abdomen. I could feel the waves of nausea rolling through me.

"Thursday?" the kid tried again.

Sheila laughed for what seemed like ten minutes. "That's not what I meant. It's Send a Flower Day."

"Oh yeah, I heard something about that," the guy said.

Send a Flower Day was a cheesy Hudson tradition where kids could pay two dollars to have a wilted carnation delivered to a classmate of their choice. For reasons that had not been made clear to me, the proceeds went to the Lower East Side Veterans Association.

"I'd love it if a flower came from a cutie like you. . . ." Her bug eyes grew big, and she cupped her hand over her mouth as if she were embarrassed. Talk about bad acting. No wonder she hadn't made it into the cast of Hudson's production of *The Vagina Monologues* last year.

"Cool." His head was eagerly yo-yoing up and down. "I'll send you one, sure."

And as he walked away, the girls waggled their fingers in a manner that I could only assume was intended to be seductive.

"Don't look so sad!" Sheila called out. I realized with a start she was talking to me. "I'm sure somebody will remember to get you a flower."

God, it was maddening. The local veterans might get some extra winter socks out of it, but that didn't feel like much consolation.

The girl who came to our homeroom to hand out everyone's flowers introduced herself as Winnie. She had long oily hair and a habit of staring at the floor while she talked.

She gave out the flowers one by one, which would have made sense had every flower not been for Sheila. After watching Sheila get up from her seat for the fiftieth time to accept a flower, I lost interest and turned my attention to *Sofa City*, a miniature comic book Ian had lent me.

A few pages in, somebody pinched my arm.

"Claire Voyante?" Winnie was saying.

"Me?" There had to be a mistake, unless Becca had bought me a flower as a joke. I stuffed the comic book into my desk, straightened my back, and went up to the front of the room to take the pink carnation. It wasn't until I was back in my seat that I opened the little envelope that was attached to the stalk.

CLAIRE, YOU ALWAYS LOOK FANTASSTIC. XX

The message was so subtle I didn't get it until the second reading. Right there, wedged between the *fant* and the *tic*, those magic three letters: *ASS*. The handwriting was loopy—definitely a girl's. My eyes darted to Sheila, but it was impossible to see her face through the thicket of flowers in front of her.

"None of you have any idea where this came from, do you?" I asked during the following period, dragging a chair over to Ian and Zach's table.

All blank expressions.

"Didn't think so."

Apart from Becca, there was only one other person at Hudson who knew about my possibly paranoid butt hang-up. I flung the flower onto a seat at the empty table next to ours. "I think I know who to thank . . . Can you believe what they're up to today?"

"I know," said Ian. "These burgers are even more repulsive than usual."

"I wasn't talking about the burgers, buddy," I said, pulling out my lunch bag. "Look at them." I gestured toward the milk station, where three of the BDLs were holding enough flowers to fill the Brooklyn Botanic Garden. "They were outside school this morning like sleazy politicians, practically trading kisses for flowers."

Zach turned white.

"You *totally* bought them flowers," Ian said. "You are an ass."

"Not true," Zach said in a falsetto.

"Zach," I said, "can you help me understand something? Are those girls even attractive to you or are you just suckered in because they deign to talk to you?"

"Can I get back to you on that one?" Zach asked.

"Let's not blame the victim here," Ian said. "He'll learn. But while we're on the subject of your friends, check this out." He zipped open his suitcase and slid something over to me.

"No way!" It was our English assignment—the "Evil Radish" comic book we'd started the other night. I couldn't believe how awesome it looked fully illustrated. I flipped through the booklet's sixteen pages, following the evil radish as she and her yoga-pants-and-hoop-earrings-wearing evil radish clones spend a day on the farm intimidating scrawny little alfalfa sprouts into paying them radish compliments. My favorite part was the end, where the evil radish and her gang get their comeuppance and are chopped up and tossed into a huge mixed salad.

Or at least, I thought that was my favorite part, until Ian showed me the back cover, where he'd drawn a police lineup of radishes next to a sign that said CHARGE: INDECENCY. VERDICT: GUILTY. And then I noticed he'd added tutus, just like the ones the BDLs had worn to school that day.

"I work quickly when inspired," he explained.

Even though the handiwork was all Ian's, the story line had been all mine, and I felt enormously proud. All through English class I was excited for Mr. Bunting to wrap up his fascinating lecture on the inherent superiority of college-ruled paper to wide-ruled and collect our stories. When the bell rang and everyone woke up, Ian handed in our comic book. Mr. Bunting did a double take. " 'The Adventures of Evil Radish'?" he mumbled dubiously. "We'll see about this."

That afternoon, Louis was finally going to make good on his promise to come by Hudson and pick me up. The plan was to ride our bikes over the Brooklyn Bridge and go to Prospect Park to see some simulated refugee camp installation that he'd heard about. As I passed through the doors, I had a sinking feeling that he'd forgotten all about me, but he was across the street, between the Queen Bees and a Mister Softee ice cream truck. I was used to thinking he was slightly dweeby, but in a sea of Hudson kids, he looked almost hunky by comparison. Or maybe that was what happened when you suddenly got a girlfriend.

He was watching the BDLs, who were waving their flowers around like beauty queens and making even more noise than usual.

When I greeted him, he nodded in Sheila's direction. "Has your old friend taken up gardening or something?"

"More like she's taken up being a social terrorist." I started walking toward my bike and he followed, guiding his by the handlebars. "She and her friends bullied every boy who doesn't know better into sending them flowers. Welcome to the world of New York's . . ."

"Bravest and brightest." Louis was finishing off my last thought, completely oblivious to the fact that I was trembling.

My bike—or at least, what I could only assume was my bike—had been completely covered with toilet paper and chewed-up wads of gum. The cherry on top: an extra-large maxi pad had been stuck on the seat, and somebody had used a tube of lipstick to write BIG BUTT ON BOARD on it. As if my carnation that morning hadn't been enough. God, she was thoroughly awful.

"I'm going to kill Sheila."

"No way. This is the work of Sheila Turd?" Louis looked back and forth between the bike and the villain, shaking his head at the horror.

I ripped off the pad, crumpling it in my hand, and hopped on my bike, with Louis following close behind. I waited until we were only a couple of feet away from the BDLs to say anything more. Just as I was about to ride by the evil pack of clones, I threw my seat cushion Louis's way and yelled, "Heads up! Try sitting on it! It makes it so much more comfortable."

He reached out for the maxi pad, and instead of catching it, he knocked it with the side of his arm. Louis was too good at sports to make a mistake like this.

The maxi pad spun in the air like a disc of pizza dough, then landed at Sheila's feet.

"Ack!" Sheila jumped back like a revolted kangaroo. "What is that thing?"

"You know what it is!" Louis called back. "Keep it for the next time you want to bully somebody. More environmentally conscious that way."

{ 24 }

When Only Bubbly Will Do

It was a beautiful day for bike riding, with a clear sky and hardly any wind, but I was in too foul a mood for our original plan. Louis rode with me to my apartment building and helped me bring my bike down to the janitor's basement closet. "We'll make it good as new," he said confidently.

But half an hour later we were still scrubbing. "It's not coming off." I was heartbroken. We'd been using industrial-strength scrub pads to loosen the gum, and my arm was too tired to keep going.

Louis ran his hand over the frame. "Feels pretty good to me, just a couple of bumps."

"A couple of bumps? That's like saying Bozo the Clown only has a few hairs on his head." I collapsed to the ground.

He looked at me and ran his hand through his hair which, come to think of it, wasn't entirely un-Bozoish. "Will you stop worrying, Lemonhead? You'll come out on top."

Sitting there on the cold linoleum floor, surrounded by shelves of roach spray and garbage deodorizer, I was too demoralized to reply.

"You've got to snap out of it," he said. "Your bike's fine. You're just depressed. It's coloring your sense of reality. You won't even notice anything the next time you see it." He lifted my bike off the floor and asked me to grab his—a hunter green ten-speed that was a shiny reminder of how terrible mine looked.

I shuffled behind Louis as he rolled my bike into the storage room, and we didn't say much on the elevator up to the eighth floor.

"You sure you don't want to go on a walk or something?" he asked up by the door to my apartment. "Or I can come in and we can watch TV."

"Nah." I stuck my key in the door. "Not in the mood. Why don't you go hang out with your girlfriend?"

Louis stepped away, putting his hands in the air. "As you wish."

There are some times when even chocolate won't do. When I'm really upset, all I want is to go to Kiki's for a long almond-scented soak. We have a tub in our apartment, of course, though we use it as often as the make-your-own-marmalade machine Dad gave Mom for Christmas three years ago—that is to say, never. There would be no point. In our household it is nearly impossible to pass five minutes in the bathroom without somebody coming along to pound on the door and kick you out.

I pulled myself together and an hour later I was in Kiki's master bathroom, dressed in nothing but a robe. My folded-up clothes were resting on the marble countertop, next to a porcelain figurine of my grandparents' old dog Winston. The bath was nearly completely drawn, and the room had already filled with the lemon verbena scent of Kiki's foaming bath gel.

"You all set?" she called to me from the other side of the door.

"Yes!" I replied, leaning into the steamy mirror to remove the last of my bobby pins and my cameo. "I'm about to go under."

"Sink away, then. I'll be out in the living room if you need anything."

I could hear her television turn off and the door shut. Kiki respects my need for total peace and quiet when I take my baths.

Averting my eyes so I didn't catch sight of my naked reflection in the full-length mirror, I reached over to dim the lights and slowly stepped into the water. A warm sensation moved from my feet through my calves, and finally reached the crown of my head as I dunked all the way under.

I leaned against the clean tile wall and looked out the bathroom's picture window. The view was of another building's thirty-eighth floor and a narrow patch of sky. I sat still, watching clouds and birds and planes as they passed by, giving my head a chance to empty out. I needed to let go of my beef with Sheila and remember what really mattered.

At some point the bubbles were gone. I used the pad of my shriveled big toe to finesse the lever down and I waited for every drop of water to empty out before standing up.

The only thing that had changed between the time I'd

shown up at Kiki's door and now was that I was clean and naked, but I had developed a completely new lease on life.

I clasped the cameo back around my neck. I was going to get to the bottom of my dreams, no ifs, ands, or buts.

When I came out, Kiki and Clem were gussied up and feasting on the weirdest picnic dinner: lamb with mint jelly, carrot sticks, and gummy worms.

"I'm not even going to ask," I said.

"We're loading up on gelatin," Kiki told me.

"My beard's been looking a little lusterless," said Clem.

"Come now, Claire." Kiki patted the seat cushion next to her. "Your hair and nails will thank you."

I joined them for a little while, but I was in no mood to linger—I needed to get home and see where my reinvigorated disposition would take me. My slice of lamb finished, I wrapped a clump of gummy worms in a napkin and bid my farewells.

I was home by eight-thirty and in bed less than an hour later. I lay there forever, staring into an old pink hand mirror and trying to put myself to sleep with thoughts of boring things: kitchen sponges, instant oatmeal, pet rocks.

Ever wonder what it's like to be a worm burrowing your way underground? Well, neither had I. Turns out it wasn't at all claustrophobic—but the darkness was mildly annoying. Underground, I wriggled ahead, toward a gauzy halo of light. I followed it up to the surface. Past a cluster of black-and-white dandelions, I could make out the silhouette of Cheri-Lee standing at a podium, gesticulating wildly. A Doc Marten boot was coming toward me, so I ducked back underground.

Everything went to pitch black. I had an itch in my belly—or was it my back?—but being an earthworm, I couldn't exactly reach out and scratch it. I noticed another seductive flicker of light in the distance and poked my body through the ground again. The top layer was pebbly, and I wriggled around against the little bumps, hoping the friction would make the itchiness go away. As I surfaced and adjusted to the sunlight, I saw a stick figure pulling apart a slice of pizza. I would have stayed for more had a hungry-looking bird not been swooping my way.

I woke up in a sweat, utterly confused. What was this pink thing pressing into my eardrum? Oh, right—the mirror.

The images clanged around in my head as I picked up a wayward pillow from the floor. I had no idea what was up with the stick figure, but I knew the first person I'd seen in my dream was Cheri-Lee giving a talk.

And before I could really think about what I was doing, I booted up my computer and Googled *Cheri-Lee Vird* and *poetry conference*.

The Rogers College poetry conference site was as corny as could be, with a lilac background and a banner line of poetry across the top that changed every five seconds. I navigated away from the list of attendees and skipped around the pages for Rogers College and Poetry, Distinguished Speakers, and Registration Information.

And then, just when I was about to go back to bed, I clicked on the Rogers College: Out and About page:

Our campus is located in bucolic Rogerstown, New Jersey, the birthplace of the touch-tone phone. Come walk under Main Street's canopy of elm trees or visit the legendary telecommunications museum.

Voted the state's second-best college town by the *New Jersey Register,* Rogerstown offers the best of both worlds: a mere hour from the world-class museums and concert halls of New York City, the area boasts a quaint center with independent bookstores, two movie theaters, and several excellent restaurants with cuisines ranging from Ethiopian to authentic Neapolitan pizza.

Come see for yourself.

Pizza, you say? Well, well. I just might take you folks up on the offer.

{ 25 }

Meeting of the Minds

"**W**ho knew? I'd never taken you for a *poetry lover!*" Cheri-Lee exclaimed. "Sheila's been allergic to it all her life. I blame her father for reading the *Economist* to her when she was still a kid." She squinted against a shaft of blinding sunlight. "God, he was always so passive-aggressive."

It was Saturday morning, and Cheri-Lee's teal Honda was heading down the New Jersey Turnpike. Getting invited to tag along to the Rogers College Poetry Conference had been a lot easier than expected. When Cheri-Lee came by to check up on us on Friday morning, all I had to do was tell her I thought the conference sounded interesting. "Then you should come!" she gasped. "Gustave, lend me your daughter for the day. Best to expose them to the joys of language when they're still *whippersnappers*."

Cheri-Lee's energy level was no less frenetic at this early hour. While she waxed hyperactive about everything from the knitted-fiber jewelry course she was considering signing up for to the new drying machines in the complex's basement laundry rooms, I gazed out the window, taking in the factories and Life Saver–colored container stacks along the turnpike's southern belt. It wasn't exactly heartstoppingly beautiful, but it had a certain Zen appeal.

Careful not to appear too interested, I made sure to keep my line of questioning about Cheri-Lee's daughter to a minimum. *Where's Sheila today? Have you ever taken her to New Jersey?* Not surprisingly, Cheri-Lee didn't have any revealing answers—no news of Sheila bringing home lumps of cash or snapshots of her taking psychological hit man classes at the Learning Annex. If I wanted to advance my investigation, I was going to have to work a little harder for it.

Though the Rogers College campus was barely ten minutes off the turnpike, it might as well have been continents away, with its brick colonial-style buildings and tree-lined paths that looked like they had never come into contact with litter. The people clustered around the center were dressed professorially, and I was glad I'd worn an olive green corduroy dress, a white button-down shirt, and a chunky pair of black Mary Janes. I looked right at home.

"I knew they'd have quite the *all-star* lineup," Cheri-Lee said as she studied the schedule taped to the door of the Baselberg Student Center. She was one of fifty poets and academics who would be participating in the day's lectures and workshops. "Get ready for the exposure of your life." Cheri-Lee tugged me by the arm down a hallway. She stopped short at a doorway with a SOUVENIRS sign tacked to it. "Oh! They had the cutest Paul Muldoon tote bags last year."

I'd come hoping Cheri-Lee would let something revealing about Sheila slip, but that didn't seem about to happen anytime soon. She was way too wrapped up in the conference to think about anything else. Was it possible that the second part of my dream, the part with the pizza, was where the secret treasure was hidden?

"Actually," I told her, "I'm suddenly starving." Ever the bad actress, I made an awkward gesture in my tummy's direction. "Why don't I run to town and pick something up for the two of us? Weirdly, I'm craving pizza."

"As if!" she trumpeted. "I'm not ready to give you up just yet. Let's pick up a muffin at the café and check out the morning programs. They tend to be the best, when everyone is still fresh."

And so, after pretending to be ravenous and stuffing a bone-dry orange-cranberry scone down my throat, I sat with Cheri-Lee through two presentations—a reading by Mya Nanh, a Burmese refugee, and then a roundtable on poetry, parody, and possibility.

"Overwhelming, all of this, isn't it?" Cheri-Lee asked at the start of the lunch break. She'd just bought a vegetable sandwich from the Keats Kiosk, and we were moseying across the atrium toward an undernourished man she said she recognized from another conference.

"Gavin? Gavin!" she called his way. "It's me, Cheri-Lee!"

Fighting my way through a wave of disheveled poets, I caught up to my host, who was now at her old friend's side. The guy was definitely Cheri-Lee's type—he was wearing several tote bags on each shoulder and he had sunglasses, reading glasses, and a pair of binoculars hanging from chains around his neck. "It is overwhelming," I told her. "So much to absorb. I think I need to get some fresh air."

"I hope I haven't scared you off," she said, more for Gavin's benefit than my own. It was clear that my companionship was no longer needed. "You'll be back soon, won't you?" she asked giddily. "The panel I'm on starts at one."

"I'll be quick as a wing," I told her, citing one of Dad's favorite mangled expressions.

She laughed, and a sprout flew out of her sandwich and landed on her quilted poncho.

Once I'd escaped the building and started down the walkway, I had to ask myself what exactly I was looking for. I'd come this far and crashed Cheri-Lee's poetry conference, but by this point I'd seen all the participants, and the only new thing Cheri-Lee had told me about Sheila was that she was considering getting a belly-button ring. There was little reason to believe any of the afternoon's programs on assonance or iambic pentameter was going to further my Shuttleworth investigation. The pizza part of the dream had better work. Maybe there'd be a secret message written in pepperoni waiting for me.

The sky had begun to cloud over and the air was starting to fill with a cool mist. I zipped up my newly Kiki-bestowed green Courrèges jacket and rushed down the pathway. A sign for the Rogerstown Museum of Telecommunications led me to Main Street. It was less picturesque than I'd expected— instead of mom-and-pop stores, there were dingy franchises for places like Taco Bell and Abercrombie. There was a huge Starbucks full of college-age kids drinking enormous whipped cream–topped drinks and talking on their cell phones.

"Excuse me," I said to a crazy-looking lady on the bench

outside. She was wearing a sweatshirt with a silk-screened picture of herself on it. "Do you know where the pizzeria is?"

"There's a Domino's down the block," she told me.

"Isn't there another one? I think it's supposed to be Sicilian style or something?"

"Not around here, there isn't," she said reprovingly. "Only Neapolitan."

My heart contracted. "That's the one," I said. "Where is it?"

"It's kind of far."

"I'll be fine," I told her, feeling mildly defiant. I've often found that residents of small towns tend to have inflated notions of how large their corner of the world is.

The silk-screen lady sighed and pointed down the street. "On the left. Just keep going. And going."

As I'd predicted, Emilio's Brick Oven was only a few blocks away, and I was there in a flash.

Or maybe I shouldn't say I was *there*, because that would imply I made it inside. When I hit the corner, I could barely breathe, let alone move.

And what I saw had nothing to do with Sheila.

Though I almost wished it did. What I saw was a whole lot worse than anything I'd ever imagined. And that's saying a lot—my imagination is hardly anemic.

Seated on the bench under the Emilio's awning was an overweight guy with a tiny head and dark hair. He was dressed in standard-issue badass attire: baggy jeans, a white Starter jacket, and multicolored basketball sneakers that were open around the ankles. On his lap sat a tiny caramel-colored dog wearing a collar that perfectly matched the guy's sneakers. But the real showstopper was the girl next to him. Even though she was facing away from me, there was no mistaking whose bony back I was looking at. The guy tried to feed Rye a bite of pizza and she started making her inimitable nervous squeals.

They moved about with the familiar rhythms of two people who've known each other for ages, play-wrestling until she finally gave in and took a bite of pizza. Her head was making tiny back-and-forth motions as, I imagined, she succumbed to the feeding hour. I was so exhilarated by the thought of him force-feeding her a greasy wad of cheese, it took me a little while to note that the slice of pizza was still in the guy's hands. I moved slightly to the side. Something was making contact with her mouth, all right—but it wasn't a high-fat dairy product. She and her friend were sucking face.

Très interessant.

How had I been so stupid?

First the duffel bag dream, then the one with the fruit. And the basketball one from a while ago. Who cared if Sheila and the BDLs had been playing with a basketball in school the other day? Far more interesting was the fact that Rye had been wearing knee-length socks.

Knee-length tube socks.

Just like the socks the Soyles manufactured.

Ooh la la!

Just then another revelation dislodged from the dark side of my brain: the pregnancy dream had featured babies and mannequins. Just like what Andy had said Rye wanted to see in London. Which meant . . . the maternity dress Sheila had been wearing didn't mean bupkes. The dreams had been alerting me to Rye all along.

So she was the real baddie. As for Sheila, well, she just sucked.

My heart did a little whoop-de-whoop. And then I felt a

thud in my stomach. I knew exactly who this guy was. He fit Becca's description perfectly.

I could hear the blood thumping in my eardrums as I ran down the street and back to the campus. Breathless and elated, I arrived just in time for Cheri-Lee's event—a reading called "Beyond the Language School."

The last in a three-person lineup, Cheri-Lee glissaded up to the lectern like a movie star.

"Ground breaking," she began breathily, deep lines forming in her forehead. "Bread baking. Wheat chaffing . . ."

With all these Rye-related questions circling around in my head, it was hard to concentrate on the poem, but I could tell by the audience members' rapt expressions that Cheri-Lee's reading was a huge success. All but one of the questions during the question-and-answer session were directed at her, and she sold out of her books during the signing portion of the event.

Looked as if I wasn't the only one who was having a good day.

"I'm absolutely *drained*," Cheri-Lee said afterward. "Do you mind if I take a time-out to recuperate during the next panel?"

"Not at all." I parked the poetic star at a table in the café and told her I had to go to the bathroom.

"Do you need help finding it?" she asked, but I was already far ahead of her.

I had to get away from the crowd and call Kiki. She'd undoubtedly have some advice for me about what to do now that I'd made this breakthrough.

I found a bank of pay phones on the second floor, in a carpeted hallway off the game room. Waiting for Kiki to pick up, I made a mental note to start dropping hints her way that a cell phone would make an awesome sixteenth-birthday present.

Kiki answered after several rings, and I immediately launched into a description of the make-out session I'd seen on the bench.

"You say her beau was plump and pinheaded? Sounds like a real Valentino."

"He's no Andy, that's for sure."

"Well, well, well, there's no accounting for taste. . . . Now I should get back to Clem. He and I were just sitting down to watch *Prime Suspect*. It's lady detective hour over here."

"Here, too!"

"Helen Mirren is at the conference?"

"No! Don't you get it?" I turned around to make sure nobody was coming from behind, and I hunched over with the phone cradled in the crook of my neck. "I had a black-and-white dream about coming here, so I hitched a ride. Then I see Rye getting it on with some guy I've never laid eyes on before. And it's got to be Otto Soyle, I just know it." My speech was gaining momentum. "You know how everyone jokes about how Rye never gave Andy the time of day before this summer?"

"Yes?" She sounded slightly vexed.

"Well, this explains it. It all makes sense. Rye's an imposter! She doesn't really like him. She's just using him to infiltrate the family."

And in the five months she'd been dating Andy, Rye must have been able to pick up so many of the Shuttleworths' particulars—their travel plans, their bank statements, the contents of their kitchen cabinets, and so on. With all that knowledge, it would be easy-peasy for the Soyles to prey on my friend's weaknesses. The text messages were just the icing on the cake.

"Ah, I see. . . ." Kiki murmured a "Thank you," and I could picture Clem handing her a dirty martini. "So did you get any evidence? Did you bring a camera?"

My heart dipped. "Only an eyewitness account. But I have to tell the Shuttleworths what I saw, right?"

"Now, there's a thought." She sounded appalled. "You know the girl running around with Andy isn't in it for real. That's mystery number one. But you still haven't figured out what she's got up her sleeve. Isn't that the important question?"

"But I can just tell them to send her packing."

"You could." I could hear in her tone that she was humoring me. "But don't you think it would be wise to find out what she's up to? Even if you told them to shake her loose and they listened to you, what good would that do?"

"They'd be rid of her."

"Yes, but have you stopped to consider she might already have information that could put your friends in danger?" I was nodding, even though she couldn't see me.

"Now, if you will please excuse me, this program is heating up. Clem's telling me a dead body just turned up in the mail chute. I should go and be a good host."

"Right." I sighed.

"Don't worry, my dear," she said soothingly. "You're going to be just fine."

Easy for her to say. Just thinking about all the dreaming ahead made me tired.

{ 26 }

Our Own Happiness

Louis woke me up with a phone call on Sunday morning.

"Everything okay?" I asked. It was 7:53, a good six hours before his regular weekend wake-up time.

"Yeah, just great." His voice had a hard edge to it. "Robyn dumped me on my head."

"What? She can't do that—I haven't even met her yet."

Louis coughed. "Sorry it's inconvenient for you."

"I'm sorry. That came out wrong. . . . Look, at least now you'll have the time to hang out more. I can finally introduce you to Becca."

"Yeah, there are so many things I can do now. Make tortellini from scratch. Reread all my childhood books. Learn how to macramé."

My heart sank a little for my friend. "Louis! It's going to be fine."

"Whatever. I gotta go. I haven't slept much."

"Hold on," I said, but the dial tone spoke back.

I swaddled myself in my robe and wandered into the main room. My mind was still in a vegetal early-morning state, and the fog didn't lift for a few minutes, not until I was nearing the bottom of my cereal bowl. I was tempted to call Becca and make plans to hang out, and it killed me to think that I couldn't. Even if I didn't say anything about what I'd seen in New Jersey, I'd surely act weird.

How could I not after the Google search on Otto Soyle I'd done the night before? A picture that went along with a *New York Post* story about the steakhouse fire showed the entire Soyle family, and it was confirmed: the bloated pea-head who'd been kissing Rye was none other than the infamous Otto.

Now, how was I going to figure out what he and Rye were up to? If only my dreams came to me at all hours of the day.

And then, as I was pouring the excess milk down the drain, lightning struck. I would spend the day on the couch, watching bad TV. If I could find programming that was dozy enough, I'd drowse off—my only chance at getting answers.

Unfortunately, even back-to-back episodes of *New York on Nine Bucks* didn't transport me anywhere other than to a bialy factory in Queens. I went into my room, lay on my back with my hand mirror, and picked up Agatha's *A Murder Is Announced*. I got to page sixty without the slightest onset of sleepiness—in fact, I felt more awake than before. I put the book down and spent the rest of the afternoon staring, in the mirror at my cameo.

Soon enough the world was back to black-and-white.

• • •

I was standing on top of a tower that was easily a couple of miles in the air, a height that normally would have terrified me. But pillowy clouds were obscuring the sharp drop to the ground, and I felt perfectly safe.

I had an enormous pair of binoculars hanging from a chain around my neck. I brought them to my face. The tower overlooked a body of water, and through the fog I could make out a flock of vultures in the distance. They circled and then alighted on a giant clock sculpture across the water. I watched as they streamed into the lattice face of the clock and out through the back.

The clock's hour and minute hands rotated with no discernable rhythm, haphazardly speeding up and slowing down. And then, as the fog thickened and the sky grew a deeper gray, the hands stopped at six-thirty and the flock of birds shot away.

Finally!

Not that I had any idea what any of it meant, but I had no doubt I would soon.

I showed up for school Monday morning ready for anything, and I had my black sunglasses and digital camera stuffed in my bag. I was confident everything would work out; my only worry was bumping into Becca. What was I supposed to tell her if she asked about my weekend? That I'd hitched a ride to New Jersey to snoop on her brother's girlfriend and then devoted the rest of my time vegging out so I could envision a flock of vultures?

I steered clear of my locker and managed to avoid her all morning, but when the entire tenth grade was herded into a surprise special assembly during the last period of the day, she singled me out and plunked down in the seat next to me.

"Any idea what's going on?" She turned around to glare at the kid behind her, who was kicking the back of her seat.

"Nothing much." I tried to affect a jaded tone.

"Not with *you*, C, but *this*." She gestured at the hundreds of full seats in the auditorium.

"Oh," I said with a start. "I don't know, but it feels like we're in trouble, doesn't it?"

"Yeah," Becca said excitedly. "Maybe somebody cut class for the first time in Hudson's history."

"Could be the start of a nasty epidemic."

Biting back a smile, I watched as Dr. Arnold came to the stage and began addressing us. Turned out a Spanish teacher had taken one of his students to Miami for the weekend, and our assistant principal wanted the rest of us to come forward if any of our teachers had asked us out on a date or weekend getaway.

"Loving gestures or amorous intentions," Becca said afterward, mimicking Dr. Arnold's nasal drawl as we walked down the hall. It was only 3:35, and the atmosphere was more gray and lifeless than it had any right to be.

"If only," I said, scanning a mental index of all my teachers. "We could use a little more love and tenderness around here."

As we proceeded toward the main entrance, I could hear Ian's suitcase thumping behind us.

"So what are you up to now?" Her expression was hopeful.

"Now?" I kicked aside a pair of socks that must have fallen out of somebody's locker. I needed to buy time until I thought of an excuse. "I, uh, have to do this thing with my brother."

"Don't be angry at me because I forgot to call you this weekend," she said. "I'm sorry, I was just so busy—on Saturday I got roped into going shopping for the wedding, and then Mom's college roommate from Smith came to visit, and it was a huge production."

"Don't worry about it," I said, trying to contain my amusement. She thought I was mad at her? "So, did the whole family go shopping together?"

"Yeah, my mom wanted to approve of any final decisions, so she made everyone come."

"Rye, too?" God, I was so unsmooth.

"No, Rye couldn't make it," Becca said, choosing not to acknowledge my Rye fixation. "She was in Vermont for the weekend, meeting with her academic advisor. She said she timed her trip up to Bennington there to coincide with some secret society dinner."

"She probably made that up and just had pizza," I said.

Becca looked perplexed.

"Just kidding." My neck felt hot.

"Okaaay . . ."

We kept walking through the hall, and neither of us said anything more until we'd made our way outside.

"Why don't we just have a seat up here?" Becca's suggestion caught me by surprise, but then I understood. The BDLs were perched on the bottom of the stairs. She didn't feel like dealing with them.

But there was no escaping. In no time they were greeting us with phony smiles and waves. "It's Betty and Veronica!" taunted Sheila.

"And Dumb and the Dumbers," I said under my breath.

Now that I was sure Sheila didn't pose any real threat, I was able to see her and her friends for what they really were: a bunch of creeps. So what if Sheila had once been nice, or if she was actually sad and insecure in some hidden pocket of her true being? She was cruel to my friends and me and countless others. She needed to be stopped, plain and simple.

"Hey, Claire." Ian had caught up to us and was digging into his suitcase. "I almost forgot to give you this. Do you want to keep it?" He tried to pass me "The Adventures of Evil Radish," but Becca was quicker and snatched it away.

"Get the hell out of here," she said while flipping through the book. "You turned those bitches into a bunch of radishes!"

"Evil radishes," I added. "Wait—how did you figure out it was them so fast?"

"Could it be more obvious? How many radishes out there torment their fellow vegetables and wear tutus?"

I looked down the stairs to see that curly-haired Lauren had risen to engulf a disoriented-looking boy in a mammoth hug.

"Brilliant stuff," Becca went on. "It's too bad everyone from Hudson can't have a copy."

And then it hit me. "Why not?" I turned to Ian. "We can make copies at Kinko's and leave 'Evil Radish' piles in the halls. We can have our own Happiness League."

Ian looked excited, but only for a few seconds. "There's no way. Do you know how much color copies cost?"

"I'm sure there's a way around it." I squinted at him, wondering how he had made it this far without figuring out that Becca was a ketchup heiress.

And Becca took her cue. She tugged a folder of sheet music out of her bag and inserted the comic book in the middle. "I'll take care of it," she said. "Trust me. I have some, um . . ."

"Kinko's connections?" Ian asked incredulously.

"Exactly," Becca and I responded at the same time.

{ 27 }

Eye of the Tiger

That evening I got the full story from Louis, or as full a story you can get from somebody who's riding ahead of you on the Hudson River bike path at twenty-eight miles an hour. Louis wasn't usually amenable to last-minute invitations, but somehow I'd managed to convince him to meet me for a bike ride.

Still, the details of Louis's breakup were coming out too slowly for my tastes.

"Were you fighting?" I asked as we neared Chambers Street.

"Sort of." He sounded deflated and shot ahead. Ten minutes later we pulled over to watch a group of spandex-clad racers shoot past.

"What happened then?" I pressed.

He looked up at the sky. "Sex, okay?"

"Care to be a little more specific?" I tried to suppress a grin. Louis and I had known each other for an eternity, and yet the closest we had ever come to talking about this kind of thing was, well, never. "She didn't want to do it?" I probed.

"No, that's not it." He sounded aggravated.

"You didn't want to do it?"

"Of course I wanted to." Louis looked at me as if I should understand what he was getting at. I didn't.

"Okay," I said. "Care to lay out what the problem was?"

"We both wanted to, but then she freaked out and said she could tell the only reason I was going out with her was to use her for the experience."

"What is she, crazy?" I asked. Then I remembered they'd met at their shrink's office. Oops.

"Anyway, I found out the real story," he said, reentering traffic. "She decided to get back together with her ex-boyfriend. And she keeps calling me. It's annoying."

"That is annoying. Tell her to take a hike!" I yelled supportively and swerved out of the way to avoid ramming into a little girl who was wobbling around on her Rollerblades.

I looked out across the harbor and watched a flock of birds swoop over the Jersey City skyline. They plunged down onto the Colgate Clock, an enormous sculpture of a timepiece that faces Manhattan. I'd passed the clock thousands of times, but this time something clicked inside me. It said six o'clock.

I stared at the clock and shivered.

I had half an hour to get there before it would be the time in my dream.

"Hey!" Louis was riding back toward me. "You coming?"

"Mind if we take a little detour? I just remembered I need to do something."

He screwed his face. "Huh?"

"It's, uh, for a class. We're supposed to learn about different city landmarks. And I chose that one." I pointed across the water.

"But that's not even in the city. It's in New Jersey, Lemonhead."

"It's *visible* from the city. That counts, too." I kicked off. "There's a ferry that goes across the water. You in?"

"I don't know."

"Don't be such a girlie-man. Follow me."

We kept riding down through Battery Park until we found the Jersey City ferry stop, where a rickety-looking boat the size of a small house seemed to be waiting for us.

"Beautiful," I said.

Louis sighed. "If you say so."

The boat ride cost a dollar. It was quick, but not quick enough for Louis, who got seasick. When we docked on the other side, I left him to recover behind a Dumpster and went to find him a bottle of water.

I returned to find him back on his bike, riding figure eights on a patch of dirt just off the ferry landing. "I was trying to keep my bulimia a secret from you." He cracked a smile, though I could tell by the way he wouldn't look at me that he was a little embarrassed.

I handed him the water and smiled. "C'mon." I nudged him with my foot, then pedaled away.

Up close, the Colgate Clock was practically unrecognizable, a web of steel beams and birds' nests. The surrounding dirt lot was parched and empty, and I would have felt unsafe if it weren't for Louis in the distance, riding around on his bike. I walked along the clock's base, and when I reached the end I paused to take in the Manhattan skyline. It looked so shiny and small, like a toy version of itself.

"Hey!" I shouted back at Louis, who'd been practicing wheelies and catwalks last time I'd checked. "Come here!"

He didn't respond—all I heard was a boat horn. "Louis!" I turned around, but there was no sign of my friend.

"Louis!" I bellowed again, even louder.

From behind, somebody reached around to tap the soft spot on my throat. I felt short of breath, and my shoulders shot up like wings.

I would have screamed but I could barely breathe.

"I have come to suck your blood." Louis was affecting his best Dracula accent.

I spun around. "Do you have any idea how much you scared me?"

"Sorry, I was just playing around," he said in his normal voice. "Is it Creepsylvania out here or what?"

"We'll leave soon. Just give me another second." I walked to the middle of the platform to give the clock's face one last look. But the only thing it was telling me was that it was 6:50. There'd been nothing to speak of.

Just then I heard a low rumbling in the distance. We had company. Louis was standing on the edge of the platform, visible to anybody who entered the lot. "Psst! Get back over here!" I whispered, immediately worried. "If someone sees us climbing on the clock, we could get into trouble."

He made his way over to where I was standing.

"Okay, I'm just going to pretend there's nothing weird about any of this. Is there anywhere around here to get a sandwich?"

"For the love of Julia Child, will you please shut up?" I snapped.

Louis slouched and turned away. Oh crap. He was going to leave me there.

I reached out for his arm. "I'm sorry. I just didn't want to attract any attention. Please stay."

"You so owe me," he growled.

We remained in our hiding places behind the clock, with our bikes at our sides. When I was sure we'd been still long enough, I slowly turned my head to look through the clock's frame. A white Mercedes had pulled up about twenty feet away.

"What's going on?" Louis whispered.

"A car just pulled up."

I was still peering through the clock's latticework when a dark town car parked opposite the white Mercedes.

"Another car?" Louis asked.

"Mmm-hmm."

"What is this? Don't people have watches anymore?"

The white car flashed its lights twice. The dark car flashed back. The white door opened and out stepped the driver, holding an envelope and a tiny brown dog. He was pretty far away, but I'd have known that white puffy jacket and itty-bitty head anywhere. Otto Soyle.

"You're shaking," Louis whispered. He started to take off his jacket.

"That's okay," I told him. I was trembling from excitement, not the cold.

Otto pulled up his sweatshirt hood as he scurried over to the dark car.

I watched the driver roll down his window and hand Otto a folder. Then Otto handed the driver a manila envelope in return. It was plump as a dumpling, and judging from what the driver removed from it, it was stuffed with bundles of cash.

"Whoa." My stomach constricted tight as a fist.

Otto returned to his car and revved his engine. The other car started up, too, and they took off in opposite directions.

By the time Louis summoned the courage to turn around and look, there was nothing left to see.

I rushed to the edge of the platform and jumped down to the ground. "I know one of those guys."

"Which guys?"

I didn't have time to answer his question. "He's up to something sketchy. We have to follow him!" I straddled my bike and pushed off in the direction of the white car.

"Hey!" Louis called after me. "Wait up!"

The streets of Jersey City were dark and barren, and in the distance fluorescent light streamed through the window of a Dunkin' Donuts. Otto never showed any sign that he suspected he was being followed. After about ten minutes, he turned his car into a parking lot whose sign read RUMPS AND HUMPS STEAKHOUSE. The sign reminded me of something you might see outside a down-at-the-heels motel, with loose black letters set on a white background lit from within. Under the restaurant's name, somebody had spelled out BACK IN BIZ-NESS! PRIVATE PARTY 2NITE. A reference, I presumed, to the kitchen "accident" that the Shuttleworths had engineered a few weeks ago. I crouched on a concrete ledge behind a parked van and motioned for Louis to follow.

He obeyed me, but not without protest. "What is this, the new 'it spot' you read about in one of your fashion magazines?"

"Don't say I never take you anywhere," I whispered back.

Otto's car door slammed, and I watched him approach the restaurant with the envelope tucked under his jacket sleeve. He turned in our direction and I veered to the right, motioning for Louis to follow.

"Hand me your glasses," I told Louis. I was afraid

somebody I knew might spot me, and I removed my bobby pins and shook my head. I never wore my hair down. It was like my mother's, only instead of curls I had poof.

"Whoa," Louis said. "You look so different with all that hair."

"And you'll look different without the glasses that you're going to give me."

"Huh?"

"Trust me, I'll explain later. Now take off your glasses. Ooh, you look handsome."

Louis was so caught off guard by my compliment that he didn't flinch when I asked him to fork over his heavy coat. In return I gave him my itty-bitty green Courrèges jacket. It didn't look bad on him, even if the sleeves were way too short for his gangly arms.

As I walked over to the restaurant, it occurred to me I might look a bit insane in my chunky spectacles and man-sized coat. My fears were confirmed when I pulled the heavy door open. "We're closed for a private party," the maitre d' told me through a wild sneer.

The room was full of loud old men and bikini-clad women passing out trays of bacon-wrapped scallops and pigs in a blanket. Thanks to the HAPPY BIRTHDAY LAZARUS banners that had been tacked to the walls, I figured the party was for Otto's father.

The maitre d' cleared his throat and shot me a "Get out of my restaurant" look. "I'm sorry, but we're closed to the public tonight," he repeated, a bit louder.

"I beg your pardon?" I played deaf as I stared over his shoulder and scanned the room. There had to be something in here for me, I knew it. Just in time, I caught a snatch of one of Otto's multicolored basketball sneakers moving up the stairs. Hanging over the landing was a BATHROOMS UPSTAIRS sign.

The maitre d' picked up a pen from the stand between us and stabbed at the crease of the reservation book, clearly at the end of his very short rope with me.

"I'm so sorry to bother you," I said in my best corn-fed naïf voice. "I just need to use the bathroom." And then, disgusting as it may have been, I made a little show of crossing my legs tight. "I was riding my bike over to my friend's house and I thought I could hold out until I got there, but the thing is I drank this huge iced tea and—"

He rolled his eyes and turned his face slightly. Bladder issues, apparently, were his breaking point. "Upstairs, first door on the right. But make it . . ."

I didn't hear the rest as I loped up the stairs. Once I was safely tucked away in the bathroom, I looked in the mirror. I barely recognized myself, and not only because of the hair and specs. I was used to my reflection showing a startled duckling, not a kick-ass detective who was a hairsbreadth away from getting into huge trouble. Kiki had been right— this adventure stuff *was* good for the complexion.

Just in case the maitre d' had his ear pressed to the door, I flushed the toilet, like a good detective would. I came out to an empty corridor, and I could make out murmurs coming from the end of the hall. The smell of cigar smoke grew stronger with every step I took. I felt a flutter in my stomach when I reached the doorway, and I nervously raked a chunk of hair over my face, hoping to better disguise myself.

Not that I needed to. When I poked my head in the room, nobody turned to look at me. The walls were painted with tiger stripes and the floor was carpeted by a huge faux tiger rug, fake head and all. Eeew. An older man was making a toast, and the other two dozen or so revelers—Otto and Rye included—watched him with their glasses held up in the air.

An enormous stuffed tiger was standing on its hind legs by the door. I slid behind it and peered from under a claw until I spotted Lazarus, the short dark-haired man I'd seen on my Google search. He looked even more pinched than he did in pictures, and he'd tanned himself to the color of a penny. I fought my nerves as I reached into my bag for my digital camera. I made sure the flash was off, brought it to eye height, and ducked another centimeter to make sure the frame was free of any tiger limbs.

"And that was the first time little Lazarus got the shit kicked out of him," the old man was saying. "To Lazarus Soyle, everybody's favorite son of a bitch! Happy birthday!"

The group erupted into loud cheers, and a ginger cat jumped out from behind a curtain and scuttled across the floor.

Everybody crowded around the birthday boy. Meanwhile, Otto grabbed Rye by the elbow and pulled her over to the fireplace, closer to where I was. She was fawning over him, playing with his earlobes and placing kisses on his cheek. It was strange—with Andy she always seemed to be the epitome of ladylike composure, but in Otto's presence, she was like a tacky girlfriend you'd see in a shopping mall food court. Immune to her charms, Otto kept a straight face and produced the sheet of paper from the folder.

I was about to press the shutter when I heard the sound of somebody coughing behind me. The creepy maitre d' was standing on the other side of the tiger. Zut! What was I going to say if he found me—that I was a Winnie-the-Pooh freak and I'd found my friend Tigger? Much to my relief, he didn't notice me and floated off to have a word with the bartender.

Without a moment to spare, I pressed the shutter. Then I stuck my camera up the sleeve of my trench coat and kept watching the young lovebirds.

Rye nodded at something Otto was whispering. Then she examined the paper from his folder and wrote something on a napkin. He studied what she'd written, shook his head, and balled the napkin up, motioning for her to start over. My heart palpitated as I stared at the mantelpiece; the rejected napkin sat next to a bowl of peanut shells, just begging me to sneak out and snatch it.

Double zut!

The napkin was only a few feet away, barely within reach, but it might as well have been in Louisiana. I couldn't just step out of my hiding spot and say hi. They'd serve my rump for dinner.

And then I noticed the maid in the back corner. She was making her way around the room, placing any and all detritus on her tray. Maybe she could do my work for me? When she approached Rye and Otto, I stared at the napkin, trying to psychically alert her of its existence.

My hands slick with sweat, I dug them deep into Louis's pockets. Every passing minute felt like ten. The maid picked up an ashtray, an empty glass, and then—yes!—the napkin. Finally, she carried the full tray back toward the door. Heart thumping, I waited for her to pass the tiger statue. At the perfect moment, I tossed a balled-up Kleenex that I'd found in Louis's coat pocket toward the back of the room. The maid stopped to look in the direction of the mysterious flying white blur. And I reached and plucked the napkin ball off the tray.

Mission *accompli!*

Still crouched in my hiding spot, I straightened out

the napkin and squinted at it. It looked like a messy architectural blueprint, with dotted lines and mysterious shapes. I wouldn't have been able to figure out what it was supposed to signify if it hadn't been for a rectangle labeled DF7X. Which had to be shorthand for Dassault Falcon 7X, Becca's dad's favorite plane. I knew that the plane was kept in London, the same city where Rye would find herself the following weekend. I was overwhelmed by a dueling sense of disgust and satisfaction. I remained in place for a minute or so, concentrating on steadying my breath while I waited for a man who was lingering against the doorjamb to make up his mind and move one way or the other. And then, when the coast was clear, I stole out into the hallway.

Just as I reached the stair landing, I heard a familiar voice behind me. "Oh, there you are."

I turned around to face the maitre d'. He was looking at me darkly, and I wondered if he'd seen me slip out from under the hulking stuffed animal. "Did you get lost?" he asked with a curiosity that was in no way gentle.

I pulled the belt of my trench coat tighter. "N-no. I was just admiring your restaurant." I decided to pull from my training with Kiki. "I entertain quite a bit, and you have some beautiful rooms."

I could feel the beads of sweat forming under my arms. He let me go with a brisk nod, and when I made my way into the cool of the parking lot and back to my friend, I collapsed against the back of a car.

"Claire?" Louis said.

I looked up at the sky and ran my fingers along my necklace. I thought I just might cry.

"Hey, Claire?" he said again.

I could feel my chest expand with every breath. "I'll explain all of this soon," I told him. "I promise."

"Okay, no sweat," Louis said with such tenderness that I could tell he was also afraid. "But do you think I can have my glasses back?"

{ 28 }

How I Became a Fake Wife

Louis rested his head on my shoulder on the ferry ride back. "Pardon the intrusion," he said. "I get less nauseous this way."

"It's not a problem," I told him, though I doubted he heard. Within seconds, he'd fallen fast asleep.

I'd propped our bikes against the bench and was holding them steady with my arm. Outside the boat's dirty window, the Manhattan skyline was swelling up against the dark purple sky. I could make out the black slab of the Trump Tower and, farther downtown, the silver wedge of the Citicorp Center, one of Andy's favorites. I must have flinched, because Louis bolted up.

"You will not believe the dream I just had," he said, rubbing his eyes.

"I'm hard to shock with dreams," I said, trying to arch one eyebrow the way Becca could do so well.

"You pretended to have a school project so you could drag me to Jersey City. We hid behind the Colgate Clock while you spied on some strange transaction I won't even pretend to have understood, and then you left me to hang around on the street by myself dressed like a girl."

"Poor Louis," I said in a baby voice. "You know, you looked very good in my coat."

"Flattery will get you everywhere."

When we made our way ashore, the ferry landing was empty except for a ticket taker who was watching a movie on his iPod. An R2-D2-like sound came from behind Louis.

"Text message," he said, and removed his cell phone from his backpack pocket. He made a face.

"Is it what'shername?" I asked.

He nodded. "She wants to know if an avocado is a fruit or a vegetable."

"And you're going to answer her after what she did to you?"

"No." He glared at me and he put his cell phone back. "But what is the answer? Avocadoes grow on trees, right?"

"Louis Ibbits!" I gripped his arms and gave him a slight shake. "Don't you see what she's doing? She's asking you cutesy questions so she can get under your skin."

Louis shook himself free. "Just because I'm curious does not mean anybody's under my anything. Jeez, I'll find out myself."

The ensuing silence was awkward, and we both turned to look out across the water. I tried to figure out which one of the factories stretching along the shoreline was home to the Soyle tube sock empire.

"Now what? Wanna climb up the Statue of Liberty or . . . go get a grilled cheese?" He looked at me hopefully.

A grilled cheese sandwich had never sounded better—I hadn't eaten anything but chocolate since my ten-twenty-five lunch. If only I could. As far as the Shuttleworths were concerned, Rye was a sweet young thing, not a Soyle stooge. I had my evidence. I needed to go home and call Becca. And according to the Colgate Clock, it was already a little after nine.

"I'd love to," I told Louis, "but Dad asked me to come back before nine-thirty."

"Yeah, right." He hopped on his bike and started to fasten his helmet, then paused. "Since when did you have a curfew?"

I swallowed hard. I wanted to sit him down on a park bench and tell him everything. He might not understand, but I knew I could trust him not to tell anyone—at least, anyone who wasn't his shrink. But Kiki would kill me.

"Hey, hold up!" I called out after he started to ride away.

"What." By the way he said it as if it weren't a question, I could tell he was angry.

"The avocado, it's a fruit!"

From this far away in the dark I couldn't really see for sure, but I suspected I'd gotten a smile out of him.

I came back to a full house. Henry and his friend Charlie W.—despite the fact there were no other Charlies in their class, he still went by his last initial—were sprawled out in the reading nook, concentrating on a game that they'd fashioned out of chess pieces, poker chips, and a grid of pipe cleaners. Douglas was nestled in one of the ratty old reading chairs, listening to Dad read aloud from his latest academic paper. I ducked into the kitchen and grabbed a jar of pickles and half of a Blimpie sandwich from the fridge.

"We're working on the flow," Douglas told me when I came back out. As to whether it was flowing well, I had no idea—most of my French comes from baby talk and children's cartoons, not the language favored by French *intellos*.

Douglas must have misread my bewildered expression for one of disapproval. While Dad continued to read, Douglas got up and joined me by the coatrack Mom had decoupaged with shellac and old *Le Monde* newspapers. "He'll get better," he whispered from behind. "His flight's tomorrow night. That gives us plenty of time."

Dad was still concentrating on his paper and had given no indication that he realized I was home. I turned around to smile at Douglas. "You're a good friend," I said. "Now if you'll excuse me, I'm going to go do some homework."

"Sure you are." Douglas gave me a devious look.

Once in my bedroom, I said hello to my fish and connected my digital camera to my computer. I hadn't cleared out my camera in ages, and I had to wait for other images to upload onto the screen. I saw pictures of an artist's studio in Harlem I visited with my old Farmhouse buddies, my family picnicking in Paris's Belleville Park, and Clem and Kiki tipsily waltzing around Clem's room. It felt as if decades passed before the shot of Rye and Otto came up. I clicked the rectangle to enlarge it. I could see Lazarus in the background, and they all had a case of red-eye that lent them a demonic aspect. Part of me wished Becca never had to see this picture, but I knew if she didn't, she'd probably end up seeing something a whole lot worse.

I took in a deep breath and dialed Becca's number. She picked up, sounding dazed.

"Am I calling too late?" I asked.

"No, no," she said. "I was just watching this TV show that reveals the mysteries of cooking."

"Since when are you into cooking?" I asked. "And what exactly are the mysteries it entails?"

"I'm not. And the mysteries aren't that mysterious, because I dozed off. . . . Oh—but I did drop off the comic book at the printer. They'll be ready after Thanksgiving break."

"Awesome." I had to look back at the computer screen before I could go on. "I have something weird to tell you."

"Try me."

"I don't think Rye should go to London with your family."

"Why? You don't think she's right for Andy?"

"Um, she's the worst thing you could possibly wish on your family." My tone was deadly, but Becca just laughed.

"If you want to surprise me, you're going to have to try a little harder. No offense, C, but it's been kind of obvious from day one that you sweat my brother and you hate Rye."

I decided to let that one pass. "Rye's hanging out with Otto Soyle. And he wants her to mess with your dad's plane."

"Oh yeah?" She could barely contain her skepticism.

"I have proof. I swear."

"And what's that?"

"I have a picture of the two of them together. Rye and Otto."

"They know each other," she countered. "They grew up in the city together."

"And I have a . . . I have more proof."

"What kind of more proof?" I could just see her drawing up an eyebrow.

"A napkin." I realized how stupid I sounded. "It has some hair-raising information on it. You just have to see it with your own eyes."

She chuckled. "I'm sorry, Claire, but I can't convince my parents to skip a family wedding based on an incriminating *napkin.* Your imagination is one of the reasons I love you, but you've got to know when to give it a rest."

I was trying to fight back my tears. Becca's stubborn streak was not something I had any chance against. "Well, when does your family leave for your cousin's wedding?"

"This morning," she said. "If you need to contact them and ruin their trip with this ridiculousness—which I'd prefer you not do—you'll find them all at Claridge's. It's a swish hotel in London."

"I've heard of it, thanks." I was feeling defensive. What on earth was I going to do—charter a jet to London to hand deliver the goods? And if Becca didn't believe me, the rest of her family might not, either. I needed to show it to Rye and let them watch her try to explain. The alternative—that they might not make it back in one piece—was too grizzly to contemplate.

"Claire?" She sounded hesitant.

"What?"

"I wouldn't worry about Andy. I don't think he and Rye are going to get married anytime soon."

"That's not what this is about," I said feebly.

"Whatever you say." I could hear her rolling her eyes. "Now if this awkward conversation is over, I have a cooking lesson to get back to sleeping through."

I got off the phone feeling totally disgruntled. Becca's attitude wasn't the half of it—how was I going to reach her family when they were on the other side of the world? Then suddenly it clicked.

"*Papa!*" I screamed, shooting into the living room. "You're allowed to bring your spouse to the conference, right?"

"*Oui,*" he said with a shrug.

"I sense an agenda here," Douglas said playfully. "Where exactly are you going with this?"

"To Paris?" I replied. "It's not like we're celebrating Thanksgiving until after Mom gets back anyway. Oh please, please, please. Can you call the symposium organizers and tell them your little lady wants to come?"

"She *is* little," Douglas told Dad.

I *had* to go. London was only a few hours away from Paris by train. If I had a free day, I could shoot there and back without Dad's noticing a thing.

"And why would the little lady want to go to France?" Dad asked. "A shopping spree?"

"Exactly!" I said, grateful for any suggestion that didn't let the truth slip out. "I read in *Biba* they're selling these amazing A-line dresses at Morgan for fifteen euros."

Douglas and Dad were both looking at me skeptically. "And cultural sightseeing," I went on. "And chocolate tasting . . . And I really want to see Uncle Cédric and Aunt Ségolène. . . ."

I shot Douglas a desperate look.

"It's better for me," Douglas volunteered. "I was going to look after both the kids anyway. One's easier."

"See?" I interjected.

Douglas went on, "It will be nice to have a father-daughter trip. And Claire would be a great coach. I can make some review sheets for the two of you to go over."

"I'll help you get ready!" I ran over to join Dad on the couch, too energized by the idea of going to Paris to care whether I was being a big dork. "I'll be your coach and your muse. . . ." Sensing Dad was warming up to the idea, I moved over a little closer. "*S'il vous plaît?*"

"What about school?" he asked.

"We'll be gone Thursday to Sunday, the same days we have off for Thanksgiving," I persisted.

"How can you say no to such a pretty muse?" Douglas asked.

"And coach," I reminded them. "We'll work a lot. Just tell them they messed up and your wife is named Claire. They won't notice."

"You guys are disgusting," Henry threw in.

Dad started to get up. "I'll e-mail the organizers and see if they can change the name on the ticket."

"Yes! I'll be the best fake wife ever."

Douglas turned to Dad. "A young blond wife could do wonders for your career."

"*C'est vrai,*" I said, batting my eyelashes at hummingbird speed.

{ 29 }

Bon Voyage and Cheerio

Thursday afternoon, just hours before our flight, I ran up to Kiki's to collect the cash that my secret international plan would require. While Clem and Edie played cards in the main room, Kiki brought me into her bedroom. She climbed onto a stepstool to pull down a hatbox from the top shelf of her closet and handed me two hundred-dollar bills. "This should cover the train ticket."

"Thank you so much." I folded up the money and tucked it into my pocket.

"And take this, too." She passed a few more notes my way. "For the box of macaroons you'll be picking up for me at Ladurée."

"Same as before, pink and brown?"

"Not *brown*. That sounds so common." She steadied herself on my shoulders as she returned to floor level. "Coffee-colored."

"Right . . ." I glanced down to see she'd handed me an extra three hundred dollars. "Whoa! Kiki, how many macaroons do you want?"

"The usual. Two dozen. If you have a spare moment, I'd replace that enormous ink stain if I were you." She eyed my black and white striped bag disapprovingly.

"I'll see what I can do," I said with a smile.

"Of course you will."

I joined Edie and Clem for a quick hand of gin rummy; then I got up and let myself out. I was home by six and I was packed and out the door an hour later. I was getting good at this globe-trotting stuff.

Dad seemed much more laid-back than he normally did when traveling. He didn't stride ahead at the airport or give me any of his anal-retentive "*zeep-zeep*" action.

"Why aren't you getting impatient with me?" I asked him.

"Why aren't you running into random bathrooms?" he retorted.

"*Touché.*"

The flight was the easiest thing in the world. No nauseating choppiness, no crying babies, and, best of all, the in-flight movie was *North by Northwest*, one of my favorite Hitchcock movies (so what if I'd only seen two?).

We landed at Charles de Gaulle airport at the crack of dawn on Friday. Dad was ecstatic the minute we stepped off the plane, and insisted on filling up on espresso and a warm croissant before hailing a taxi.

"This is the civilized way to live," Dad said, indicating the row of people seated at the coffee bar. "Nobody in Paris would dream of a to-go cup." He grinned and took a final swig from his espresso's ceramic vessel.

L'Hôtel Grand Canard was in the Sixth Arrondissement, a swanky district in central Paris. After checking into our room and ordering up my cot, Dad and I decided to take a stroll through the Jardins du Luxembourg. Despite Dad's caffeine level, we were both too wiped out for conversation, and spent whatever energy we had watching the park's assortment of characters—mostly pigeons, young lovebirds, and old men reading the newspaper.

On the way back, we stopped in at a chic clothing store with 1960s film posters on the walls. I bought a canvas tote bag with an enormous leather pocket on the front. I made sure to get it in black so I wouldn't have to worry about any more exploding pen problems.

"One hundred and twenty-five euros? *C'est chèr!*" Dad exclaimed when the shop assistant wrapped my purchase in tissue paper.

"It's on Kiki," I told him, and he seemed much less troubled.

We slept away most of the afternoon, and then went to Chez René, a restaurant on Boulevard Saint-Germain, for a four-course dinner. With the conference covering airfare and taxis, Dad felt he could justify splashing out on one big meal. "Your mother would love it here!" he exclaimed when we walked into the restaurant.

All through dinner, I consulted my lap, where I'd put the review sheets Douglas had made, and quizzed my father on everything from eye contact and smiling techniques to optimal microphone heights.

I could tell Dad was bored by what he thought were superficial concerns, and by the time the crème brûlée had come out, he had completely lost interest in Douglas's notes.

"*Papa*," I said sharply, "I know you're thinking about how much you miss Mom and how stupid this is. But getting your much-deserved due from the academic community is not stupid, is it? You've been preparing for this moment since I've known you."

"Since before that," he corrected me.

"Exactly. You have to make a good impression. Don't blow it."

He looked at me as if he'd never heard anything so poignant and called the waiter over to order a chocolate soufflé. In the twenty minutes it took for our second dessert to arrive, we went through Douglas's Dos and Don'ts all over again, and Dad started to get the hang of things. Night had fallen by the time we left the restaurant.

Back at the hotel, Dad spent some time on the phone with Mom before going into the bathroom to wash up.

"Are you going to trim your mustache?" I asked when he stepped back out.

"*Pourquoi?*" He touched the fringe above his lip.

"It's just looking a little messy." In truth, it was fine, but I needed to buy a little extra time so I could call the Shuttleworths.

My father turned and headed back into the bathroom and as soon as I could hear the water running, I fumbled with the phone, trying to figure out how to get an outside line. It proved more complicated than I'd expected, and it was a miracle that Dad was still humming "Clair de Lune" to his reflection when the reception desk at Claridge's put me through to Mr. and Mrs. Shuttleworth's room.

I had no idea how nervous I was until the ringing sound started. I felt as if I was going to die of heart failure.

Becca's mom picked up. "Claire?" Her voice was edged with dread as soon as she identified me. "Is everything okay?"

"Absolutely. I'm just in, um . . . My dad and I are in London, and I wondered if you wanted to get together?" I felt weird planning a playdate with my friend's mom, but I couldn't think of any other way to proceed.

"Oh! You are!" She sounded confused about whether she should be flattered or concerned. "You know Becca's not here with us. . . ." Clearly she felt weird, too.

"Oh, I know—she told me. It's just that my dad's really busy with his conference, and I thought it would be fun to hang out." My ears went hot—had I just told my friend's prim and proper mom I wanted to "hang out" with her?

She chuckled. "Well, I'm flattered. Where are you staying?"

"Oh, this little place called the . . ." My eyes shot over to the antique print of a duck hanging over Dad's bed. "The Spotted Duck."

"I can't say I've heard of it, but it sounds lovely."

"It's, um . . . it's sort of on the edge of town," I sputtered.

"As if that means anything to me. London is such a labyrinth. . . . Do you want to come by tomorrow, for breakfast?"

I told her that might be a little rough. "We have an early thing we have to go to."

"Can you do lunch? Oh wait, we have a meeting with some antiques dealer at one. What about tea? They're famous for their tea here."

"In London?"

"Yes," she giggled. "But more specifically at Claridge's."

We made plans to meet in the hotel lobby at two-thirty, and I was off the phone by the time Dad came back out.

"You like?" he patted his freshly trimmed mustache.

"Much better," I told him.

Dad turned on the news and helped me set up my cot. I crawled in and pretended to be sleepy, though my heart was still bumping around too much for me to relax. Eventually I slipped into a dreamless sleep—evidence, surely, of how exhausted I really was.

In the morning, I helped Dad pick out a bright green shirt (Rule #4 on Douglas's list: Wear cheerful colors) and listened to him practice his speech.

"Sounds perfect." I hoped he was planning on leaving soon so I could get going on my own journey. "So will I see you for dinner tonight?"

"Under normal circumstances, yes, but I'm trying to be like Douglas. I'm going to the participants' dinner to practice his networking moves."

"Bravo," I said.

"If you put on a fancy dress, you can come and play with the other wives, real and fake."

"No thanks," I said. I couldn't look at him straight on—I would've cracked and let my mission slip out. "I have a big day. I'm going to visit Fauchon for chocolate, and I want to go to the Galeries Lafayette and try their food court. I hear they have a superb dinner platter."

It was partly true; I did want to go there. Ever since I was a kid, I've loved visiting their lingerie department. The floor is filled with racks of unaffordable wisps of ribbon and lace, and the dressing rooms have day and night light switches for customers who need to know how their underwear will look at high noon as well as in the soft glow of a bedroom.

"Shopping, shopping." Dad rolled his eyes. "You're lucky your grandmother likes you so much."

"What can I say?" I told him. "She has excellent taste. Now, let me take the elevator down with you and wish you *bon courage* at the door."

"In your pajamas?"

I picked yesterday's dress up off the floor and threw it on over my jammies. "It's the tunic look," I explained. I saw him to his taxi door. I could tell it gave him immeasurable pleasure to say to the driver, "À la Sorbonne!" and I beamed as I blew Dad one last kiss. He was going to do great, I just knew it.

Once Dad's car disappeared around the corner, I ran back upstairs to get ready. Remembering how Kiki always complained that people didn't know how to dress for traveling these days, I put on the nicest dress I'd brought—a wool magenta number with gold details at the wrists—and my special black suede wedge boots that Kiki never lets me wear in the rain. Then came the hair and makeup. My hair was looking especially bird's-nesty, and I made a note to spend the rest of Kiki's money on a decent haircut. Finally, I double-checked my bag to make sure it had my essentials: water bottle, photos, Rye's discarded napkin, and *Murder on the Orient Express*.

I was set.

Or so I thought. My taxi dropped me off at the Gare du Nord nearly an hour early, but just as I had settled on a stool at the station coffee counter, I spotted a woman carrying a chic leather passport case.

Passport.

How could I be so stupid?

"*Oui, mademoiselle?*" the barista asked me, wiping my portion of the counter clean.

"*Pardonez-moi . . . j'ai un petit problème!*" I sprang off my seat and raced out to the taxi stand. There were about twelve people waiting in line in front of me. When my turn finally came, I was so nervous I'd miss my train, I could barely return my driver's snaggletoothed smile. With my eyes darting between the window and the dashboard clock, I kept reminding him how little time we had. *"Vite! Vite!"* I cried as he drove me to the hotel.

I ended up making the nine-twenty train, but the passport ordeal still took its toll; I could barely stop sweating during the three-hour train ride.

We pulled into Waterloo Station a little after noon. London was gray and rainy, nothing like the mild and sunny Parisian weather I'd left behind. I had no idea where I was—or where I was going.

I went to a drugstore and bought a map and an umbrella. With two hours to kill, I decided to take a little stroll, hoping my suede shoes wouldn't be ruined by the rain. I made my way down crowded streets, passing stately-looking buildings and pubs. Most of the people I walked by were blond, or at least dirty blond. It was almost liberating—for once, I was in the majority! Was it possible they told dumb brunette jokes here?

An hour later, I sat on a wet park bench and tried to locate Claridge's on my map.

"Need any help?" asked a bag lady who was feeding the pigeons.

I doubted she'd know where the hotel was, and barely enunciated its name.

"A lovely hotel, that. Best to take the tube," she declared, scattering crumbs at my feet. "Bakerloo line to Mayfair. Just a hop away."

"Sounds right," a passing man said. "And watch your

shoulder," he said, which I guessed was his way of saying "Take care"—I'd heard about English people and their weird sayings.

"Okay," I said, smiling at his wacky parting words.

It figured that Mayfair was a fancy-beyond-belief neighborhood, with flowerpots outside every doorway and store windows filled with cashmere and five-thousand-dollar—and pound—trophy handbags.

I found the hotel on a quiet street, and a valet in a top hat guided me through the front door. The lobby was the polar opposite of my own apartment building's, with sweeping ceilings, a spiral staircase, and a black and white marble floor that looked like an oversized chessboard. I settled into a plush armchair and smelled something funny.

Crap!

Literally, from a pigeon. All over my right shoulder! So that explained why the guy in the park had told me to watch my shoulder.

I felt my face turning bright red and I dashed to the bathroom and used one of the hotel's monogrammed washcloths to scrub away the yuck. By the time I'd successfully cleaned my shoulder and drenched the entire top half of my body in water, I realized Becca's mom was probably looking for me in the lobby. Kiki would be appalled that I'd kept her waiting.

I raced to the hotel's main hall and looked everywhere, but Becca's mom was nowhere to be found. A film of sweat was moistening my palms when I finally spotted her standing next to a bowl of lemons. She must have just come in from the rain; her hair was covered with beads of water. Fastened to her cashmere sweater was a jet-shaped pin. It was made of diamonds and it looked like an incredibly ritzy cookie cutter.

"I'm so sorry I'm late," I cried, rushing over to her.

"Don't worry," she said, combing her fingers through her hair. "There's no better place for people watching than a hotel lobby."

"I could not agree with you more." My thoughts traveled back to all the hours I'd spent sitting in Kiki's lobby.

"Now are you ready for the best tea on earth?" She lightly touched my back and led me down a hallway, under a succession of the most gorgeous chandeliers.

As we were being seated, we watched a waiter bring a triple-tiered stand of sumptuous miniature sandwiches and confections to the next table.

"We've all become addicted," Becca's mom told me. "Even Rye's been eating the cucumber sandwiches . . . well, without the bread." She smiled. "And leave it to D.K. to have already discovered the bite-sized hamburgers. He's not really a tea sandwich kind of guy."

"Do you think that's a ketchup-related thing?" I asked.

"What isn't?" Her green eyes sparkled.

Becca's mom was a master at conversation, so despite the foreign setting, I didn't feel all that weird sitting across from her sans Becca until she asked me what school was hosting Dad's conference.

"Oxford," I said, naming the first English university I could think of.

"And they're putting you up in London? Oxford is hours away."

"It is," I said, pretending to search for something in my new bag. "But it's at a satellite campus."

God, was I an imbecile!

"I didn't know there was one," she said without the slightest trace of suspicion. "If you have a chance, I recommend making it out to the real Oxford. It's just beautiful."

"I'll see what I can do." I needed to change the subject. "And how was your niece's wedding?"

"It's not until tomorrow. We're all looking forward to it, though Andy's developed a little problem. His tux seems to have grown a little too small around the waist." Her voice held an edge of amusement. "Oh—speak of the devil!"

I turned around to see Andy and the rest of the gang sailing into the room. Becca's dad was wearing a Big Bird yellow blazer and a huge, crooked smile. Rye was in all black, except for a maroon tasseled handbag. My stomach was in a knot. It was all happening faster than I'd expected.

"They took a field trip to D.K.'s British offices," Becca's mom informed me. "I find it so boring, but Rye was terribly interested in seeing them."

I'll bet.

"How did *you* get here?" Rye asked me by way of greeting.

"I took the train," I said.

"You mean the London *tube*?" she asked in a pretentious English accent.

Andy rolled his eyes at me and I felt a wave of warmth.

After about ten minutes of small talk, the table was brimming with porcelain teapots and minihamburgers and a tower of scones and sandwiches. I hungrily eyed the cluster of chocolate chocolate chip cookies on the middle tier and waited for somebody else to start.

"Do you want anything, Claire?" Andy pointed at the tower. Was it that obvious?

"Yeah, thank you." I took a watercress sandwich and two chocolate chocolate chip cookies.

"I'm going to have half of a cucumber sandwich," Rye said, "and then I really have to go upstairs and take a nap. I'm so knackered from today."

"Hard day?" I asked bitingly, but she was too busy taking apart her sandwich to understand my meaning.

I had to hurry up and get to the point before she excused herself.

"Say," I said to Becca's mom, "I love your pin."

"Thank you," Becca's mom replied. "It *is* special, isn't it? D.K. picked it out for me yesterday. I never would have thought to buy it myself." Her tone suggested she was still coming around.

"Yes, you would have," Andy said through a mouthful of cake. "You think to buy everything."

"Now, now." Becca's dad shot his son a stern look.

Before I knew what came over me, I turned to Rye. "I bet you like it, too. You're a big fan of airplanes, aren't you?"

I wasn't used to being so bold, but I had to say, it felt good.

She glared at me. "Sure, I like planes."

My cheeks starting to heat up, I devoured a chocolate chocolate chip cookie in one bite.

"We were looking at some planes today," Andy filled in, his green eyes glowing kindly.

I set my focus on Rye. "Is that all you did, look at them?"

Rye blinked hard and turned the color of a tomato.

I took in a deep breath and clenched my fists. Was there any subtle way to tell a table of people that somebody they're taking tea with is assisting in their murders?

I fished the evidence out of my bag.

"I know Otto Soyle was hoping you'd have a more hands-on experience." I stared hard at Rye. "According to this diagram that I witnessed you draw, it was the Dassault Falcon 7X he was interested in you getting to, right?"

"Let me see that!" Rye shrieked, but I'd already passed the napkin to Becca's dad.

"Why—that sort of resembles the plane hangar!" he said, clearly confused.

Andy read the napkin over his father's shoulder. I'd never seen anybody look more shocked. "That looks sort of like your handwriting, Rye."

"Otto Soyle showed her the lay of the land," I explained. "He gave her a map of the hangar and she sketched it on the napkin."

I gave Becca's mom the picture of the couple scheming at the steakhouse. "If you look closely, you'll see another familiar face in the background."

"It's not possible," she denied, pushing the picture back at me.

I didn't flinch. "Take another look."

She put on her reading glasses and stared harder. "You're with Lazarus?" she asked Rye. The corners of her mouth were trembling.

"I have no idea what any of this is," Rye growled at me, "other than evidence of your insanity."

Becca's dad rose from his seat and placed his clenched fists on the table. The only one to keep her cool was Becca's mom, who picked a piece of lint off her pantyhose and asked Rye, "Did you go on the plane today, yes or no?"

Rye hiccupped and squealed. "We all did."

"What is wrong with you?" Becca's dad demanded. I could see that he was becoming livid. "And what on earth were you trying to do to my plane?"

"I wondered the same thing," I cut in. "Of course, there's no way to be sure what she was told, but I went online and I'm guessing it had to do with the control computer. Any nitwit could press a few buttons and throw off the entire system."

"I am not—" Rye protested.

"Shut up." Becca's mom's tone was icy. "Just tell me this: did you go near the computer?"

"She did!" Her husband seemed astonished by his own memory. "She must have been setting it up for a crash."

"That's not what I was doing!" Rye broke down. "I swear, it's not." Now she was sobbing. "They said it would just destabilize the plane so it wouldn't take off, okay? Nobody was going to get hurt. The Soyles found out through their spies that your family planned to take over their steakhouse empire, I don't know, something about shares and a hostile takeover, and Andy, I'm sorry, I'm really sorry, but Otto pushed me into doing it." Here she broke down, not bothering to wipe the black mascara tracks under her eyes. "I shouldn't have done it."

Andy shot Rye a disgusted look and moved over to his parents' side of the table. "You try to kill my family and all you have to say is 'sorry'?"

"I wasn't trying to do that!" Rye wailed, reaching out to grab a handful of cookies. "They told me it was a little prank. Just a stupid prank." She stuffed three cookies in her mouth and swallowed them whole.

"And what about the text messages?" I asked her.

"What text messages?" She sounded so dumbfounded I actually believed her.

"The ones to Becca. The ones about whatever she was wearing. The ones that scared her shitless." I looked over at the Shuttleworth parents. "Pardon my French." They didn't seem to mind. Or notice.

"They did that?" Rye blinked hard and shook her head incredulously. "I was supposed to tell them what Becca was wearing every day, but they said it was so they could start a fashion line based on her look. They said it was their one chance at recouping their los—"

"And just how did you find out about all of this?" Becca's dad asked me, speaking over Rye.

I took another deep breath. "Last week I was in Rogerstown, New Jersey. That's where I saw Rye kissing a guy on a bench in front of Emilio's pizzeria. It wasn't until I got home that I realized it was Otto Soyle. I Googled him and I found his picture from the *Post* story on the steakhouse fire."

"Why didn't you say anything?" Becca's mom was sheet white.

"Because I didn't have proof, and I was afraid nobody would believe me. I'd look like a jealous idiot." Whoops. I hadn't meant to say that. I glanced at Andy, who didn't seem especially startled, then down at the floor. I went on, "A few days later I was biking through Jersey City with my friend Louis. I saw Otto get out of a car and go into Rumps and Humps Steakhouse. A sign in front said there was a private party, and I was curious, so I snuck in and poked around. I found a private room where Otto was showing Rye something in a folder and she was taking notes on a napkin. I assumed it wasn't a curriculum-based meeting." I glanced in Rye's direction—I couldn't help myself—and continued, "Lucky for all of us, she discarded the first try, and I made sure to get my hands on it. I could tell it was a map of something, and when I saw 'DF7X,' I realized that it was your plane. Becca had told me about it."

Andy's green eyes started to melt and, like an idiot, I began to cry.

His father, who hadn't moved a muscle thus far, suddenly began typing something into his BlackBerry. Then he waved a waiter over to the table. He stood up and said something in a low voice. In less than a minute, hotel security had arrived and the Shuttleworths all fell back.

It seemed like a good time for me to leave as well.

I was in such a state of shock as I walked out of the restaurant, I barely felt connected to the blond girl who was walking away from the Shuttleworths' table. My heart was on the verge of breaking. Even though I knew I had done the right thing, and everyone was safe now, I was sure the Shuttleworths would send Becca away again, and maybe Andy, too. On the outside, I was just a crying and trembling Claire, but I had changed far more than that. In only one day, I'd aged many years.

I still needed to get back to Paris in time to make my pilgrimage to Fauchon. A shiny pink bag of the world's most incredible chocolates would keep my story straight with Dad, and never had a girl been in such need of truffle overdose.

{ 30 }

Rocky Rentrée

"**Ma** chérie, ma chérie!" Dad cried when he returned that night. He took off his jacket and started twirling it around as if he were a ballroom dancer.

My first thought was that he must be drunk, but when he sat down on my cot and removed his shoes, I was sure the only thing he smelled of was duck à l'orange.

"So? It went well?"

"More like . . . superbien. Magnifique! And guess the best part. An editor from Université de Sorbonne Press said he is interested in seeing my book. He tells me Zola is in vogue again." He waggled his eyebrows.

"And you knew he would be all along!" I said. "That's terrific!"

"*Pas mal.*" He padded off toward the desk. "Let's call your mother."

After he'd been murmuring sweet French nothings into the headset for a few minutes, he handed it to me. Mom immediately launched into a monologue about how much she wished she were in Paris.

"So how's it going in Florida?" I asked at last.

I heard her take a glug of water. "Not exactly the French thirty-five-hour workweek." Her voice lowered to a whisper. "They're slave drivers down here."

"They are?" All along I'd been picturing her sunbathing on the docks and getting ogled by leathery fishermen.

"You would not believe how seriously they take things at the *Planet*. I'm glad I'm coming home soon. When I get back, all I want to do is take a few days off and play housewife, just help Henry with his homework and cook seven meals a day for my family."

"Anytime," I said.

"Oh, stop pretending you don't miss me."

Yet again she'd mistaken my raspy voice for sarcasm.

"Mom." I tried not to sound peeved. "I do."

My business in Paris over and done with, I was ready to get back home and see Becca.

Our flight was at six the next night, meaning we had a Sunday in Paris to ourselves. After our morning newspaper and croissants, I dragged Dad to Ladurée to pick up Kiki's macaroons, and then to the Lanvin boutique, which was just around the corner. Some of the gowns were made of nothing but tulle and bows. They looked like spun sugar, and as far as I could tell, their only flaw was that my derrière would never fit into them.

The last thing on my list was a French haircut. Dad and I found a cute-looking salon, and before I knew it, a man named Sylvestre was hovering over me. And within less than an hour, I had said *au revoir* to four inches of hair and had suddenly grown Emmanuelle Seigner–ish cheekbones. The look was going to take some getting used to, but I knew it had been a good call when Dad got misty-eyed and started rambling on about my growing up so fast.

Flying back home is always less fun than starting out on a trip, and this time was no exception. The flight felt twice as long as our previous one, and instead of Hitchcock, the movie was some cheesy melodrama about a supermodel who puts her career on hold to teach at an inner-city school. Yeah, right.

Everything felt kind of weird when we got back to New York on Sunday night. My three days sneaking around Paris and London had been a whirlwind, and now the adventure was officially over.

A small creature popped out from Henry's bedroom to greet us. He was wearing a pillowcase with a green extraterrestrial face drawn on it.

Douglas smiled at Dad and me. "He overheard me discussing a paper I'm giving on existentialism and alienation in Camus, and he whipped this up."

"I got alienated today!" Henry whirred around and made a beep.

I planted hello kisses on Douglas and my alien brother and went back to my room. I hadn't even unzipped my suitcase when the phone rang.

"I bet it's Becca!" Douglas called out. "She's been looking for you."

I raced over to the phone. I couldn't wait to hear her voice.

"Hello?"

"Well, there you are, Nancy Drew!"

"Hi! I tried calling you from Paris but it went straight to voice mail."

"Paris? I thought you were in London." She chuckled. "What kind of a private eye are you if you don't know I called you a million times?"

I felt a smile tug at my mouth. "I literally just walked in the door."

"Oh right, you were busy running around the world. Listen, I can't believe you tried to tell me about Rye and I didn't get it."

"Well, a paper napkin isn't exactly the most convincing evidence. . . . Anyway, you okay?"

"Sure, I guess. I'm just in a state of shock. And I hate the idea of having to go through life second-guessing everybody I meet, wondering how much they tell me is true, you know?"

My stomach tightened. How would she take it if she were to discover the truth about my special talents? Had I been lying, or just holding back? And, really, what was the difference?

"We shouldn't talk about this on the phone," she said. "You never know who's listening. I just wanted to say welcome home. And I owe you. Big-time."

The next day was cold and damp. At nine fifty-five sharp, Becca and I met up with Ian, Zach, and Eleanor outside of school. Becca ran over to give me a huge hug and raked her hand through my new hair. "Wow," she said approvingly. "From Betty to babe."

"Here it is!" Ian alerted us.

A white Kinko's van came rolling up the street. While Becca signed something, the rest of us formed a human chain to unload all the boxes into the building.

Change doesn't need very long to take effect. When the bell signaling the end of homeroom rang, I stood at my locker, pretending to be searching for something, and watched the pile of "Evil Radish" diminish until there were no copies left. And when I overheard one girl scream, "Oh snap! I know which stuck-up bitches this is about!" I tipped my hat to Ian. How many artists can make a bunch of radishes resemble a specific gaggle of girls?

At lunch, nearly everybody was absorbed in the comic book, myself and Ian included (we didn't want to give ourselves away as the creators). Our ultimate triumph came midway through the period, when a few of the BDLs rolled into the cafeteria. They pretended to be in on the joke, waving and smiling, but we'd got them—and how!

I was feeling pretty pleased with myself until I went to my locker after lunch and saw Sheila and her minions waiting for me. Her eyes were clouded over, and I wondered if she'd been crying.

I said hello, but she was in no mood for pleasantries.

"Sixty-five?" she asked. "I would have given you a better grade."

I opened my mouth to ask her what she was talking about, and she thrust her copy of "Evil Radish" into my hands. I now noticed, for the first time, that Becca had put a blurb on the bottom of the cover: "65%. Needs Improvement—Mr. Bunting." She must have thought his disapproval was a funny badge of honor.

"You're in Bunting's class, right?" Sheila asked, a few BDLs fanning around her. The only one who wasn't glaring at me was Janice. She looked mortified.

"It's—it's just a comic book," I stammered nervously, and I could hear how deep my voice was. "All about a bunch of radishes who aren't very nice."

"I don't need your synopsis," Sheila told me. "I already read it. Very impressive, especially the part about Evil Radish's summer with her friend Little Lemon. Funny how the comic book didn't get into the part about how Little Lemon stole Radish's boyfriend."

There was no convincing her that Hayden and I were just friends, was there?

"How many times do I have to tell you?" I cried, exasperated. "Nothing ever happened between Hayden and me."

Sheila's shoulders heaved. "And now there's a book about a radish insisting that all her little admirers come to Sammy's Noodle Shop?"

"Maybe," I said, summoning all my courage, "if those radishes didn't torment the boys—I mean, alfalfa sprouts—there wouldn't be comic books like this."

"Maybe you're right," she said in a baby voice. "Maybe the radishes need to learn a lesson."

She began to walk away and her cronies followed closely behind. I couldn't remember how to breathe as I watched their figures recede down the hallway. I wasn't cut out for this having an enemy business.

"Or maybe," Sheila turned around to face me again. "The radishes will stop tormenting alfalfa sprouts and set their sights on"—she squinted and looked me up and down—"sour little lemons. For the sequel."

"Can't wait to read it!" I yelped, trying to sound brave. The truth was, I was petrified. Say what you would about Sheila, but she wasn't stupid. And now she was about to bump me up to the number one spot on her list of foes.

I trudged down the hallway with my head hanging, like a sad horse. But when I went outside at the end of the day, I saw how much the ecosphere I inhabited had changed. A suddenly popular Ian stood front and center of the crowd, showing his sketchbook to a tangle of enamored classmates. Meanwhile, Sheila and the rest of the BDLs were nowhere to be seen. I could only assume they were off in somebody's living room, scheming their revenge. Oh, the thrills that lay ahead! It was a welcome surprise when Becca came up from behind and pinched my back pocket.

"Talk about a brilliant redesign," she said, surveying the scene. "I can hardly wait to get going on our next big project."

And that was when it hit me—going back to Farmhouse suddenly didn't seem all that desirable. As much as I'd loved it there, as much as I missed taking hoedown dance classes and working in the bunny garden, there was no denying it: that was all in the past.

Henry Hudson was my home now, like it or lump it.

Becca went on, "If we actually spent a real chunk of time planning something, it could be major, right?"

"Depends if I'm still alive," I said, and told her about my run-in with Sheila.

Becca winced. "The Bunting quote. She knew you were in his class. I'm so sorry. I didn't think it through."

I draped my arm around her back and led her away from the building. "It's not your fault. She would have figured it out anyway."

"Really?"

I nodded. "You know the part about how the evil radish calls her ex-radish boyfriend and tells him he can't dump her because one day she's going to be so popular she'll get her own show on MTV and he'll regret it?" Becca nodded intently. "It's based on a true story that Hayden, her ex-boyfriend at camp, told me."

Becca was grinning uncontrollably. "Whoops," she said. "So much for your career as an undercover operative."

"Very funny."

"So, wanna get mushroom slices at Sal's?" Becca asked.

"Let's go somewhere without other Hudson kids."

"Oh, will you stop being embarrassed already? Who cares if you wrote a really funny story about somebody who deserves it? Let's catch up on your trip."

We ended up going to Dirt, a vegan tea shop on Rivington Street. The interior was cave-dark, and the only other customer was a woman with dyed-red hair and a dolphin tattoo that took up most of her back.

I told Becca pretty much what had happened, minus the weird dreams.

"I can't believe Rye was behind the freaky text messages," Becca said.

"Don't give her full credit," I reminded her. "She was just feeding them information."

"No wonder she was always complimenting me on my outfits and asking me questions about where stuff came from," Becca said, breaking off a piece of her dairy-free banana bread. "The thing I don't get is how did all this information fall into your lap?" She looked at me suspiciously.

"It was just a freak encounter," I said, and gave her the explanation I'd prepared in French class about how Louis and I had stumbled into Rye and the Soyles totally by accident.

"Still," she said, "you've got to admit that's too strange. You'd think there were higher forces at work or something."

I started to change color. Thank God the restaurant was so dark.

"Dad had one of his security employees interrogate Rye," Becca said.

"And?"

"It's as she said. Otto put her up to it. Turns out the two of them have been on and off for years and she's hopelessly in love with him."

"That is totally bizarre," I said, bringing my teacup to my mouth. "Have you ever seen him? He looks like—"

"A fat drowned rat in baggy clothes, I know. But he's a total jerk, and some girls love that kind of thing. I guess she was wooed by his evil streak. . . ."

All these pieces were coming together: Rye, planes, the tasseled handbag, Otto's ugly little dog. Wait—could it be?— she was the girl on the plane coming back from Paris last summer. My vision back then hadn't been so stupid after all!

"So what was she doing on the plane?" The words were rushing out of me. "Was she telling the truth when she said she was just jamming it so it wouldn't get off the ground?"

"That's what she thought she was doing. That's what the Soyles told her, and she didn't ask any questions. They had her pour water on the computer. Just enough to make the system sick."

"How sick?"

"There's no way to know. It was possible that the plane wouldn't take off." She shrugged. "It was also possible it would go haywire thirty-five thousand feet in the air." Becca put her vegan dessert back on the plate and stared over my shoulder. I could tell she was sadder than she was letting on.

I put my hand on top of hers and squeezed tight. "It's okay. The Soyles aren't going to get to you guys. You're safe. They're in the hands of the police."

As if on cue, the door opened and a couple of cops ambled inside. Becca motioned for me to lower my voice and proceeded to speak in a whisper. "Shall we move on to another topic?"

I smiled and the two of us sat quietly, sipping our tea.

"All things considered," Becca broke the silence, "we're fine. Except for Andy."

"He's totally heartbroken?" I asked, trying not to look too sad.

She paused. "More like Jack Nicholson crazy, sweeping through rooms and banging everything around. But he'll calm down soon enough. And then he'll be single. And he'll be dying to get revenge on that bitch." She gave me the eyebrow. I wasn't entirely sure if she was trying to let me know that she would now condone my going out with her brother, but I didn't press the issue.

"Well, tell Andy I send my best," I said hesitantly.

"He needs more than that. Let me know if you can think of any good distractions."

Could I ever.

"He's welcome to come over to our place on Thursday night for fake Thanksgiving." I was startled by my own words. Kiki's refrain about how it's up to the gentleman to do the asking ran through my mind. "You know," I said pathetically, "he always said he wanted to see the nutty-professor complex. Everyone will be there: Kiki, my mom, Douglas, Louis, Cheri-Lee, maybe even Sheila." I made a funny face.

Becca stood up and started fiddling with her coat. "I'll pass along the message." Her face was long. "Sounds like fun." Only now did I realize that she wasn't upset that I was angling to see her brother. She was just feeling left out.

"Don't be ridiculous," I said, fighting back laughter. "You're invited, too, obviously."

{ 31 }

Crowded House

With this year's Thanksgiving celebration occurring a week late, Mom and Dad were hoping Kiki would be so aghast with our household's ineptitude that she would decline their invitation. But Kiki was a stickler for tradition—and a fan of eating great big meals. She was thrilled to have two Thanksgivings.

When I arrived to pick her up, she gave me a big kiss and congratulated me again on my work in Europe.

"A job well done. You're off to a most promising start."

"I could use a little rest first." I handed her two boxes of possibly stale macaroons. "As requested."

She quickly devoured one cookie and appraised my new hairdo.

"This is a good thing," she declared, circling me to see it from all angles. "We might have to figure out a way to get you to Paris more often. Now be a dear and set these on the table, will you?" She put the boxes of cookies in my hands.

Then she disappeared to get ready. I sat at the table, and I'd flipped through an issue of *Vanity Fair* and eaten an entire rain forest's worth of nuts by the time she emerged. Her pale hair was up in a tortoiseshell headband, and she was wearing a blue wool dress that emphasized her heft.

"How do I look?" she asked.

"Beautiful." I needed to butter her up—the better her mood, the better our Thanksgiving. "Like a million bucks."

"You sound as convincing as a cheap politician."

Kiki was in a testy frame of mind, so I remained quiet in the cab ride downtown. I didn't react when she asked for an update on a rip in my apartment's couch she'd found particularly fascinating last Thanksgiving. And when she pressed me about how the family had gotten on with Mom in Florida, I lied and told her it had been smooth sailing.

"Aren't you little Miss Positive Outlook?" She sounded disappointed.

"Aren't you the one who taught me you catch more bees with honey than vinegar?" I reminded her.

When the cab stopped outside our complex, I helped her out and kept hold of her arm as we inched down the Washington View Village walkway.

"Aloha!" I shouted when we entered the apartment, a warning to everyone to stop talking about the controversial houseguest.

"We'll be right out!" Mom called from the kitchen. "The potatoes got a little unruly and . . . we're sort of messy. . . ." She and Dad erupted into giggles.

Kiki struck the pose of a penguin, flapping her arms out at her sides. Henry scurried over to remove her coat.

"Hi, Kiki!" he cried.

"How nice it is to be waited on by a handsome young man." She whispered something into his ear and, when she thought nobody was looking, slipped his fifty-dollar "tip" into his hand.

"Whoa!" If only Henry's head could have spun all the way around.

"Welcome, Kiki!" Dad stuck his head out of the kitchen. "You look lovely. Can I bring you a—"

"I'll get it myself," Kiki thundered, making her way to the bar to fix herself a martini.

"The couch," I whispered at Henry. "Did you remem—."

I looked into the living area and saw that he had draped Mom's green crocheted throw over the busted cushion.

When Kiki, her martini, and Henry were safely situated on the couch, I ran into the kitchen to check on everything. Apart from the mashed potatoes splattered all over the counter and my parents' aprons, the scene looked pretty promising.

"Is this okay?" Mom asked, pulling off a piece of roast chicken for me with her tanned fingers. "Can you tell?"

Mom's one act of subversion on Thanksgiving was to serve chicken instead of turkey, which she said she found too dry to give to guests. "It's great," I told her, "but you should probably cook it longer. It's still really moist."

"But its supposed to be a little tender." Mom pouted.

"It'll be fine," Dad whispered, coming up from behind to kiss the back of Mom's neck. "I'll make sure Kiki has a few martinis before dinner."

"Oh—would you?" she asked him. "I'll be just a second,

Mom!" she yelled into the main room. "I just need to check the vegetables!"

Even though the kitchen was far too small for three of us, I stayed to watch my mother kneel down and pull out an oven rack of *légumes en papillote*—a French dish of diced vegetables cooked in parchment paper. Using a wooden spoon to poke open one of the packets, she prodded at the mound of diced peppers, onions, and eggplant, all as bright and fine as confetti. How I was related to somebody so good at cooking was a mystery to me.

"Henry," Kiki could be heard saying. "Will you tell your parents they need to get this couch reupholstered? What if the Queen comes over one of these days?"

"I think she just got here ten minutes ago," Dad whispered.

I had to suppress my laughter.

Mom sighed dejectedly and turned to my father. "Tell me everything's going to be—"

"It will." He kissed her on the tip of the nose. "More than fine."

In a rare effort to be nice to my parents, Kiki called out, "I saw a fabulous show at the Met. All about the fashions of Paul Poiret. You had quite the talented fellow countryman, Gustave."

"Poiret?" Dad confessed he'd never heard of him.

"You've never heard of anyone," Mom teased him. "You wouldn't know Karl Lagerfeld from Kmart."

Feisty! I guessed all those hours at the *Planet* would sharpen anyone's wit.

At last, the other guests started to arrive—first Douglas, then Becca.

"No escort?" I asked her.

Becca frowned. "Andy said he wasn't feeling up to it. I think he went to the movies, but he said he might come by for dessert."

"And what's the chance of that happening?"

Becca shrugged and turned to fix her hair in the mirrored Renault poster.

I was feeling bummed but perked up when Cheri-Lee entered the apartment, bearing what appeared to be a pineapple with hundreds of shrimp sticking out of it on sparkly toothpicks. "That's amazing!" I exclaimed. "How on earth did you do that?"

"Toothpicks are our friends. You can attach anything with them—shrimp, pineapple, *radishes*." And in case I hadn't picked up on the colossal hint, she added, "You know who helped me with it? Your friend Sheila."

That was my cue to open up about my relationship with her daughter. Sorry, but I wasn't going to bite.

"Let me get that for you." I tried to relieve her of the fruit-seafood sculpture.

She pulled away. "I'm fine."

In the shade of the coatrack, we played a game of tug-of-war. "I know you're upset with me, but I need to tell you that you don't know the whole story," I told her. We were both clinging to the pineapple, our faces barely three inches apart. "It's not as simple as you think."

My voice had slid to a softer version of its normal self. I'd always wanted Cheri-Lee to understand why I wasn't her daughter's biggest fan, but at this moment everything else in the world ceased to matter. I had to get through to her.

"And maybe it's not as simple as *you* think, either. The last thing Sheila needs is any more grief, with her father leaving and all. This hasn't been an easy time for her."

While I was biting down on my lip and feeling guilty, she yanked the pineapple out of my grasp. "She's still very bent up over that Hayden incident, you know."

"Hayden and I were only ever just friends."

Cheri-Lee eyed me incredulously.

"It's *true*." I steered her and the shrimp sculpture back to the crowd. "Just let us work it out on our own. We will."

"You'd better." Over the cherry-colored frames of her glasses, she eyed me sternly. "You're two of the sweetest girls, and I'm sick and tired of your *shenanigans*, both of you."

Our tussle appeared to have gone unnoticed. Everybody else was clustered by the couch, where they were listening to Becca. The scene was reminiscent of a kid telling ghost stories in the middle of the night—the crowd was captivated, and the only light sources in the apartment were a handful of candles stuffed in the necks of empty wine bottles.

"I was waiting outside my voice coach's studio—which is really just another word for *office*," Becca was saying. "And I could hear him practicing scales. All of a sudden, I heard a horrible noise inside and I opened the door. He'd collapsed from stomach troubles. Something went wrong with his gastric bypass surgery."

"Dear Lord!" Kiki hooted, clapping her hands together.

"What did you do?" Henry asked.

"That's the amazing thing—I didn't have to do anything. Apparently this kind of thing happens all the time at the opera house. All these guards came out of the woodwork and rushed him to Beth Israel. He's fine, back on his feet." She popped a grape in her mouth and grinned. "He just might need to alter his diet a little bit."

Kiki turned to me, "Speaking of diets, would you kindly remind me when we're supposed to eat?"

"It should be very soon," I promised her. "Do you want to try one of Cheri-Lee's shrimp?"

Mom scurried out of the kitchen with flour in her hair. "Why doesn't everybody sit down?" she asked nervously.

Kiki wasn't the only hungry one. There was a mad rush for the table, and hands were flying into the bread basket before every seat cushion had been sat upon.

Henry's construction-paper-and-feather place cards had Becca sitting as far from me as possible, but she didn't seem to mind. And I wouldn't have been much use; she and Douglas were chatting away about some reality fashion show I'd never seen.

"This is marvelous, Priscilla," Cheri-Lee said, scooping a helping of walnut-sausage stuffing onto her plate. "You should go to Florida more often."

Mom patted the top of Dad's hand. "I don't think I'm allowed to do that again."

Kiki took a small bite. "Not bad," she said, grabbing a raisin pecan roll out of the breadbasket. "Though rather moist for turkey, isn't it?"

Mom looked immeasurably grateful when the sound of knocking came at the door, distracting everyone from the question. Out of the corner of my eye I saw Kiki glance around to make sure it was safe to stuff the ball of bread into her mouth. For some strange reason, she hated letting other people see her use her hands to eat.

"Sheila said she might be swinging by," Cheri-Lee said. "Why don't you go and see, Claire?"

"Bliss," I grumbled to myself as I got up from the table and trudged over to the door.

But instead it was Louis, with his tennis racket slung over his shoulder.

"It's you!" I gushed.

"Sorry I'm late." He'd misinterpreted my statement. "The match was never ending. We played to 7–6."

"Did you win?" I asked, watching him kick off his tennis shoes.

"I would have. My racquet was messed up."

"Well, you came to the right place." I dragged him into the main room. "You can eat away your sorrows."

"I'd rather eat a burger."

"You all know Louis, right?" I looked around the room, and then my eyes alighted on Becca. She was sitting straighter than usual, appraising him as if he were an animal that had trespassed on her territory. "Everyone but Becca."

"Why don't you sit here, Louis?" Douglas asked, clearing his place. "I have to be at the soup kitchen at eight."

"You do know Thanksgiving was a week ago?" Becca asked. She didn't want Douglas to give his place to this alien interloper.

"I offered to help prepare tomorrow's breakfast," Douglas told her. "Soup kitchens are open every day of the year."

Becca looked down at her plate, slightly ashamed.

"Not necessarily," Kiki came to Becca's rescue. "Sadie Lindenquist and I used to host the most fabulous dinner for the needy at the Colony Club on alternate Thursday nights."

At this bit of information, Mom put down her fork and smiled. "I didn't know you fed homeless people, Mom."

"Well, to be perfectly honest, they were artists, but by the way they blew about from one apartment to the next, they were practically homeless."

Kiki tucked into her supposed turkey and left everybody else at the table to exchange wide eyes and suppressed smirks.

The rest of the meal proceeded smoothly—plenty of wine

and chocolate. Very few awkward silences. And no more glares from Cheri-Lee. But the best part was watching Becca. All this time, I'd known her to be the paragon of composure, sometimes a little high-handed, but after ten minutes of sitting with her back to Louis, she started to warm to him. He brought out her girlishness, a side of her I'd only seen when we were alone together. Becca was acting alternately coy and effusive, and enjoying herself more than I ever would have thought possible. They were talking about horror movies and entertaining each other with impressions of bad zombie acting. Everything was going perfectly until he leaned in to take an uneaten spinach pie off her plate. The plate snatching didn't bother her, but he inadvertently knocked the pitcher of gravy onto the floor, splattering her beautiful embroidered velvet flats.

Louis disappeared under the table, wiping her shoes with a napkin. "I'm sorry!" he kept saying. "I'm a spaz!"

"Don't worry about it," she said, leaning down to him. "I didn't like these shoes anyway." She kicked them off and sat cross-legged. "Much more comfortable. I'm starting to get why everybody makes a fuss about going barefoot around here."

Kiki and I exchanged a look.

It was funny, I thought. I'd always meant to introduce the two of them, but never in a million years would it have struck me to set them up. But now that they were inches apart, I could see that I'd blocked out the obvious. I had two sarcastic, privileged, and, yes, not-bad-looking best friends. How had it not occurred to me to bring them together?

Becca barely said anything to me until dessert, when she passed me her cell phone and frowned. "Looks like Andy's not coming after all."

DIDN'T REALIZE IT WAS A DBL FEATURE.
TELL CLAIRE I'LL MAKE IT UP TO HER.
I OWE HER A FIELD TRIP. I'LL MAKE IT XTRA GOOD.

My heart quickened. I nearly dropped the phone when I was handing it back.

"He's an idiot to miss out on this. Let's make him jealous." Becca got up and pointed her cell phone at the table. "Everyone, say cheese."

Since cheese makes me wince, I said "Chocolate" and tried to duplicate one of Mom's bewitching smiles for Andy.

"Looks like you've done more good for that Shuttleworth clan than you might recognize," Kiki said after dinner. We were in the backseat of a taxi that was headed uptown to the Waldorf. She was right—I'd never seen Becca smile as much as she had at the end of the meal when Louis made a point of telling her he wanted to see *Valley of the Dead*, the movie she'd been talking about wanting to check out earlier in the evening.

"I don't know how I didn't think of it before," I told her. "They'll make a lovely match," Kiki said "and we can be sure neither of them is using the other for their money."

"That's a romantic way of looking at things," I said dryly.

"I'm just being practical. I do want the best for everybody." She rolled down the window and took a deep breath of fresh air. "Especially you, my dear." She gave me a funny look. "Time to get cracking."

"What's that supposed to mean?"

"You're not supposed to use the cameo to achieve things only for yourself. But if there are other people involved, well, that might be a different story. You're on the verge of something. . . ."

"I am?"

"Do I have to spell it out? *A-N-D-R-E-W.*"

It took me a second to realize what she meant. Andy. I was struck by a gut feeling of my own—it was as if a thousand tiny fish were swimming around my stomach. I was slammed with every emotion under the sun—terror, anxiety, ecstasy, and that's only two percent of the things I was feeling. I leaned back in my seat and looked out the window, pretending not to have grasped what she was driving at.

"Pull yourself together." Kiki gave my knee a double pat. "He's just as scared as you."

I was riding my bike along a path in Washington Square Park when I saw him. He was sitting on a bench and reading the newspaper. His brow was furrowed and his long legs were carelessly kicked out.

I pulled up in front of him and tapped his foot with my own. He smiled at me, and next thing I knew, my bike was leaning against the bench and we were sitting side by side and my heart was beating so hard I was afraid he'd hear it. He was running his finger around my wrist, then up my arm, and somehow he was tugging at my earlobe, and playing with the part of my ear that met my neck. It tickled, and I wasn't sure exactly what was happening—only that I felt warm and safe, as if I were floating above everything I'd ever known until now.

It was all in black-and-white, but when I woke up the next morning, I felt a wave of calm. I knew everything would be colored in soon enough.

The author would like to thank Christy Fletcher;

Ben Greenman, Sarah Fan, and Eden Edwards, readers extraordinaire;

The Mechling caravan, and, alphabetically, Stacy Abramson, Vanessa Bertozzi, Pooja Bhatia, Andrew Bujalski, Anne Dodge, Gail Ghezzi, Kitty Greenwald, Matt Herman, Jamie Irving, Steven Jack, Jessica Johnson, Laura Moser, Lisa Oppenheim, Tim Rostron, and Jake and Daniel;

And Krista Marino, dream editor.

Tobias Everke

LAUREN MECHLING is the coauthor of all three 10th-Grade Social Climber books. She has written for the *New York Times, Jane,* and *Seventeen.* She lives and writes in New York City. You can visit her at www.laurenmechling.com.